The Words of Bernfrieda
a Chronicle of Hauteville

THE WORDS OF BERNFRIEDA
A CHRONICLE OF HAUTEVILLE

THE CHRONICLE OF THE LIFE OF FREDESENDA
WIFE OF TANCRED OF HAUTEVILLE AND
MOTHER OF ROBERT GUISCARD DUKE OF
APULIA AND ROGIER COUNT OF MILETO FROM
HER BIRTH IN 1000 ANNO DOMINI AT
GRANVILLE IN NORMANDY UNTIL HER DEATH
AND BURIAL AT THE ABBEY OF SANTA
EUFEMIA IN APULIA IN 1063 ANNO DOMINI

THE WORDS OF BERNFRIEDA BY HER HAND
WRITTEN AT THE ABBEYS OF SANTA EUFEMIA
IN APULIA AND SANTA AGATHA IN CATANIA
BY THE GRACE OF GOD

A NOVEL BASED ON CONTEMPORARY ACCOUNTS AND HISTORIES OF THE
NORMANS IN FRANCE AND ITALY

GABRIELLA BROOKE

EWU
P·R·E·S·S
Eastern Washington University Press
Cheney, Washington 1999

Library of Congress Cataloging-in-Publication Data

Brooke, Gabriella 1947-

The words of Bernfrieda: a chronicle of Hauteville: the chronicle of the life of

Fredesenda wife of Tancred of Hauteville and mother of Rober Guiscard . . . / by

Gabriella Brooke.

p. cm.

"Novel based on contemporary accounts and histories of the Normans in France

and Italy."

ISBN 0-910055-49-1 (pbk.)

1. Fredesenda, 1002-1063—Fiction. 2. Tancred, de Hauteville, d. 1047—Fiction.

3. Robert Guiscard, Duke of Apulia, Calabria, and Sicily, ca. 1015-1085—

Fiction 4. Normandy (France)—History—to 1515—Fiction. 5. Normans—

Italy—History—to 1500—Fiction.

I. Title

PS3552. R65767W6 1999   813'.54—dc21   98-42114

CIP

Book and cover design by Scott Poole

*To my mother and to my husband
and to the memory of Luigi Biancheri*

CONTENTS

INCIPIT LIBER
DE VITA FREDESENDAE

(The book about the life of Fredesenda begins)

Robert Guiscard arrived, the best of all his brothers, leader and glory of all Normans, for he was an example of chivalry and courage, a man of great strength and heart . . . and Mars, god of war, marveled at Robert's daring. Athena, goddess of knowledge, marveled at Robert's wisdom, and Mercury, god of speech, marveled at Robert's eloquence.

Robert Guiscard, having found that his marriage was within the prohibited degree of kinship, dissolved his marriage to Alberada and married Sichelgaita, sister of Gisulf, Prince of Salerno.

— Amatus of Monte Cassino: *Ystoire de li Normant* (circa 1075)

CAPUT PRIMUM

The Abbey of Santa Eufemia
On the eve of the Feast of Saint Sabbas (April 12)
In this year 1061 from the Incarnation of our Lord
The words of Bernfrieda

E ven now, that in spite of my sex I have learned to write as well as any monk, I interrupt my work and stare when Brother Gaufredus begins a new manuscript. I watch my teacher, fascinated by the care he takes with the first letter. How painstakingly he traces it, fills it with red ink and embellishes it with drawings. His quill glides on lambskin scraped so smooth that even the smallest follicle has disappeared.

After Prime, at daybreak, when the shepherd crosses the courtyard with his bleating herd and heads toward the hills, I am blind to the play of the lambs. Fredesenda and I often sit on the steps in front of the church, waiting for them to pass. She likes to watch the young ones as they stumble by their mothers. I can only think of what Brother Gaufredus told me about lambskins my very first time in the *scriptorium*: "The younger the animal when its skin is harvested, the smoother the parchment it produces. The skin of a newborn lamb, or one still in the womb, is to be prized above all, Bernfrieda. Its skin is naturally smooth and unmarked and does not need all the scraping and bleaching."

When I repeated that to Senda, she raised an eyebrow and inclined her head to the right, as she does when she is puzzled. Pointing at a lamb that was bleating furiously for its mother, she said, "How could anyone wish to turn such beauty into a dusty old parchment?"

I did not argue with my half-sister, for she does not understand my love for the *scriptorium* and the peace I find there. I love the musty smell of parchment so thick that I can almost taste the ancient dust. Senda thinks me daft for liking it. In the spring it mingles with the scent of lavender and thyme that wafts into each cubicle of the *scriptorium* from the herb garden facing it. The occasional cry of a sea gull swooping down the fluttering waters of the Tyrrhenian sea and the tolling of the monastery bell are all that break the day's quiet.

As I write on the virgin page of this vellum, I am well aware of the treasure I behold. The lambskin is among the finest I have seen — surpassed only by the missal of Queen Emma that is kept at the Abbey of Saint Evroult in Normandy. The man who supplies the *scriptorium* could offer no less to Senda — the mother of Robert Guiscard, Duke of Apulia. Had he known that the parchment was a gift for me, her handmaid and half-sister, he might not have brought his best. He assumed, like the monks, that Senda ordered the sheets as a gift to her son. What other use would an illiterate woman have for something so precious?

Before I begin Senda's story I must explain how I, Bernfrieda, daughter of the Lord Mauger of Granville and his handmaid Alsinda have come to know the written word. I will also tell what prompted me to begin this work and the reason Senda and I retired to this half-finished Abbey so far removed from the comfort and excitement of the court of her first-born in Melfi.

May God assist me. Should I make a mistake, the scraper and goat tooth (to smooth the page) are on my desk ready to use. Marring a page that rivals in touch the velvet wings of a butterfly is what I fear the most. I vowed to see each paragraph in my mind before setting it down on vellum.

A year ago last November, Senda decided to leave Melfi and the court of her first-born Robert to retire to Santa Eufemia. I encouraged her with enthusiasm, looking forward with delight to the *scriptorium* I would find there. In spite of her dark mood — for she did not leave Melfi willingly — Senda thought it amusing when I told her I wanted to learn to write. "Why did you ever dream of doing what monks do?" she said.

I smiled and shook my head, unwilling to tell her that my desire stemmed from our visit to Saint Evroult, sixteen years before. I saw Queen Emma's Missal there, and the memory of that lovely manuscript had stayed with me for years.

"To whom would you write, Bernfrieda?" Senda asked when I told her my wish, just after we settled at Santa Eufemia. "You have no family other than me." But she asked the Abbot (who denies her nothing) that I be allowed to learn. Though I was well over sixty when I began a year ago, I learned well and now am quite accomplished. Time is slow at Santa Eufemia. Senda needs little attention and I practice at will.

Each day in the early afternoon before I go to the *scriptorium* for another lesson, I practice on my green wax tablets at the desk in the window alcove of our room. Senda sits next to me in her chair as I work, but faces the sea. She leans forward, her elbow on the carved lion's head at the end of the armrest. The few strands of golden-red hair mixed with white that always escape her wimple caress the side of her face as they are lifted by the breeze from the sea.

She can spend hours just staring outside, watching the breeze and the sun play on the water below. She says it helps her think of the past, when she was happiest. I can see why she enjoys it. Today she is honored because she is the mother of Robert Guiscard, Duke of Apulia, and of Rogier, Count of Mileto, the two most powerful men in southern Italy. But she is lonely. Her sons are busy fighting each other and rarely come see her. Senda is alone, save for me, her handmaid and half-sister.

When I began to learn, my goal was to take Brother Odo's place and take care of Senda's correspondence. But when I felt accomplished enough to suggest it, just after the almonds were harvested last fall, Senda shook her head. "You can't have learned all that Brother Odo knows in such a short time, Bernfrieda. What if the signs with which you fill your wax tablets are not understood by my sons' scribes? I can't chance a mistake. Especially now." She picked up her embroidery and began to work. When I looked up, ready to argue, she was frowning. *She is thinking of her sons.* She suffers grievously each time they are warring. She forgets her sorrow the moment they make peace, and then she plunges into despair again when they break their truce. And they have broken it many times during the last three years.

Senda thinks that I suffer with her when her sons are at war. Because we shared the same father, she assumes that I feel as she feels. I feel only anger when Robert and Rogier begin another fight. I saw Senda's pain when they were born. She still lets them torment her. Her sons are men now. Senda should learn to ignore what she can't control.

Anger drove Senda to Santa Eufemia. She could not bring herself to accept the annulment of Robert's first marriage to the Norman Alberada and his marriage to Gaita of Salerno. In the two years we lived in Melfi after arriving from Normandy, Senda had been the true Lady of Robert's keep. Alberada had been awed by her mother-in-law, even entrusting her with the keys to the larder of Robert's keep.

But Gaita was different. Her father, the Prince of Salerno, had taken her with him on the battlefield from the time she was a child, and she was accustomed to lead. I knew the moment the new bride asked Senda to surrender the keys to the larder that they would never be friends.

Gaita arrived in Melfi on a lovely June day three years ago. When the sentries on top of the walls shouted that the bridal party was approaching, Senda and I had hurried into Alberada's tower room. We stepped up to the small window alcove where Alberada was already scanning the wheat fields below, and together we crowded to catch a glimpse of the woman who was to take her place. The wedding party pushed forward slowly in that sea of gold, broken here and there by a bright splash of red poppies or a silver olive tree. Even as the column began the climb to the keep, we still could discern no jewel-encrusted litter, no train of ladies-in-waiting. Only foot soldiers, an old woman — much too old to be the bride — and several mounted knights followed Robert and the knight by his side.

When the column entered the keep, we climbed down from the tower, crossed the great hall, and hurried into the bailey where we joined Senda's youngest son, Rogier, and much of the castle household. An admiring murmur rose from the crowd as Senda's formidable first-born dismounted. Robert pushed back his mail hood, and ran his fingers through the flattened blond hair that reached almost to his shoulders. Wearily he smoothed his short red beard, as he waited for Rogier to meet him.

"Welcome, Robert!" Powerful and warm, Rogier's voice rang through the courtyard. He quickly walked the few steps that divided him from his brother and embraced him. Against Robert's massive torso Rogier looked much younger than his thirty years. He wore his brown hair cropped well above the ear and was clean-shaven. I often wondered why he did not grow a beard; for it would have made him look closer in age to his brother, more of a match for Robert. As it was, Robert and Rogier looked more like father and son than brothers. Senda beamed as she watched them. I could only bite my lip and hope the peace of the greeting would last.

Robert turned to his riding companion, who had made no move to dismount. Moments later cries of surprise rose among the crowd as the "knight" pushed back the hood of the dark travelling coat to reveal a thick golden braid that fell to her waist. Clad in a man's mail coat and short green tunic, the Lombard Princess Gaita looked more like an Amazon ready for battle than a new bride. She dismounted, smiled at her husband and then faced Rogier. She put her hands on his arms as he kissed her and I held my breath in surprise, for she was almost as tall as he was. She returned Rogier's kiss and then gazed at us. In

spite of her fearsome size Gaita was pleasingly proportioned.
Her face was large, with wide cheekbones, unmarked skin, and a
long straight nose.

Senda gasped when she saw her new daughter-in-law.
Alberada let go of her small son's hand. Mark ran happily toward
the party, calling his father. He ended in a soldier's arms, but
Robert called to his son and then proudly introduced the little
boy to Gaita. She surveyed him with unsmiling blue eyes; she
would have a hard time producing an heir that could match
Robert's first-born. At four, Mark was a small replica of his father, taller and sturdier than most boys his age. He had his
father's bright blue eyes and nothing of Alberada's face or meek-
ness. Senda offered her cheek to Gaita's kiss. Then Robert introduced his new bride to Alberada.

"Lady Alberada is my beloved sister," Robert said in a boom-
ing voice, so everyone in the hushed crowd could hear. He
turned to face them and repeated what he had said. Senda
looked at her former daughter-in-law as he spoke, but Alberada's
face was blank.

"Our marriage was a mistake of which we were both innocent.
As soon as we learned that our marriage fell within the prohibited degree of kinship, we agreed to ask for an annulment. From
that moment on we vowed to love each other only as brother and
sister. And as my beloved sister I introduce her to you, Gaita, my
only wife in the eyes of God."

Robert was so convincing that many had tears in their eyes.
When he finished Alberada walked to Gaita and kissed her on
both cheeks. The members of the household cheered wildly;
only Senda and I knew her true feelings.

Just two months before, before leaving for Rome, Robert told
Senda that he had discovered he and Alberada were related
within the seventh degree of kinship and an annulment was im-
pending. After Robert left she stormed into Alberada's room.
With an imperious sweep of her hand, she ordered Alberada's
women to leave.

"How can you let Robert do this to you and your son?" she asked, her voice quivering with rage. "He can't have the marriage annulled if you oppose it!"

Alberada looked up at Senda as if she had not heard. Then she rose and walked to the window and looked down at the wheat fields surrounding the keep.

"These Church rules," Senda grimaced, "they change so often. Think of Duke Guillaume and his wife. Every Norman knows that they are cousins within the fourth degree, more closely related than you and Robert! Yet the Pope was happy to recognize their marriage after they vowed to build two cathedrals as penance."

"Robert promised to honor me as a sister, and to provide for Mark in a way fitting to his rank." Alberada said, without turning from the window.

"His rank! That of a bastard!" Senda spat.

Alberada turned to face her. "You know only one side of Robert," she said quietly, her small round face troubled. "He is driven, Mother. He is consumed by his passion for land; nothing is as important to him."

"But —"

Alberada raised her hand. "When we were first married I was terrified of him — Robert gained much from our marriage, in land and soldiers. But I understood from the beginning that it was not enough, that I, and even Mark when he was born — we were never enough. Now he wants Salerno and he can get it by marrying Gaita. He will have both, Mother, whether I resist or not. If I do not agree he will find ways — he could take Mark away, imprison me in one of his keeps or even —" she looked at the floor. "I know how he is."

After kissing Alberada, Gaita received the greetings of the rest of the household. Afterward, Gaita and Robert went up to Alberada's former chamber to prepare for the wedding feast. The smell of roasting meats from the kitchens outside filled the hall and the servants began to set the tables for the wedding banquet. Alberada waited until the wedded couple disappeared upstairs and then she too left the hall.

⚜ ⚜ ⚜

Two weeks ago yesterday Brother Amatus of Monte Cassino came to visit Senda. He came to question her about the childhood of Robert Guiscard to fill in the chronicle he is writing. Early the morning after he arrived, as we shared a breakfast of cold mutton and bread, Senda told me to return from the *scriptorium* after the hour glass had emptied only once instead of thrice, so that I could attend to her when the monk from the Abbey of Monte Cassino came for his visit.

I was disappointed that I could spend so little time in the *scriptorium*, for I had just begun copying from the life of Saint Agatha. Anxious to finish the first page, I begged Senda for an early leave and rushed to the *scriptorium* to do as much work as I could. By the time Brother Gaufredus entered the cubicle I had worked for three quarters of the time allotted and had used up most of the ink.

"The great Amatus arrived late last night, Bernfrieda!" Brother Gaufredus eased his slight frame into his chair, hooked the writing board to the forked stick on the side and adjusted it to a comfortable distance from his eyes. Having done all this, he acknowledged my greeting with a quick nod. His normally pale face was flushed, and he was so excited he made no effort to pick up his vellum and quill. "Amatus retired immediately, for he was weary from his journey and wanted to rest well before he met with your Lady." Brother Gaufredus looked at me through pupils no bigger than an embroidery needle. *He is expecting me to tell him how Senda feels about this visit. His curiosity about my mistress is the driving force in his life. But I learned long ago that silence is the best defense.*

As Gaufredus spoke, I kept glancing at the page I had almost finished. The margins of the two columns of writing were within one letter of being perfectly aligned. Blue and red alternately colored the enlarged first letter that began each new paragraph, and the overall effect of the page was very pleasing. Still to be finished were the details on the letter that began the page, a large *Q*, beginning the phrase *Quis es?* I drew it inside a small square, as Gaufredus had suggested.

"Are you ever going to speak, Bernfrieda?" Brother Gaufredus's thin voice was laced with envy. "You seem indifferent to Amatus's visit. Perhaps you are too accustomed to important visitors to mind." He drummed his fingers on the writing board. "Your penmanship is so good that at times I forget that you are a woman. Why should the implications of his visit interest you? Like most women you only care about simple things."

It was not the goading that moved me to respond but the rare praise. "Do explain those implications to me, Brother Gaufredus, since I have a simple mind."

"You can be humble, Bernfrieda, and that is good." I bowed my head to hide a little smile. "Word is that your Lady's son, Robert Guiscard himself, commissioned Amatus to write the chronicle of his conquest of Apulia. Don't you see? What your Lady says about her noble son will live through the centuries in Amatus's chronicle. Oh, lucky Amatus to find such a patron! To write down history as it unfolds, to record the truth about events that will inspire future leaders to greatness!"

Brother Gaufredus clasped his hands against his chest.

"How can Amatus record the truth if he only hears Robert's side?" I asked as I began the last paragraph of the page I was copying.

Gaufredus looked at me, his eyes round with puzzlement. "What other side should he hear? Of course Amatus will record the truth. He is not simply relying on what Duke Robert tells him, he is gathering information from those who know the Duke best — your Lady for example, the Duke's own mother. Who else would he speak to? The Duke's enemies perhaps? How, pray, could the infidel Greeks and the heathen Saracens help Amatus arrive at the truth?"

"When we read the chronicles of Thucydides together you pointed out that they are highly partisan, Brother Gaufredus."

"Of course they are, Bernfrieda! Thucydides was a Greek, a pagan. What do you expect? But if a chronicle is written by a man of the cloth and if its subject is a man devout to our Holy

Church like Duke Robert is, how can the truth elude the chronicler? It will pour from his words like pure water from a spring!" Brother Gaufredus shook his head. "I had not realized that you had misinterpreted my lessons so grossly. This proves once more that women should leave the written word alone. For what good are reading and writing without a mind capable of discerning what is important from what isn't?"

I quickly sought to distract Gaufredus, for I knew he would complain again about how the Abbot forced him to teach me. He never forgave Senda for it.

"Well, Brother Gaufredus, if learning from Brother Amatus means so much to you, why don't you ask him to let you assist him during his visit to my Lady? You could help take notes or make yourself useful in other ways."

"Did you think I had not thought of it?" My teacher's face was gloomy. "I begged my Lord Abbot to let me help. But the great Amatus wants only his own helper around when he works." Gaufredus slouched in his chair like a child.

Having finished the page, I put the quill down, blew on the ink to make it dry faster and then put a linen cloth over it. It was time to go back to Senda.

"Do not fret, Brother Gaufredus," I said. "Since Amatus's words are so important to you I will take my leave right now and return to my Lady's chamber. I will record everything Amatus says to her and come back to report to you . . . if you finish the illumination on my page."

Gaufredus's face lit in a rare smile. "You will? Oh Bernfrieda, do hurry! Do not worry about the illumination — it will be done by the time you come back."

Once outside the *scriptorium*, I stopped a moment to admire the orderliness of the plantings in the cloister and inhale the fresh morning air. Gravel in the form of a cross separated four major planting areas in the center. Two of these held herbs, flowers and medicinal plants, while the others were reserved to vegetables. Two novices were weeding the beds and looked up as I passed them. The scent of the sea from the nearby Gulf of Santa Eufemia invigorated me as it always does. Jasmine and honeysuckle climbed upon the rows of white stone columns all around the cloister, creating an enchanting island at the heart of the Abbey.

I hurried down the east side of the cloister, heading south toward the Abbot's hall where Senda's apartment was located. Her rooms — the best in the Abbot's house — were upstairs. Out of breath, I pushed the door open and crossed the antechamber.

Through the large window alcove across the room, the sea shone green. Whipped by the breeze, white foam capped the waves. The sea has been a constant in my life. Angry, and dark, it marked each day of my youth on the Cotentin; placid and transparent, it marks now the days of my old age. *Now, as in the past, it reflects my mood.*

Senda sat in her chair facing the sea. She was leaning forward, her elbow on the carved lion's head at the end of the armrest.

"Senda?"

Her eyes as green as the sea, Senda turned and looked at me. Before she could acknowledge me, a knock interrupted us and I retraced my steps to the door. I stood aside to let the two grey-bearded monks in.

"Brother Amatus of Monte Cassino is here to see your Lady," the shorter of the two said.

I nodded and led the visitors into Senda's chamber. Senda stood up and took a few steps toward us. The monks held their breath when they saw her and bowed deeply. Even with the coarse woolen mantle she favors, no one mistakes her rank. Senda carries herself — her back straight, her pace unhurried and yet determined — as one who knows her place in the world. I too hold my back straight, yet strangers do not defer to me the way they do to Senda. Perhaps it has to do with her coloring. In this land of dark small people, she stands out with her light skin and blue-green eyes. And she is tall, a gift our father Mauger denied me.

The stout, grey-bearded monk strode toward her and bowed again. "I am Amatus," he said in a ringing voice, "from the Abbey of Monte Cassino, my Lady. Your son Robert sends me."

Her face blank, Senda nodded and motioned him to follow
her into the great window alcove. The whole wall overlooking
the Tyrrhenian jutted out almost five feet, graced by three elon-
gated windows arched at the top and separated by slender columns. Stone benches lined the space below, leaving enough
room for Senda's lion-head chair in the middle, my loom, and a
small desk to the right of the chair. Amatus raised an eyebrow,
surprised, I assume, at the simplicity of the rest of the room.
Though they may pretend to despise it, I know most monks are
fascinated by the trappings of wealth. As Senda is the mother of
the Duke of Apulia, the most powerful man in southern Italy,
one could easily picture her in clothes woven of gold thread and
trimmed in ermine, her chamber laden with rich tapestries, her
chests inlaid with enamel and jewels. Amatus took in the green
woolen curtains tightly drawn around the modest bed across
from the window alcove and Senda's old mantles hanging on a
pole. His gaze finally came to rest on the only token of luxury in
the room — a gift from Robert's first wife, Alberada — an exquisite silver decanter and matching cups, which rested on a
large oaken chest at the foot of the bed.

I led Amatus to the wooden stool by the desk, where he sat
with his back to the sea, facing Senda. I chose the stone bench
on Senda's left where I could work on the tapestry we are embroidering. Although the weather is mild at Santa Eufemia,
walls sweat here too. The tapestry would help a little. I wove it
of heavy linen last summer and it will hang from the top of the
wall over her bed. Senda treasures it already, for we have recorded the high points of her life on it.

Amatus noticed the tapestry as he sat down; it is so large that
one can hardly ignore it. His eyes kept returning to it as he explained his mission. Robert had asked him to write a chronicle
of his campaigns. The Duke wanted all he had accomplished to
be preserved in writing for future generations. I could tell
Amatus was greatly flattered at having been chosen for the task.
He smoothed his beard in a self-satisfied way several times as he
spoke. He had travelled to Santa Eufemia to gather from Senda's

lips whatever gems she could offer about the Duke's childhood. Senda frowned at his flattery.

"Do you want to compose an Italian *Chanson de Geste*, Brother Amatus?" she asked sarcastically.

But Amatus smiled, flattered by the comparison. "I am only a humble scribe, my Lady, I only record facts. But perhaps someone will be prompted by my chronicle to compose a *Chanson*." He chuckled.

"It would only be fitting. Roland *was* Robert's hero."

Senda told Amatus that when Robert was very young — five, six perhaps — he shared everything with the ragged band of serfs' children that he led. They loved him, and not just for the food he shared with them each day. He was a big child and a natural leader; children deferred to him then as adults do today. And he took his leadership seriously. Once he refused to touch food for days because Tancred had ordered the hall cleared of his small friends. "They are my charges, Father," he said, after Senda begged Tancred to reason with him. "Just like your knights are yours. They can't do my bidding if their bellies are empty." Tancred had roared with laughter, and relented, as he always did with Senda's sons.

Amatus scribbled furiously. But I could tell by the way he kept asking about Robert's early years that he was not pleased with what she said. What had happened at Father's house, and later at Hauteville, had been events momentous only to women's lives, mine and Senda's, hardly the stuff of a *Chanson de Geste*.

Amatus asked much about Tancred and his children by his first wife, Muriella. Senda looked past him at the sea when Amatus mentioned Guillaume *Bras-de-Fer*.

"Guillaume trained at my father's house, Brother, but I barely knew him then." I looked up sharply from my embroidery. Would her response make Amatus suspect her secret?

"You should talk to his widow Yolanda. I understand she still lives in Sorrento." Senda betrayed nothing. I could have been misled too, had I not known her true feelings for Guillaume.

"What about your other stepchild, our beloved late Count Onfroi? — may God keep his soul!" Amatus crossed himself.

Senda told him an episode that had happened when Onfroi was sixteen and Robert only seven. Onfroi had come back from the hunt and was riding in the bailey, toward the stables, when Ansgot, one of the serfs' children, had darted in front of him. Onfroi's horse had reared. Paralyzed with fear, Ansgot had stood rooted to the spot while Onfroi struggled to calm his mount. Furious, Onfroi jumped off his horse and began whipping the child. Within moments Robert threw himself against his stepbrother. Enraged, Onfroi turned on Robert. Lashes shredded Robert's linen shirt and split the skin open on his arm and back. Senda threw herself between them, and Onfroi had to lower his whip. The lash had slit open Robert's right eyebrow — a mark he bears today.

I could tell Amatus thought the story unsuitable. After all, it was hardly flattering to Onfroi. *He will make something up. Memories can be changed — if they are retold often enough in a certain way.*

Amatus asked nothing *about* Senda, save Father's name (whom he must have judged noble enough to be worthy of mention). He didn't ask about the circumstances of Senda's wedding to Tancred, but he was delighted by the account of how Tancred had slaughtered a wild boar. He had heard the story before — what Norman has not heard it? — but he asked Senda to retell it. He kept asking for details, seemingly unaware that Senda had not even been alive at the time. She complied, indifferently retelling the story we had heard so many times during the long winter evenings at Hauteville. That story must have compensated him, I suppose, for the otherwise meager pickings of his visit.

I went to the *scriptorium* after Amatus left. Hunched over his desk, Brother Gaufredus looked like a giant spider ready to ambush its prey. He nodded briefly when I entered his cubicle. Without looking at me, he gathered the folds of his black robe between his knees to make room for my chair.

Carefully, I removed the white linen cloth that covered my parchment. Inside the *Q* Brother Gaufredus had drawn a tiny Saint Agatha in her cell and Saint Peter just outside it. The woman looked fixedly from behind tiny bars. Two red spots marked where her breasts had been torn off. Saint Peter, looking vacantly ahead, seemed more concerned about the impression he would make than in the bleeding girl in front of him. But the illumination was exquisite and I said so aloud.

Gaufredus blushed. "It is your turn, Bernfrieda. Do tell all that Amatus said!"

I filled the cow horn with ink, chose a new quill, tested its sharpness on the back of my hand, and began to trace the first word on the new page. Gaufredus did not speak, but when I raised my eyes and saw the expectation in his eyes, I felt a little ashamed and I began to tell all that had taken place in Senda's room.

Amatus's chronicle will barely mention Senda. His readers will never know of our life at Granville — how she came to marry Tancred.

The realization came as a jolt and I made a mistake. Annoyed, for I was normally very careful, I asked Gaufredus for the knife to scrape the parchment and for a goat's tooth to smooth it. He wrapped a finger around a curl in his beard and drew his thick dark eyebrows down but did not speak until I asked for both again. "Did Amatus's visit upset you, Bernfrieda?" Brother Gaufredus asked. He held his quill in midair and looked at me.

I hesitated, but I saw no harm in telling him what was on my mind. Nothing that happened at the Abbey escaped Brother Gaufredus anyway.

"Brother Amatus never even asked about my Lady's early years."

"Why should he?" Brother Gaufredus put down his quill, leaned back in his chair and massaged his forehead with inky fingers. "The past is interesting only when it foreshadows greatness. The only greatness in your Lady's life is the fact that she is the mother of our beloved Duke, and this fact Amatus will record. Why should a chronicler be interested in your Lady's past beyond that?"

"You do not know my Lady, Brother Gaufredus," I said. "You have never even talked to her. Aren't the seeds of her children's heroics in her past too?"

He shrugged. "You mean in their father's past, Bernfrieda. We all know that Tancred killed a wild boar with a single thrust of his sword when he was just a boy."

"But they are also part of Senda," I said. "She too was their teacher."

"What can a mother teach a male child?" He gestured toward the bleeding Agatha. "Did your Lady perform saintly deeds? Has she been a paragon of piety? What can a woman do that her children's children would want to read about?" He shook his head. "You have learned your letters well — yet after all the time you spent here with me, you still can't sort out what is important from what isn't. If you feel there is something notable about your Lady's past, embroider it on your tapestry, Bernfrieda."

He too does not think Senda important beyond the fact that she is the mother of Robert Guiscard and the wife of Tancred of Hauteville. Brother Gaufredus picked up his quill and began to work. I started to correct my mistake, scraping gingerly with the knife lest I cut into the parchment. *Had Senda been saintly she may not have had the same children, or any children at all for that matter. Apulia would be ruled by someone else, and Amatus would not have his task. How can Brother Gaufredus be so sure that Senda's grandchildren would be interested only in saintly deeds? Saints' lives are dull. Even the gore of martyrs' deaths becomes tiresome. I know it well, for all that Brother Gaufredus has ever allowed me to copy have been the lives of female saints.*

I will record what happened — but not on my tapestry! No matter how faithful the colors, how careful the stitching, embroidery yields only stick figures. How can I portray the haughtiness of Senda's mother, Lady Mathilda, on cloth? How can I describe with thread what I felt when I saw her ride by my father's side? No, not with a needle but with my quill I will record Senda's story!

I stopped, and looked in Gaufredus's direction. I felt so excited I almost told him.

"What now, Bernfrieda?" He pursed his thin lips so that the corners of his mouth turned downward. I shook my head and lowered my eyes again, pretending to have trouble erasing the *f* that looked too much like an *s*.

He loves writing but he would not understand. I can almost hear his mocking words: "You? Write a chronicle? Oh, that would be perfect, Bernfrieda! Why don't you write a Chanson *instead?" He'd roar with laughter and then he would scold me. "If God intended women to write he would have set up the world differently. Don't forget God made you from a rib, Bernfrieda, not exactly the site of a man's intellectual gifts!"*

I won't write a Chanson de Geste, *but I can write a chronicle. My goal will be modest: to tell what happened so that Senda's children's children may know what will be left out by Amatus and the other chroniclers.*

I could barely control the desire to run back to Senda's room. *I will tell my half-sister that I'm bored with my wax tablets and need some parchment. She'll tease me, but she'll buy all the parchment I need from the man who supplies the Abbey. I'll write as often as I can before I come to the scriptorium. And when I finish, I shall ask Senda to have these loose sheets of vellum bound into a codex and have her ask the Abbot to preserve it.*

Time changes everything. Perhaps all that Senda and I know so well today will be forgotten tomorrow. My manuscript will be as mysterious to those future eyes as the writings of the ancients are to us today. I must strive to make everything plain.

No one knows better than I what happened then, and what was in my half-sister's heart and mind. Didn't I spend my whole life watching her?

DUCHY OF NORMANDY
997-1057

In 829 the Frankish bishops, while remaining intransigent on monogamy, declaring that a man might have only one partner, were prepared to tolerate concubinage as a poor substitute for full marriage. They could hardly do otherwise if they did not want to destroy society and there were advantages to this dual system. Precepts could be applied more flexibly. A priest might be refused a wife but allowed to keep a concubine. A noble might drop his concubine in order to contract a "lawful marriage" and yet not commit bigamy.

— Georges Duby, transl. Barbara Bray: *The Knight, the Lady, and the Priest*

CAPUT II

The Abbey of Santa Eufemia
On the eve of the Feast of Saint Justin Martyr (April 14)
In this year 1061 from the Incarnation of our Lord
The words of Bernfrieda

Granville, 997

Massive and forlorn, Father's wooden tower stood on a small promontory overlooking the English Channel. The wood of the tower and the palisade that surrounded it had weathered to a silvery grey by the time I was born. From the sea, and from the green river valley on the other side, the keep looked like a great hawk resting on its pole after the hunt. The Viking Rollo gave the land to Haremar, my father's father, shortly after he led our people south to Normandy from the homeland in the North. Haremar built his square tower upon a large mound and dug a deep moat as a further defense. Haremar boasted that no enemy could ever take Granville, and he was never proven wrong. The promontory jutted into the sea and was connected to the Cotentin by a thin strip of land, which made it easy to guard and defend. A well, dug within the palisade, supplied the keep with clean drinking water.

The older knights often told of the long siege by an angry neighbor. Haremar and his men had slipped out of the tower one night and taken the enemy's son. A truce ensued and then peace, sealed by Haremar's marriage to the neighbor's dark-eyed daughter Geva. After his marriage Haremar enlarged his keep by adding a courtyard surrounded by a fortified wooden fence. His married knights built their quarters within the compound, as had the smith, the carpenter and other skilled workers. Most of the animals left the main hall, too, housed in stables and in the peasants' huts, though Haremar's stallion continued to share the hall with us until it died.

Haremar's son and heir was my father Mauger. My mother, Alsinda, was the illegitimate daughter of one of Haremar's brothers. They grew up together, and my father took Alsinda to his bed when she was twelve and he fifteen. He had two sons by her and then me. I remember little of my early childhood, but I do remember that my mother laughed often. I was awed by my father, who did not come home to our cottage in the bailey at night like other fathers. I knew my father was the most important person in the keep after Lord Haremar, and that no one ever crossed him. I used to envy my two older brothers, for he always kept them by his side and spoke to them often. Sometimes, my mother and I were invited to join my father on the dais in the great hall. I cherished those occasions because I felt important. Even the visiting priest tolerated my mother and father's illegitimate union, but Haremar had other plans. A few months before he died, when I was five, my grandfather negotiated with a neighbor lord for a bride for his son.

One late spring night, I woke up at the sound of my mother crying, and heard my father say that his marriage to Lady Mathilda would not change anything. I was surprised that Father came to our cottage instead of summoning mother to the keep. Lady Mathilda's name became etched in my mind. I listened carefully after that, whenever her name was mentioned. I understood that Lady Mathilda was to come to live with us and sleep in my father's bed. There was such excitement about this event among the people in the keep that my curiosity was heightened.

Father and his men went hunting from dawn to dusk for days, to provide fresh game for the wedding. For the first time since Lady Geva's death two years before, the great hall was swept of debris and a mountain of dry straw and grass was burned in the bailey. I followed the women to the woods down the hill and helped carry fresh reeds and leaves for the floor. Servants sprinkled the hall with lavender and thyme from the garden. The cooks were busy for days, adapting Lady Geva's recipes for soups and stews to serve at the wedding feast.

I was standing in the bailey at my mother's side one summer afternoon when the new bride arrived. The open kitchens were located in several wooden huts that adjoined the keep. The aroma of game roasting on spits and bread baking in the ovens mingled with that of fresh hay, and overcame for once the stench of dung that always hung in the bailey.

Lady Mathilda's blond hair was kept in place by a golden circlet and fell loosely on her back. Her red mantle fell in rich folds around her body and over the flanks of her white mare, which kept pace with Father's black stallion and didn't miss a step. She turned toward us as she passed, and the setting sun made her hair look like red gold. *She is like a little sun herself!* I was suddenly conscious of how I looked. The dark coloring I had inherited from Lady Geva seemed as ugly to me as did my drab brown tunic. More than anything at that moment, I wished I could be close to Lady Mathilda, touch her hair, feel her clothes.

"She is too thin, Alsinda — and so young!" the smith's wife whispered to Mother. "Why, she can't be more than twelve. She won't last the first lying in!" I looked at Mother, but she did not reply. Her face white, she stood rigid as Father and his bride went by. Perhaps she sensed that Father already was taken with his bride and that nothing ever would be the same. In any case, the smith's wife was proven wrong, for Lady Mathilda gave Father three children: Adeliza, less than a year after their marriage;

Fredesenda, two years later; and Mauger, Father's namesake and heir, almost six years later.

That day, as we followed the bride and groom into the great hall, I purposely fell behind my mother. When I was sure she was not watching, I inched toward my father. Because I was so small, I easily squeezed through the crowd and finally stood only a few feet from him and his bride. They were sitting on the two oaken chairs on the dais surrounded by knights, vassals, ladies-in-waiting, and servants. Though I knew I was not to address him so in public, I whispered, "Father." As he did not seem to hear me, I raised my voice. "Father!" I called. He turned toward me then, and frowned, staring at me as if he did not know who I was. Stricken, I looked away from him and realized I was surrounded by strangers.

Lady Mathilda, who had been talking to the ladies standing behind her, turned toward me. She stared at me for a moment — the corners of her shapely lips turned downward, her blue-green eyes unsmiling — as if I were the runt in a litter of pigs. Lady Mathilda raised her eyebrow then, glanced at my father and turned to her Lady-in-waiting, whispering something.

"Take the child away and make sure she does not come back," Father ordered. Someone took me by the arm and dragged me toward the entrance. I sat on the dirt, just outside the hall, hugging my knees and shaking, cold in spite of the mild summer evening. Later Mother found me. As we walked to our cottage, she scolded me for leaving her side.

"Father does not like me," I said. "He sent me away."

Mother did not look at me. "You had no business going to him, Bernfrieda. Your father was busy." She turned and entered the cottage. This further betrayal was more than I could bear, and I started to cry and didn't go inside. She came to me then and held me tightly. I buried my head against her soft breasts, comforted by her scent of smoke, garlic and sweat. I realized she also was crying: my father had hurt her too.

Father did not come to see us for a long time, at least until Lady Mathilda was heavy with child. After that he returned often to see my mother. Mother stopped smiling and shunned the visiting priest when he came, for she understood full well, as I soon did, that she was in mortal sin now that Father was married. He still favored my brothers, and they were with him as often as before, but I stayed away. I did not want to be near him or the new bride whom I perceived to be the cause of my father's change. He never asked for me. When he came to the cottage I left, and made sure that he was gone before returning home. I found a small hiding place in the hall behind a huge beam that rose to meet the rafters. From there I had a good view of the dais, the wooden platform where my father sat with his wife and their little Adeliza. Often, I would huddle there watching them hungrily, thinking of the times my mother and I had sat by him.

After Fredesenda was born, Lady Mathilda summoned Mother and me to the keep to serve her. We had to leave our cottage and sleep in her antechamber. I was to help with the baby while my mother was given the meanest chores — helping wash dirty linens, scouring the grease and soot from the pans in the kitchen, emptying the chamber pots. Lady Mathilda hardly spoke to us. Mother could never please her. In the evenings, I would huddle with Mother on my pallet and pretend we were still at the cottage, shutting out the long hours of chores that awaited us during the day. Of all the changes Lady Mathilda brought to my life, being separated from Mother during the day was the most painful and the hardest to accept. But accept we did, for there was no recourse. "He won't cross his Lady, Bernfrieda," Mother said one night. "Nothing will ever be as it was!"

I was eight at the time. It took me two years to accept my mother's words. I felt sure my father didn't know about our suffering, so one day I resolved to speak to him. I knew that he walked through the bailey to the stables after breakfast, so one day I waited for him just outside the hall. "Father!" I whispered, realizing I had not spoken to him since the day of his wedding. *Please O please Father let everything go back to the way it was before.* He glared at me, like that other time. I almost turned and ran, but then I thought of Mother.

"What is it, Bernfrieda?" he asked. "You know I am busy."

"It is just — O father, I hardly see Mother anymore and Lady Mathilda has so many things for us to do and is never happy with our work and Mother is sad and she cries every night —" He stopped me with a gesture.

"Lady Mathilda knows what needs to be done in the house, Bernfrieda. She is in charge there. Everyone must work hard so we may prosper. You and your mother must do your share. You can't cling to your mother's skirts, Bernfrieda. Look at your brothers — they both work hard, they serve my dinner, follow me in the hunt, take care of my horse — yet they do not complain! Do not ever bother me with this again." He turned and walked away. I never called him Father again.

The baby Fredesenda had a large mouth, flat nose and a long thin body. Watching her in the cradle, swaddled tightly so that only her unsmiling eyes could move, I wondered how she could be so homely. When I realized that she did not please her mother or father, I began to like her. Soon she became the only source of joy during my days, for Senda loved me from the start. Shortly after she was three, Senda's nurse died and she took to sleeping with Mother and me.

After Senda was born, Lady Mathilda changed. Not yet sixteen, she took to wearing long dark tunics that accentuated her pallor and boniness. She became devout. I often saw her on her wooden *priedieu*, frowning slightly, her eyes closed. The tiny chapel she had built in her chamber had become her refuge.

When the visiting priest came, she spent hours closeted with him in her room. I sat with my mother outside the circle of women who crowded around the large brazier in winter, listening to Father Raoul as he preached. He always ate before he did so, and the fat from the roasted pork he favored made rivulets down his beard and stained his black robe. When he finished, he would wipe his mouth with his hand as he peered at the crowd of women, unsmiling. The oldest laundresses, Pega and Sieburge, would flinch and exchange glances as he trailed his greasy hand across the front of his robe. Lady Mathilda would spend her day listening to him, and she made my mother stay and listen too.

The first time that happened was the day after Mother and I were made to leave our cottage and move to the antechamber. Before that, Mother shunned the priest when he came to Granville. But that day, I was sitting by my mother away from the warmth of the brazier, for Lady Mathilda's women had crowded us out. Father Raoul peered at us as he preached about the Ninth Commandment. I could barely follow what he was saying, but I knew my mother was uneasy. She fidgeted on her bench, glancing in the direction of the stairs.

"And do you know what is going to happen to those who defy God's law?" he asked in a terrible voice. I huddled closer to my mother and realized she was trembling.

"Think of the last burning you saw — the nauseating stink when the hair catches on fire, the way the eyes explode, the scorching heat that devours the flesh but does not kill right away. Imagine the pain, and now imagine suffering it for eternity." He glared at my mother. "That is what awaits you, Alsinda, if you do not change your ways!"

There were beads of sweat on my mother's forehead and her hand was clammy. I hated Father Raoul. I couldn't understand why God wasn't angry with my mother before Lady Mathilda arrived. In my mind, she was the one who should burn. At night my mother had nightmares. She cried in her sleep while I clung to her. To this day if I close my eyes I see the black terror in her dark eyes.

This scene was repeated often, up until the time my mother died in childbirth, six years later. I grew up hating the priest and all he stood for. God was an alien being who hated my mother and was going to let her burn for eternity. How could I love Him? I learned to disguise my feelings and stay away from the priest as much as possible.

My mother died in autumn, two months before I turned fourteen. The morning she died Lady Mathilda called Pega and bade her gather all the filthy linen and clothing and go down to the river. Mother was part of the laundry team; she was not as strong as the other laundresses but she was very good at getting rid of food stains, which she treated with a mixture she had

learned from Lady Geva. I watched that day as Mother asked
Pega to be excused. Pega's large face was sympathetic, but Lady
Mathilda overheard Mother's plea.

"We all have our duties, Alsinda." She stood up from her
chair and walked toward Mother, taking in the swollen belly.
"Pega and the other women need help." She turned away. "Had
you listened to Father Raoul, Alsinda, there would be no need
for this conversation."

I stood up from the circle where I was holding Senda and
walked up to Lady Mathilda.

"I beg you my Lady, please let me take my mother's place today." My throat was so dry that the words came out as a hoarse
whisper. Senda's mother looked at me, as if considering my offer,
then shook her head.

"It is clear that watching Senda is not enough work for you
now that she is older. I am glad you brought it to my attention,
Bernfrieda. From now on you'll help Ragnhild with her cheese
making. Report to her immediately. You can still look after my
daughter while you make yourself useful."

Mother wobbled after Pega. Senda followed me in silence as I
led her to the shed by the stables where the cheese was made. A
steady, icy drizzle began to fall. Inside the shed a great brazier
filled with coals kept the enclosure warm. When we stopped to
eat, I begged Ragnhild to let me go to my mother. She said that
I could leave as soon as I finished so I kept working, cutting
large squares from finely woven linen cloth and forming them
into pouches. Then I tied the pouches to a pole that hung hori-
zontally over large wooden troughs, and filled each one with
milk. This process allowed the whey to separate from the curd,
and made the soft sweet cheese that Lady Mathilda favored for
breakfast mixed with just a little honey.

I worked as fast as I could. Senda tried to help. While I finished tying a pouch, she took the large iron scissors and tried to
cut the next square, and ruined it. I scolded her. Hugging her
arms, Senda marched into a corner and sat down. I paid no attention to her, for the men kept pouring fresh milk into the
wooden barrel by my side. It took most of the afternoon to fin-

ish. As soon as I was done I left Senda with Ragnhild and flew down the hill.

The women were rinsing the last of the laundry in the river. The wooden troughs where the laundry was soaked in wood ashes and caustic soda were empty. The sticks the women had used to beat the linen tablecloth and sheets were carefully heaped by the troughs. I saw Mother in the distance, bent over a rock, alongside the others, her elbows deep in the icy water. I knelt by her side and touched her cheek. She turned slowly, her lips bluish and her face red from the cold.

I took a step back. Mother acted as if she had had too much wine. She gave a silly laugh and her lips cracked. Blood began to trickle over her chin. I helped her get up and held her arm to steady her.

"Pega, oh Pega, let me take her place!"

Sieburge, and Himiltrude, who had grown up with Mother, looked up with sympathy, their hands in the icy water. Rozala, who had come to Granville with Lady Mathilda, fished out the sheet she had been rinsing and began to squeeze the water out.

Pega hesitated, glanced at the women and then at Mother, and nodded. As I stepped up toward the water, Mother put her hand on my arm as if to hold me back. She opened her mouth to speak, and fell to the ground. I knelt at her side and called her, rubbing her hands between mine to revive her.

"Sieburge, Himiltrude!" Pega called, and rushed to Mother's side.

Sieburge put her strong arm under Mother and began to lift her; Himiltrude gripped Mother's knees.

"She is bleeding, look how she is bleeding!" Himiltrude screamed. Blood had soaked through the back of Mother's brown tunic.

"Rozala!" Pega called to the last laundress, "Put wings under your feet and fetch Aelis! We'll take her to the stables."

"Aren't we taking her to the keep?" Sieburge asked.

Pega shook her head. "She is losing too much blood; she will be better off in the stables . . . and she has no friends at the keep." I felt numb. Aelis was the midwife; but the baby was not due for another two months. "It will be born on your birthday, Bernfrieda," Mother had promised. "Give me your hand!" She put my hand over her side to feel the baby kick, and smiled. "It won't be so lonely when the baby comes," she had murmured.

Pega hastily spread out some hay and made a pallet by throwing a mantle over it. Over and over I cried my mother's name. Rozala arrived with Aelis, who rubbed Mother's hands with vinegar, and she revived.

"Too soon, Aelis," she whispered to the woman who had helped bring forth the three of us. Aelis shook her head and muttered something.

"Bern . . . frieda!" Mother whispered. I rushed to her side. "Don't . . . not like me." She sighed and closed her eyes.

"Pega!" Aelis called as she took the meat hook from her pouch. I knew the baby was dead. She motioned to Sieburge who took me firmly by the arm and marched me out through the wooden doors. Mother screamed once and I turned to run back. Sieburge tightened her grip on my arm but I tore free.

The stench of blood, urine and feces hung over the stall where my mother lay dead. Even her black hair was matted and bloodied. Her eyes were half-closed. Next to her, the midwife was shaking her head. Then she put her tools away, and stepped around the pool of blood.

"No point in waiting," Lady Mathilda said when she was informed. "Alsinda was in mortal sin and Father Raoul can do nothing for her." They wrapped Mother in a rough brown sackcloth, placing the baby the midwife had cut out of her body over her breast. I was the only one to follow the two serfs who buried her later that same day.

Mother was buried on the hill behind the keep in an unmarked grave. No one spoke of her. Not Father or my brothers, whom I rarely saw, nor Rozala, Sieburge, Pega or the other women. Often, during those first few weeks after her death, I felt like screaming at all those calm faces. It was as if she had never lived.

I noticed that Senda too was lonely. Her parents doted on her older sister Adeliza, who was uncommonly pretty. But her out-

ward grace was not reflected in her character; she taunted Senda
often. This realization strengthened my bond with Senda — until I realized that she still saw me as a servant.

I had trouble sleeping that winter. The pallet I shared with
Senda lay against the right wall, on the side closest to Lady
Mathilda's chamber. Adeliza and Mabille slept across from us,
on the left. Three more pallets lined each side and accommo-
dated the other women. Often I lay with my eyes open listening
to the women's breathing as Senda slept next to me, only a few
months since my mother had been by my side.

One night in the middle of winter, Father visited Lady
Mathilda for the first time since my mother's death. He left the
door to her chamber ajar and tremulous light and resinous
smoke from the torch he brought with him filtered into our
darkened antechamber.

Their voices soon were raised in anger.

The noise awakened Senda, who sat up. Her mother's voice
was shrill, more piercing than usual. I too sat up in the semi-
darkness and pulled Senda close. Within moments the door
burst open, and Father strode out yelling that he would have the
priest hanged when he came again. His short mantle brushed
against Senda as he made his way to the narrow wooden steps
that led to the hall, but he did not see her. Senda shivered, and I
pulled a sheepskin over her shoulders. She began to cry. "Will
Father burn in hell, Bernfrieda? Will his whores and bastards
seal his fate?" She had heard what her mother was screaming.

I stiffened. "Oh, she did not mean you, Bernfrieda. You were
born before my father's wedding. Even Father Raoul said it was
not a mortal sin."

"Father loved my mother."

"How could Father love a servant, Bernfrieda?"

I looked at her, stricken.

"Oh, Bernfrieda! You are not a servant, not really — you have
my father's blood —"

"So did she." I wrapped the coverlet tighter around my shoulders. "He laughed when he was with her."

Senda sighed. "Father never laughs when he is with Mother,"

"He continued to see my mother even after his marriage, though he knew that then it was a mortal sin," I whispered.

"That is why the whore died." Adeliza hissed. Her words burnt like hot tar. She propped herself up on her elbow, lifted her chin and looked down her nose, the way her mother did when Father forced her to attend a drunken feast. "Mother said that was the reason your mother could not bring forth another live child. Her death was a punishment for her sins, and she is burning in hell."

🌿 🌿 🌿

Father had loved my mother. I clung to that thought. He continued to see her after his marriage — discreetly at first, openly later — often summoning her during the day. But he did not defend her from Lady Mathilda's anger. He never crossed his wife when she dealt with the servants. Was that how he saw my mother after all? Or was she a pawn in his struggle with Lady Mathilda?

That night we witnessed the first of many quarrels. I held Senda close when I heard him coming, and kept my eyes shut until he went away. I believed then that Lady Mathilda had changed toward Father because she could not forgive him for loving Mother. I shut my eyes also to the respect with which he always treated Mathilda in public and to the fact that he trusted her judgement in all household matters. Even when I learned the true reason for their fights, I still needed to believe he loved my mother.

Lady Mathilda had asked Father not to sleep with her any more. After all, she had conceived three children and given him a healthy heir. Marriage was above all a spiritual union, Father Raoul had told her. I believed that Father simply wanted to spite his wife with his frequent visits. How could I have accepted then that it was Lady Mathilda he really loved and desired?

It was during one of the loudest quarrels that I resolved never to love a man. I made sure that I was with Senda or with another woman whenever I had to run errands for Lady Mathilda. I shunned the young knights who had begun to smile at me. It was difficult, especially after they were drunk at special feasts, but my brothers watched over me, even though they rarely acknowledged me in the hall. When my mother and I still lived in the cottage, they often came to see us at night. They would sit in the room, hardly speaking, and they never stayed long. Armand, the oldest, brought us food; Henry, who liked to carve, often fashioned wooden dolls and birds for me. He even carved a falcon's head on the side of my pallet one day and laughed when I clapped with delight. It became a habit for me to trace the bird with my finger before I fell asleep. After we moved to Lady Mathilda's antechamber, we rarely saw them. After her chores were done, Mother used to creep into the hall to get a glimpse of them.

I never thought they paid any special attention to me until one day after Lent when the cooks had gone out of their way to provide a feast for the household. I was fifteen then. My decision about men kept me close to the other women. There was much drunkenness and joking among the knights in the hall; Father did nothing to curb it. Then Lady Mathilda rose from her chair.

"Where are you going?"

She looked down at Father, her lips turned down. "To my chamber, Mauger. I am tired."

"I am tired, Mauger." Father mimicked. She turned to go. We rose to follow her, but Father stopped us with a gesture.

"Oh no, Mathilda," he chided, "*you* may go with the children and the hags." Pointing at Mabille and Pega, he said, "But the girls stay!" His knights applauded. Mauger roared with laughter.

Mathilda tried to argue, but in the end she could only gather the children and leave.

Slowly I sat down again with the other maids. One by one, they were claimed by Father's knights. The unwilling cried and tried to resist, but that only increased the merriment of the men. One of the younger knights, Alferio, staggered toward me. He pushed away the girl by my side and straddled the bench.

He pawed at my right breast. "Come," he said in a thick voice. "Smile at me, Bernfrieda."

I shoved him away but he pushed me down against the bench. I could hear the men laughing. I kept struggling; Alferio slapped me hard across the face. My mouth filled with blood.

Suddenly his weight was lifted from me. Henry held Alferio's hair from behind and was pulling him backwards. Then he was slamming Alferio's face against the table, over and over again.

I called him — "Henry! Henry!" He stopped and let Alferio go. Alferio tried to stand, then doubled over, vomiting. His nose was broken, and his front teeth.

My lips were swelling; yet I felt a curious mixture of elation and disgust.

"Leave Bernfrieda alone," Henry hissed to Alferio, "or I will kill you next time."

I felt dizzy; Henry's brown tunic mingled with Alferio's saffron leggings, the green of Father's mantle and the surprised wine-reddened faces of the older knights in the background. Father exploded in long peals of laughter, and soon the hall filled with yells and taunts, and merrymaking resumed.

"Go upstairs now, Bernfrieda," Henry whispered. "Quickly. Father won't mind."

Mauger was kissing Enid, the young servant girl who poured the wine. Quickly I turned and ran to the safety of Lady Mathilda's chamber.

After that night, I treasured the knowledge that Henry cared for me, that I was important to him.

Years passed, one like the other. Father sent young Mauger to the household of his overlord, the Bishop of Coutances, to train. Lady Mathilda grew more and more devout, and Adeliza more spiteful.

Senda was growing up. Lady Mathilda's women had often told her that she would change when her flux began, become prettier, like Adeliza. Senda awaited anxiously for that to happen, and when it did in the summer shortly before her twelfth birthday, she could hardly contain her excitement. She fidgeted all morning as she worked at the loom in her mother's chamber, longing to run to the quiet pool by the river, where she could study her reflection while the women washed the clothes.

Adeliza arched her brows several times that bright summer morning while watching her sister.

When she could, Senda ran straight to the river. When she bent to see whether she had changed as we told her she had, Adeliza managed to slither behind her. Senda recoiled, but Adeliza grabbed her neck and forced her to lean over again, her face next to Senda's. There was a struggle. Senda turned her face to one side. Adeliza pushed her toward the water. Senda did not fall in, but bruised her cheek against the bank. Adeliza laughed. "You should thank me Senda, for now there is color on your face."

When I think of what I saw by the river that day, I think also of my young self, kneeling at my mother's grave, crying because I couldn't remember her face.

Between two castellans, though a technical relation of Lord and vassal might exist, it was never one of domination and dependence. Between a castellan and a knight, it was: the knight was legally and socially inferior. Yet his subordination at that time and place was typically moderate. Usually he still owned some land outright and did not depend on land granted by the Lord.

— Frances Gies: *The Knight in History*

CAPUT III

The Abbey of Santa Eufemia
On the eve of the Feast of Saint Leonidas, Martyr (April 22)
In this year 1061 from the Incarnation of our Lord
The words of Bernfrieda

How curious that people live in my mind as they were at a specific time in their lives, not necessarily as they were the last time I saw them. Adeliza, for example, is always fifteen when I think of her. Father Raoul never aged in my memory either, though I have seen him in old age.

Guillaume I remember as the youth with raven-black lashes who captured Senda's heart. At fourteen he had an intense face with eyes that the light, and his mood, could turn dark and black or light and green. When he talked to someone he weighed each word, be the subject light or serious, and never spoke until his interlocutor had said all he meant to say. This patience earned him many friends and a reputation for wisdom well beyond his years. His smile was sudden, a rare reward, an affirmation that a thousand words would not accord to the speaker. He was not tall, just a hair more than Senda and — unlike most other knight apprentices of his age — his skin was unblemished.

Words are flowing on my parchment. It is late and I should go to bed, yet I cannot. The bundle of candles is within reach. I cannot stop now. Memories are too pressing.

Granville, 1014

Senda liked Guillaume from the time he arrived at Father's house to train, even though she was months younger than his seven years. She soon started following him everywhere, to the great merriment of Father's knights. She followed him in the great hall where he helped the servants set the trestle tables for dinner. She followed him into the bailey where he was learning to groom the horses. She soon realized, however, that she was being watched. Soon, she learned it was prudent to follow him only with her eyes.

It took Guillaume years to do the same.

Often when Guillaume was training, Senda would stroll on the drawbridge that linked the tower with the bailey and sit on the wooden planks, feet dangling over the brownish-yellow moat, apparently engrossed in the frogs swimming in the water. When she thought herself unnoticed, she watched Guillaume charge the dummy in the middle of the bailey with his lance or practice with the sword against another apprentice knight.

Adeliza soon understood that Senda was in love.

One summer day she strolled on the drawbridge with her women, Mabille and Pega, and waved gaily at Senda as she passed. Senda's love was dueling with Alferio that day. Guillaume was solidly built and very strong; he earned his nickname, *Bras-de-Fer* (Iron Arm) then and it remained with him until his death.

Holding his sword broadside with both hands, Guillaume hit his adversary flat on the chest. The wind knocked out of him, Alferio stumbled and fell. Guillaume paused to give him time to recover.

"Guillaume, watch out!" Senda screamed as Alferio threw a handful of dirt aimed at Guillaume's eyes. Guillaume leapt aside, then with a fearful roar, swooped over Alferio and put his foot on his neck. Adeliza, Mabille and Pega cheered.

"Well done, Guillaume!" Adeliza shouted, clapping her hands. His face was flushed when he took off the leather helmet and face guard. His hazel eyes gleamed; he shook out his straight brown hair, and bowed his head quickly in her direction.

"Thank you, Lady Adeliza," he said, looking past her to the bridge, where Senda was holding her hands tightly clasped against her chest. He smiled then.

Adeliza gathered her mantle and turned away. Her lips pursed, she made her way to the tower, followed by her women. As she passed on the drawbridge, Senda dropped her an exaggerated curtsy. Looking straight ahead, Adeliza quickened her pace so that her women had to break into a run to keep up. Then they disappeared under the raised portcullis.

☙ ☙ ☙

The summer was short and hot that year. After practicing, the younger men often swam in the river upstream from the women who were laundering. One day, Guillaume did not stay long with his companions, but pulled on his shirt and breeches and left unnoticed to wade downstream till he found Senda.

Later that day, she kept going over her meeting with Guillaume, delighted when she remembered yet another sliver of detail to tell me. She had gathered the hem of her skirts inside her belt and was sitting by the pool, splashing her feet. She was startled when Guillaume came upon her, but she did not cry out. They stared at each other without smiling. Guillaume climbed onto the bank and sat by her. They looked into the pool without speaking, aware that the sudden intimacy changed something between them. She glanced at his profile, then turned away, her cheeks burning. His brown wet hair stuck to his head; his shirt clung to the muscles of his torso.

"Some day I shall go to Italy," he said. "I'll make a fortune with my sword, and then I'll return to Normandy."

"Where is Italy?"

"I am not sure. When I visited my father's house three years ago, a knight came to see him. He said Italy is rich with silver and gold for the taking. The people of Italy do not like to fight, he said. They pay well for protection."

"You will go there, Guillaume?" She turned and looked at him.

"As soon as I finish my training — three — four years, at the most." They watched the water for a little while, listening to the boys shouting in the still afternoon.

"I'll miss you." Senda said. She wanted to sit there with him, her bare feet almost touching his. She was afraid someone would call for her or one of the boys would splash downstream and find them.

"I must leave. I have nothing of my own. My father's land will go to his first-born, Serlo — not that I care," he added quickly. "I would not want Hauteville anyway. I want to travel . . ." He stopped and looked at her. "But I'll come back to Normandy one day."

"What if I am not here? What if my father sends me away?" She did not mention a marriage.

He smiled, and Senda stared, fascinated by his white teeth, slightly crowded in front. No other man in the keep had better. She recalled how her mother's women often said how his flashing smile and long eyelashes were wasted on a boy.

"I'll come for you, wherever you are."

They looked at each other. She put her hand on his.

"Guillaume!" His friends' voices were not far. He jumped up and looked in their direction. "I must go," he said. He smiled at her again before sloshing back up river.

They met other times by the river that summer, knowing full well that they would not have the chance to be alone as soon as the weather turned bad. She came upstairs one day, her face radiant. I knew right away that something had happened.

"What is it, Senda?" I asked. Slowly she opened her hand and showed me a silver brooch. The contours of the etched lion ravaging a deer were almost worn smooth, but the surface was shining as if it had been polished often.

"Guillaume gave it to me," she said. "He will marry me some day, Bernfrieda." She looked up to see my reaction. "After he makes his fortune in Italy."

I shook my head. "It will be years before Guillaume can afford to marry. Look at how many of Father's knights are still not married!"

"Then I'll run away with him. I'll follow him to Italy."

Oh Senda, you'll find out soon that your desires count for nothing! I thought, feeling sad as she blushed prettily.

That fall, Father promised Adeliza to Richard de Walchelin, son of Rollo, whose lands adjoined Father's. As Richard was only eight, seven years Adeliza's junior, they were not formally betrothed. Still, Rollo and his son visited often and Adeliza was flattered by the attention she received as future Lady of her own keep.

Richard was a handsome child. Short for his age and a little overweight, he favored sweetmeats and honeyed pastries, and was much more interested in them than in his betrothed when he came to visit. In spite of his jocund appearance, he had a nasty temper, which he did not bother to conceal. And he was cruel. I discovered it long before Adeliza, for one day I was walking to the stables and caught him tearing at a small fox he had brought back from the hunt.

Richard was kneeling by the animal as it twitched in agony. I saw him turn the fox on its back and slowly tear at its belly with a knife. He gouged one eye out, then the other. He licked his lips as he looked at the bloody, trembling heap. He was so involved in his cruel game that he did not see me approach. When he did, he stood up and smiled, as if challenging me. I turned and ran to the keep.

❧ ❧ ❧

The following Christmas, Richard presented Adeliza with an intricately-wrought gold pin for her mantle. He had received it from one of his father's knights, who had returned from a pilgrimage to the Holy Land. That evening Adeliza came upstairs and sat on her pallet. Showing the pin to Senda, she said, "What do you think of my pin? Isn't it beautiful? Rollo said that I'll have more women than Mother's when Richard and I marry."

"I am glad for you," Senda said. She sat on her pallet so I could undo her braid, and we exchanged a glance.

"Of course Richard is only eight, and insufferable," Senda added. "I hope for your sake that he changes by the time he finally marries you." The soft red-golden mass of her hair fell over her shoulders. She bent her head as I began to comb it.

Adeliza turned red. "What difference does it make whether he changes or not? I'll be mistress of a keep grander than Father's; I'll be received at court in Caen. Could your precious Guillaume offer you as much, even if he could marry you?"

Senda's head jerked up. Adeliza's brown eyes were half-hooded and there was a slight smile on her heart-shaped mouth. "Of course you may not marry at all. Father Raoul told Mother that the nunnery in Fleury would be a perfect place for you." Senda sat very still. I wanted to laugh at Adeliza but I was afraid of her too. Senda sent to the nunnery? What would become of me then?

Adeliza smiled and called Mabille to help her get ready for bed. I dug the bone comb deeper into Senda's hair, forcing myself to follow its steady course to her waist. Later in bed, Senda buried her head on my shoulder. She was trembling. I held her tight. Neither of us slept well that night.

⚜ ⚜ ⚜

When Father Raoul came back, Senda lingered with the other women. She kept glancing at the priest and then at her mother. Anyone could see she was afraid of something — anyone but Lady Mathilda, who was too wrapped up in her devotions.

Adeliza knew. She kept glancing at Senda throughout the day, a half-smile on her lips. *If I could only strike that mouth and make it bleed!*

There were few people Senda disliked more than Father Raoul. She never slept well after his visits, terrified by the visions of hell he could conjure so vividly. He was thin, his black robe stank of sweat and old urine, and his feet were encrusted with dirt. Lady Mathilda herself insisted on washing them, using her precious bar of Castilian lavender soap. She called on a different woman to help her each time, but she was the one that gently lifted each filthy foot, lovingly wiping it with her soapy hands. Father Raoul would close his eyes and smile. The dirt slowly melted under her methodic wiping while the water in the basin turned black. She had a servant change the water twice, and took her time before she finally called for a soft linen towel. There was an animation about her that we rarely saw when the priest was not there.

That morning Lady Mathilda called on Senda to assist her with the washing of the priest's feet. Senda paled when she heard her name. Father Raoul sat in Lady Mathilda's chair, his feet in a shallow basin of warm water. With an expectant smile on his grimy face, he waited for the weekly ritual to begin.

Lady Mathilda lifted Father Raoul's foot, hesitated, then looked at her daughter. "Take my place this time, Senda," she said reluctantly. "I shall assist you."

Senda froze. She feared she would vomit. Could her own mother not see that? When Lady Mathilda handed her the soap, she shook her head. Her mother stood still, staring at her.

"Do as you are told! Our Lord Jesus washed the feet of beggars. Are you better than He?"

Senda shook her head again. Her lips pressed together, her eyes fixed to the rushes on the floor.

"You are a willful one," Father Raoul frowned. "It is clear that your pious lessons have not touched this child's heart, my Lady." His voice became rich and rose as it did during his sermons. "This child needs more than your loving guidance, my Lady, for her soul is hard and there are only pride and willfulness in her heart. I beg you to consider the nunnery for her. The Abbess of Fleury might still succeed in teaching her the humility she lacks."

Senda looked like a doe surrounded by hunters. "Do not send me there, Mother!"

Lady Mathilda looked at her daughter with distaste, and pushed her away. She knelt in front of the priest. "Watch! You may have to do this often at the convent." She began the ritual of washing Father Raoul's feet.

She kept Senda by her side all morning, releasing her only to go to confession. When the time for supper came, I had to take Senda's hand and steady her down the steps into the hall. She sat by me at the lower table, as she often did, since she was never missed at the high table. I smoothed the tendrils that always escaped her thick, golden-red braid.

"Here, Senda, eat this." I took a spoonful of the *blanc-manger* a servant had ladled into our bread trencher and brought it to her lips. Father favored that dish, prepared with Lady Geva's recipe, chicken paste blended with millet and boiled in almond milk, seasoned with honey and garnished with fried almonds and anise. It was much simpler and more satisfying than Lady Mathilda's elaborate version, the one reserved for special feasts. On those occasions, Lady Mathilda's cook cut the chicken breasts into small pieces — rather than pounding them in a paste — boiled them quickly, fried them in lard and finally simmered them in a white sauce of almond milk, rose water and millet flavored with cinnamon, nutmeg and coriander.

Senda turned her face from the food, but the scent of anise was hard to resist. She took a bite. I watched as she cleaned the bread trencher, and even started to nibble its edges. I too brought a spoonful to my lips, but the dish reminded me of the times when my grandmother, Lady Geva, insisted I sit by her side and share her trencher.

"Even Lady Mathilda cannot send you to the nunnery without Father's approval," I told Senda as the servants were clearing the table. "And he may well have other plans for you."

"Father never crosses Mother," she said.

I could not kill Senda's hopes. "He hates Father Raoul, Senda. Remember?"

"He has often threatened that he will bar the gate in his face." Senda brightened.

I nodded. But Father Raoul always found his way in. Father may have hated him, but he, too, was afraid for his soul. That day the priest was sitting between Lady Mathilda and Adeliza at the high table. Father, who sat to Lady Mathilda's left, was engrossed in his conversation with his guest, Lord Rollo de Walchelin. Richard had chosen to sit by young Mauger, who was home for a short stay, rather than by Adeliza. The two boys had placed Lady Mathilda's favorite monkey between them and were feeding it chunks of food from their trencher.

The lower tables were set on the dirt floor, among the rushes, and extended from each end of Father's table. Senda and I were sitting at the left end, well out of Father's hearing. The meal was almost over and the white linen tablecloths were stained with wine and littered with food. Father's hounds were growling and snapping over a piece of roasted hare. The sudden flapping of wings caught everyone's attention. Father's hooded falcon had again lost its balance. Guillaume raised the *T* shaped stick on which the grey falcon normally perched, to help the bird regain it. In a moment all went back to normal and Guillaume stood again behind my father, his eyes fixed on the bird.

Even if Father had other plans for her, they wouldn't include Guillaume. He was poor, the second son of a knight of modest means. *Oh if I could only help you, Senda,* I thought. *But I am as powerless as you are.*

❧ ❧ ❧

Weeks passed, and then months; yet Lady Mathilda did not mention the nunnery. Senda lived from day to day, like a condemned prisoner awaiting execution. Her mother never asked her again to help when Father Raoul came to visit, but made sure she stayed in her chamber all day. During the rest of the week, life went on as usual. Lady Mathilda spent her time supervising the servants and instructing Adeliza and Senda about housekeeping. She was mainly concerned about Adeliza, since her oldest daughter would be Lady of an important keep some day.

Since my main duties revolved around Senda, I often joined them. At times, however, I was assigned to heavier labor. Lady Mathilda took her daughters to the kitchens, showed them how to teach her recipes to the cooks and make sure they would follow them faithfully. She took them with her when she supervised the seasonal tasks, drying the meat or storing the grain. She alone had the keys to the larder, and she made sure her daughters understood how important it was for a Lady to know all that was used in her house. She took them with her to watch as we other women sheared the sheep, washed the fleece and carded the wool with thistles. Adeliza and Senda sat with us and combed, spun and weaved the wool. When the carts delivered flax to the keep, Lady Mathilda divided the women in teams. We steeped, washed and beat the flax and then wove it into linen. Senda and Adeliza joined us when it was time to dye the bolts of cloth with woad, madder or vermilion. She made sure they could weave a mantle and sew a tunic, shirt or linen drawers so they could properly instruct servant girls. Adeliza and Senda were by her side when she supervised the cleaning of the rushes. Unlike other keeps, where the same rushes were often kept more than one year, the floor of our hall was swept clean and then strewn with clean hay and foliage every autumn. During the year Lady Mathilda made sure the servants removed all debris they could, and that they sprinkled dried herbs to overpower the stench of the rotting food and animal feces in the rushes.

Senda changed. Slender now, rather than thin, her height had become an asset. Her golden-red hair, which she kept in the maiden's fashion, fell in a thick braid below her waist. Beautiful she wasn't, not even pretty, like Adeliza, yet she was striking and people began to notice her — including Father.

Shortly before her fourteenth birthday, Senda and I were preparing to leave her mother's chamber. Lady Mathilda was kneeling on the wooden *priedieu* near her bed and did not hear Father enter. He stood leaning by the door looking at her, his arms folded against his chest. Finally he cleared his throat and walked to the chair by the brazier. He sat down, stretched his long legs toward the coals and unfastened his short mantle.

Lady Mathilda jumped up like a hare when she heard him, then stood by the *priedieu* without speaking. Senda and I waited against the wall between them for Father to give us leave to go.

Father's face was relaxed, his eyes half-open as he looked at Senda. "Fetch some wine," he told her, smiling, and she hurried to a small chest. "Senda is growing up," he said. "She looks much like you did when I married you, Mathilda."

Senda flushed. Never before had Father said anything flattering about her. Her hand trembled as she handed him the silver cup.

Lady Mathilda also stared at Senda, as if noticing her for the first time. "She is almost fourteen," she said, half to herself. She looked at her husband. "You must soon decide what to do with her, Mauger. She is a willful child, in sore need of discipline."

Father sipped the wine and looked at Senda. She stepped back to me and found my hand.

"Father Raoul suggested that we send her to the nunnery in Fleury. She could learn her letters, become Abbess someday —"

"The devil take that priest!" Father sat up. "If it were up to him all the women in my household would be nuns. By the blood of Saint Denis I won't have him dictate what goes on in my house."

I squeezed Senda's hand.

Lady Mathilda paled and hugged herself. "Father Raoul only wants what is best for Fredesenda. What could be better than to be the Lord's bride?"

Father laughed. "Perhaps the nunnery would be a fitting place for you, Mathilda. Not Senda! She will marry some day."

Lady Mathilda's eyes narrowed; her voice was low. "I wish my father had given me the choice to enter the cloister when I was her age. I would have gladly taken it over this life."

Father's knuckles were very white around his cup. He laughed uneasily. "That is not what you told me when I first took you to my bed, Mathilda. You were happy then to become my bride. Yours was a late vocation — but you have managed very well to follow it."

Senda dropped my hand and slowly edged along the wall toward the door, watching her parents.

"I did not know what you were like then. To share my husband with a common serf — to have your bastards underfoot every day —"

Father shrugged, then got up and walked toward her. She stepped back. He grasped her hand and pulled away her wimple, laughing. Her beautiful blond hair fell loosely to her shoulders. Senda crouched against the wall. She had never seen him touch her mother with desire.

Lady Mathilda looked younger, defenseless. She was still as beautiful as she was when she rode into Granville by my father's side.

Father took a handful of her hair and pulled her to him. I glanced toward Senda but she was no longer there. Where was she? Then I spotted her. She had sunk to the floor and was crawling toward the door.

Father turned toward us just as I helped Senda up. He frowned and let his hand drop. "Go now!" he shouted. "Tell the women to set their pallets in the hall; your mother won't need them tonight."

I opened the heavy oaken door and led Senda out. She ran past me down the stairs. As I hurried to shut the door I glanced in. Unsmiling, Father and Lady Mathilda were facing each other, enemies, ready to give battle.

*And the mother of these five young noblemen having died,
their father [Tancred], not wanting to live in sin, took a
woman named Fredesenda for his wife who was no less
noble and virtuous than the first one.*

— Gaufredus Malaterra, transl. John Julius
Norwich: *Historia Sicula*

CAPUT IV

The Abbey of Santa Eufemia
On the eve of the Feast of Saint Sigismund (May 1)
In this year 1061 from the Incarnation of our Lord
The words of Bernfrieda

Granville, 1014

Fall came and brought a livid light that shrouded Father's keep in shadows. Each day was marked by the rhythmic breaking of the waves against the rocky coast below Father's keep. Their monotonous battering was broken at times by the clanging of swords in the bailey, and by the sharp cries of seagulls. The sun rarely shone and the sea was deep grey.

Word came from Hauteville that Guillaume's mother had died in childbirth, and that Tancred would soon visit Granville. Though Guillaume had returned home only once in the seven years he had lived at Father's house, he was deeply affected by the news. For weeks his laugh did not resound in the hall, and he would often sit alone, shunning the games and chatter of the other men.

Lady Mathilda did not mention the nunnery again after the night when Mauger had pulled her wimple off. Father also seemed to have forgotten Senda, who became livelier and wandered in the bailey, looking for Guillaume.

One such time, late in the fall, Senda crossed the bailey and walked to the stables, where Guillaume was grooming Father's stallion. She sat on a bundle of hay next to where he worked. After he was done, he sat down next to her and hugged his knees. The smell of horse dung and straw pervaded the place, she told me later that night, and the heat from the horses made the place warm. "What was your mother like, Guillaume?" Senda asked.

He frowned. "You are the first to ask me. She had dark hair, like me. And she was small. The last time I went home I was taller than her, and I was only ten."

"You are almost taller than I am," Senda said.

"But I am almost fourteen now. You are a big girl."

"I'll never be beautiful like your mother." Senda said.

He looked at her for a moment. "No, you are not like her at all. But you are beautiful."

"No one else thinks so."

He took the end of her braid and wrapped it around his index finger. "Feel how soft it is," he said.

She touched her hair. It was as soft as her mother's saffron silk tunic, the one she wore on great occasions.

"And your eyes are the color of the waves of our northern sea on a warm summer day."

She flushed and looked away.

"Are you glad your father is coming?"

Guillaume beamed. "Yes! My father is strong and kind. And loved by all that know him."

"I hope I will like Guillaume's father when he comes to Hauteville," Senda said to me that night — and left me puzzled for a month.

❦ ❦ ❦

It was a late November morning when Tancred of Hauteville rode into the bailey. A freezing wind battered the keep and huge billows broke against the cliffs. The hall was dark because the servants had laid heavy pelts over the wooden shutters in an effort to shut out the wind. A few oil lamps cast sparse shadows on the walls; the hall was a huge cave. In spite of their fur-lined clothing, Father's knights crowded noisily around the glowing braziers. Senda and I also huddled in our favorite corner which offered a good view of the dais and Father's chair. When Tancred was announced, Father rose to his feet and ordered more light to be brought in the hall. "Guillaume!" he called, "come here on the dais by me. You — !" He took a servant by the arm. "Put another chair next to mine — and get some more coals. Lord, it is freezing today!" He stomped his feet and rubbed his hands together. "And bring food!" he yelled at the departing servant.

Senda watched Guillaume. His eyes darted from his Lord to the entrance, and he seemed unaware of all else. The last time he had seen Tancred he had been a boy of ten.

The guard announced Tancred as he strode into the hall, followed by two men. The three halted, temporarily blinded by the darkness. They wore long hooded brown fur wrappings and leggings. Tancred was the biggest man I had ever seen, and his furs made him look frightening. The shadow he cast on the wall could be that of a mighty ancestor who raided faraway coasts and returned to the ancient homeland loaded with booty. Haremar used to describe them, just so. I glanced at Senda and saw my amazement reflected on her face. Guillaume was standing by his Lord, a wide smile on his face.

Tancred pushed his hood back as he strode to the dais. His reddish mane fell loosely upon his broad shoulders and mingled with a thick long beard of the same color. Haremar and his knights had worn their hair like that, but few now did. Everyone followed the Caen fashion, beardless, with the hair shaved almost to the crown at the back. He looked like Haremar's description of Rollo, the leader who brought our people to Normandy from the Northlands.

Father stood up and came down into the hall to meet him. He shouted his welcome and took Tancred by both hands as he led him onto the dais. Tancred climbed on the wooden platform and for a moment he stood by Guillaume and his Lord, towering over both. When Tancred bowed and started to kneel, Father stopped him. "Tancred!" he repeated, and they embraced. I had seldom seen my father so excited.

"Guillaume does not look like his father," Senda murmured. Holding his son at arm's length, Tancred studied him, smiled, hugged him and then followed Father's invitation to sit by him. He loosened his mud-splattered fur and leaned back in his chair. Father called Adeliza to bring wine, which she set with three goblets on a trestle table beside him. I glared at her, more envious than ever. I should have been in her place. Her mother displaced mine, and now she was standing close to Father's handsome guest, her back to the delicious warmth of the brazier.

Father patted his guest's arm. "By Saint Denis, Tancred, it was time you showed your face — how many years has it been since I last saw you? Five? Seven?"

"Too many, my Lord," Tancred replied.

"Call me Mauger, as you did while we were growing up in Caen. Have you forgotten all that we went through together?"

Tancred smiled.

Adeliza's green woolen tunic was cinched tightly at the waist with a saffron belt. Her thick, dark braid kept falling over her shoulder as she refilled the wine, and she kept throwing it back, aware that the movement strained the cloth outlining her breasts. Father drank from his goblet and looked somberly at Tancred. "I am sorry about your loss, my friend."

Tancred nodded gravely. "Hauteville is empty without Muriella — but she has been buried four months, Mauger, and I have two young boys still at home and a baby now who needs a mother — it is the reason I came — you are my Lord and my friend. Help me find a wife. I was married for too long to be celibate again."

Father tilted his chin up and raised his eyebrows. He studied Tancred for a moment, then laughed.

"Take a serving girl to your bed, Tancred! Why a wife? You already have an heir and four other healthy sons — you do not need marriage —"

"No, Mauger," Tancred broke in, "temptation is strong but I shall not live in mortal sin. Those times in Caen, it was so exciting to be at court, and I thought my life would last forever." He leaned forward. "I have changed, Mauger. Years ago, after Serlon was born, Muriella insisted that we go to Saint Evroult, to thank the saint for our first-born. Abbot Thierry spoke to me. I am not at all like I was. He made me realize that Muriella . . ." His voice trailed off.

Father was silent for a while. He looked into his empty goblet and motioned Adeliza for more wine.

"Well, Tancred, you may have changed, but my friendship for you hasn't. If it is a wife you want, a wife we'll find for you! Drink and rest now. Adeliza, fetch your mother."

Adeliza nodded and started toward Lady Mathilda's chamber. At the base of the stairs, she gathered her skirts for the climb and looked back. Tancred smiled at her, and she returned the smile, then ran swiftly upstairs.

"Adeliza likes him," Senda whispered and I nodded. I felt confused and elated when I looked at him. Senda pulled on my sleeve. "Let's walk around, Bernfrieda, perhaps Guillaume will talk to me."

For the evening meal, Senda was summoned to the high table on the dais, to sit with her family, while I sat below the salt with the other servants. Father introduced Senda to Tancred, who surveyed her with interest, but he soon turned toward Adeliza who was sitting by him, sharing his trencher.

Tancred sat on his Lord's right. I had not seen Father in such a good mood for some time. He laughed like a young boy as he recalled their days at the court of Duke Richard the Magnificent in Caen where they had been raised. As Guillaume filled his Lord's bread trencher with a savory mix of stew and vegetables, Father retold an episode we had heard many times.

While on a boar hunt in the ducal forest, Tancred had become separated from Father and the other hunters. Alone, he had followed the barking of the hounds and had come upon a boar. The dogs had cornered the beast at the foot of a cliff, and the forest echoed with his grunts and furious barking from the dogs. Attempting to escape, the boar charged, impaling the closest dogs on his tusks and sending the others flying into the air.

Two of Tancred's best dogs were closest to the beast. He drew his sword, but hesitated; only the Duke was allowed to kill game in his forest. But the boar gored one of his prime hounds, and Tancred could stand it no longer. He approached the beast, and when it charged him, he struck it with his sword and pierced its skull.

Fearing for his life because he had broken the game laws, he turned and ran without retrieving his sword. He did not go far, however, for Duke Richard arrived at that moment with his men. After the hunters recalled the hounds, the Duke dismounted and examined the long sword that still quivered in the boar's skull. Many recognized it as Tancred's; the Duke asked for him. When the guards brought him forward, Duke Richard praised the blow and awarded him the boar's tusks.

Tancred waved dismissively. "That happened long ago, Mauger."

He spent the evening dividing his attention between Father, Guillaume — and Adeliza. He would whisper into her ear and she would smile and blush. He kept refilling her goblet with wine and offering her the choice morsels from their trencher on the point of his dagger. I saw her lean against him at one point and laugh loudly. Lady Mathilda turned sharply toward her daughter and glared at her. Instantly Adeliza was sitting properly on the bench again, her face deeply flushed.

Guillaume's face was also red with excitement as he turned to serve his Lord and then his father. Engrossed as he was, he did not look toward Senda all evening.

I was sharing my trencher with Mabille. I was not hungry and the sight of Mabille slurping soup made me even less so. Intent on stuffing her belly, Mabille nevertheless noticed Adeliza's lack of appetite.

"The Lord Tancred likes Lady Adeliza," Mabille mumbled. She gummed a piece of meat. "Such a pity she is promised to a child."

"He is handsome," I said.

Mabille raised an eyebrow and surveyed me. "Smile to him then. You are pretty enough, and he has been a widower for some time. He'll take you to his bed if you let him know you like him. It would be about time you slept with a man, Bernfrieda. No other girl of your age is still a virgin, except for Katrin, who is meant for the cloister."

I felt myself flush and lowered my eyes, but I did not answer her taunts.

What if I did smile at him? I would be as pretty as Adeliza if I could wear better clothes, a few baubles, comb my hair with bone and not wood . . . I looked down with dismay at my drab brown woolen tunic. *Twenty last summer, perhaps I am too old to attract a man.* Tancred glanced in my direction just then, and I looked into his brilliant blue eyes. He smiled, but he could have smiled at any of the dozen or so people around me.

Mabille shook my arm. "Look, he smiled at you! He may court Lady Adeliza but he is a man, let him know you want him, go to his bed. He may even take you away, if he likes you enough." I stood up to move away from her foul breath, pushing on the bench so violently that I almost overturned it. Mabille swore and the two people on the other side of me looked up in surprise. I looked around for an empty spot further away from the high table, so I could be left alone until it was time to go upstairs.

After dinner the servants moved the tables against the walls so they could be used as pallets for the night. Tancred and Father remained in their places; Lady Mathilda called the women upstairs.

"I wish Guillaume had looked at me tonight," Senda whispered wistfully, as we lay on our pallet. "But he had eyes for his father only. He will leave soon however, and then all will be like before."

"Did you like Tancred, Senda?" I whispered.

"He is so big," was all she said, as she began to drift into sleep.

Adeliza was having trouble going to sleep. She tossed and turned until finally she propped herself up on her elbow and shook her maid awake. "Mabille, Mabille, wake up — I can't sleep."

"My Lady, what is it?"

"I can't sleep," Adeliza murmured. "I have never felt like tonight — I keep thinking of Father's guest."

"He is so handsome, my Lady — and you must have captured his heart, for he looked only at you all evening," Mabille whispered hoarsely.

"He needs a new wife. Perhaps I could be the one!"

"My Lady! You are promised already!"

"Not formally, until summer. It is only an understanding with Rollo de Walchelin. Richard is so young. I do not want to be old when I marry."

"But my Lady, Lord Tancred has only ten knights, and he has an heir already. Lord Richard has over sixty men — and your son will be Lord."

"But I like Tancred!" Adeliza whined. "Senda could marry Richard."

"But you are the first daughter, my Lady — "

Adeliza slapped her, a sound like a board snapping in the darkness.

"Why do I waste my time talking to you? Ready my green tunic and a length of silver ribbon tomorrow. I attend to Father's guest at breakfast."

Mabille sobbed quietly for a while, then all was silence. *Walchelin will not settle for a second daughter. Adeliza is foolish if she thinks her wishes will make a difference. I can't wait to see her face when she finds that out.* With that sweet thought I drifted into sleep.

❧ ❧ ❧

In the morning I woke Senda. Adeliza and Mabille were already downstairs. I brought Senda's saffron tunic, and took my time combing her hair, admiring the soft red-golden tresses as I braided them. My black hair was longer, for I had never cut it, and very straight. I doubled my braid and pinned it at my neck and I could feel its weight there.

What will Father decide? Tancred is a modest knight and he already has five boys — his new wife's children will receive nothing — Father cannot possibly consider him a good match for his legitimate daughters. But what about me?

Grey light filtered through the narrow windows. Father and Tancred were already seated as they had been before, talking animatedly while Guillaume cut up cold roasted quail and bread and Adeliza poured wine. We sat at a table below the dais. Guillaume looked down and smiled happily at Senda, then went back to his task.

Father saw us too. He turned to his friend.

"I thought about your request that I help you find a wife. What better way to show you my favor than to give you my daughter in marriage?"

Whom does he mean?

"Mauger!" Tancred grinned and looked at Adeliza, who stopped the pouring, a radiant smile spreading across her face.

Father quickly understood.

"Adeliza? I have already promised her to Richard de Walchelin. I meant Fredesenda. Senda!" he called.

Fredesenda!

Tancred turned away from Adeliza, trying to hide his disappointment. And managed to nod graciously enough at Father's words. He looked around for Senda.

Adeliza stood as if carved in stone. I watched Senda as from a long distance. *Father could easily have found a better match for her.* Senda stared at Father without moving, beads of perspiration on her forehead. She had lost all her color, and the saffron tunic gave a yellowish tinge to her skin. She reached for my hand and held it for dear life. That was enough to stir me.

"Senda, stand," I muttered. She stood up; a gentle push set her walking to stand before them, dazed, eyes lowered.

"Fredesenda!" Father said, not unkindly. "You are to marry Tancred." She looked up at both of them.

Tancred's eyes widened as he appraised her. He smiled. *His front teeth are worn; they show his age.* She looked away. "It shall be Fredesenda then, Mauger," Tancred said, very pleased. Father laughed.

"So be it, Tancred. Senda, fetch your mother!" Senda nodded and turned towards the stairs. She glanced at Guillaume as she left; his face was a stone mask of grief.

I followed her. *I will not think of Tancred. Not now, there is too much to do. Later. I'll think of Tancred later.*

❧ ❧ ❧

After Lady Mathilda had hurried downstairs with her women, we were alone. Fredesenda was sitting on her pallet, next to me, shaking in spite of the fur coverlet I had wrapped around her shoulders, when Adeliza appeared on top of the stairs.

"You think you are going to be a great Lady, don't you?" She stopped in front of Senda.

"Tancred is old," she continued, "as old as Father. And he has sons already. He won't care for your children. And when he dies, Hauteville will go to his first-born. Your children will have nothing." She laughed. "You can have him, Senda!" Then she whirled and stamped downstairs.

Adeliza need not have spoken at all. We listened to her mother and the women downstairs, making excited plans for Senda's wedding. It was decided that the ceremony would take place the following week, when Father Raoul came back to visit. Tancred was anxious to return to Hauteville. "He seems kind, Senda." She pushed me away, her first forceful reaction since Father's announcement.

"How can I marry Guillaume's father?" She stood up and paced the antechamber. "I shall send word to Guillaume. We could run away —"

"Senda! Go against Father's will? You would disgrace yourself — and Guillaume too — how far do you think you could go be-

fore you were recaptured and brought back in shame? Guillaume
would be killed!"

"Father would not kill Guillaume!" she whispered.

"You would be made to watch while he was hanged from the
tower. Father would kill you too — or bury you in a convent."

She stopped pacing and stared at me. She was silent for a long
while. Her voice was still a whisper when she finally spoke. "You
are right, Bernfrieda, I could not ask Guillaume to betray his
Lord. I do not want him to die!" She burst into tears and she fell
on her knees, and I held her again.

"I'll miss you," I said, thinking of what my life would be when
she had married, serving Lady Mathilda and a vengeful Adeliza.
Senda looked up, her eyes still full of tears. She took my hand
and held it tightly.

"You must stay with me, Bernfrieda," she said. "I can't leave
you too. I shall ask Tancred." We knew full well that our wishes
meant nothing. We knelt for a long while there in our awkward
embrace.

That evening, Senda traded places with Adeliza. Tancred was
silent at first. But he saw to her every need, cutting meat and offering it to her on the point of his knife, breaking bread and
handing it to her. He looked at her often, unsmiling. Senda sat
by him rigidly, aware that Guillaume too sat in silence across
from them. "Are you afraid of me, Fredesenda?" Tancred asked
quietly,

She shook her head but kept her eyes on the trencher.

"Then why don't you look at me?"

She was silent for a moment, then gathered her courage.
"There is something I must ask you, my Lord."

I leaned forward. Mabille put a hand on my arm. "What now,
Bernfrieda?" I shook my head, my eyes riveted on Tancred.

"What is it?" He looked at her intently and the small lines
around his eyes became more noticeable.

She fidgeted. "I don't want to leave my half-sister, Bernfrieda,
my Lord." She pointed at me and Tancred glanced in my direction. I felt my cheeks burn and I lowered my eyes.

"The Lord Tancred just looked at you, Bernfrieda," Mabille chuckled. "He would not need to do more to have me come to his bed. O, but Lady Adeliza is brokenhearted over her sister marrying him."

"Would your father consent to part with her?" Tancred asked Senda.

"I do not think he will object."

"Then I shall ask him."

Senda and I were both surprised at how easily he had agreed. Shyly Senda smiled at him and he smiled too. For the first time since that morning, she seemed more at ease.

Father consented to Tancred's request. He was very pleased with the marriage arrangement because Tancred had not asked for a large bride portion. And since the wedding would take place in a matter of days, he did not have to worry about an expensive wedding feast.

During the following few days, Senda seemed lost. She stared into space or looked anxiously for Guillaume. He avoided her now and did not smile if their eyes met.

She was grateful to Tancred for interceding on my behalf. Slowly she became accustomed to his quiet attention.

I too was grateful. No, I must be honest; I wanted him to notice me. After Senda told me that I could stay with her, I decided to thank him. I approached Tancred as he crossed the frozen bailey one afternoon.

"My Lord." He stopped and turned toward me.

"I — am Bernfrieda — I — wanted to thank you," I said. He raised an eyebrow as if trying to recall, then smiled. *His teeth are pitted and worn and the lines around his eyes deep. But his skin is fresh and unblemished, his face kind and strong. What would it feel like to be held by him?* Ashamed, I lowered my eyes.

"I am glad you are coming to Hauteville, Bernfrieda." He extended his hand and I took it. Blood came to my cheeks as I bent to kiss it.

"You are a handsome woman, Bernfrieda," Tancred said. "Five of my knights are still unmarried. Perhaps you could choose the one who pleases you the most."

Again I blushed as I bowed to take leave. I wrapped myself tighter into my cloak and I hurried into the keep.

After that I avoided Tancred, for I had begun to realize that he moved me as no man had moved me before. He was not young and he was not looking for fleeting pleasure. What I felt confused me. At times I let myself think of what it would be like to live at his house, see him each day. When I thought of this, the drudgery of my tasks, the pettiness of the women — even Lady Mathilda's temper — seemed unimportant. Even a glimpse of Tancred as he strode in the bailey or sat down to eat gave me joy, which I immediately regretted. *But you take nothing from Senda — she does not love him.*

I should have trembled for my soul instead of worrying about Senda. "To indulge a sinful thought is as evil as the sin itself," Father Raoul often said. "To desire another's mate is a sure way to the flames of hell." Those words made me shiver. How could I ever forget my mother's downcast face as he berated her? But the memory also brought back the feelings of rebellion and bitter hatred I felt for Father Raoul and the pitiless, cruel laws he stood for. It would take me decades to make peace with God.

Lady Mathilda was shaken into frenzied activity by the closeness of the wedding date. She gave Senda three of her tunics, several pieces of linen to use as bedding, a feather-filled quilt covered with wool, two feathered pillows and an embroidered coverlet. She had the women sew little packages of seeds from her summer garden and spent a whole afternoon lecturing Senda on the proper way to plant one. She also gave her a fair supply of cinnamon and nutmeg for cooking, and two new pieces of her treasured Castilian soap. She kept Senda constantly at her side during those last few days. She reminded her of how to supervise the drying of the meats and the stocking of the larder, and had her memorize recipes for potions and ointments. Busy with all the hurried sewing and mending, I hardly saw Senda during the day, but when night came and we huddled under our bedding we held each other and whispered. Sometimes she cried about Guillaume. Often we drifted to sleep talking about Hauteville, wondering what our new home would be like.

The day before the wedding, Adeliza spit her venom once more. She lingered behind while the women went down for breakfast.

"Are you content to marry an old man, Senda?" she asked. "Tancred does not even own a keep — just a miserable house." Senda looked at Adeliza but did not say anything. Adeliza came closer.

"Guillaume must be delighted to have a new mother," she said, and smiled when she saw Senda wince. I put my arm over Senda's shoulders to lead her away but she pushed me back and faced her sister.

"Tancred may be old, Adeliza," Senda said, keeping her voice calm, "but at least I won't have to be a mother to my husband. And I'll be a bride tomorrow while you must wait. I'll be mistress of his house, and I'll have children soon while you must wait for Richard to reach manhood. If he ever does."

Adeliza threw herself on her sister, trying to rake her fingers over her face. But Senda was taller and stronger, and she pushed Adeliza to the floor with little effort.

"Come Bernfrieda. I won't make Tancred wait." Senda turned toward the stairs.

*Not far from the marriage chamber a large crowd kept up
a long and noisy party, having gathered to certify the
physical union, to rejoice at it, and through its own
brimming pleasure to capture the mysterious gifts needed
to make the marriage fruitful.*

— Georges Duby, transl. Barbara Bray: *The Knight,
the Lady, and the Priest*

CAPUT V

The Abbey of Santa Eufemia
On the eve of the Feast of St. Boniface, Martyr (June 5)
In this year 1061 from the Incarnation of our Lord
The words of Bernfrieda

Granville, 1014

Senda sat tightly wrapped in a blanket near the brazier in her mother's room. She watched as I poured crumbled lavender, mint and sage into the padded wooden tub. Servants had filled it almost to the top with buckets of both steaming and cold water.

She had scarcely slept the night before. Today she would be the first in the tub; in the past she had loathed bathing in the lukewarm water which had already served her mother and Adeliza. "It is ready, Senda," I said. She nodded and cautiously approached the tub. Climbing on the small stool by its side, she put her toe in. Hurriedly she withdrew it and almost lost her balance; the water was so hot it burned. She tried again, and eventually stood up in the tub, discarded the blanket and lowered herself into the water. She sat on the padded bottom of the tub and inhaled the scents of mint, lavender and sage. She told me that nothing, nothing at all she had known compared with this new feeling of complete warmth.

"Turn around, my Lady." Mabille began to scrub her skin with a piece of cloth and Lady Mathilda's soap. I unbraided Senda's hair, which I had washed two days before, and let the red-golden mass fall outside the tub. I untangled each shiny strand carefully as I combed it.

Mabille left to ready her wedding clothes and Senda closed her eyes. The servants had prepared the wedding chamber by partitioning off the far end of the hall with drapes. The next day, the soft feather bedding in the makeshift chamber would follow us to Hauteville along with the rest of her belongings.

What would happen tonight? Senda had clung to me fearfully the night before. Lady Mathilda had not told her much about what to expect from her groom, but Senda knew about coupling. She had often observed dogs mounting bitches and Father's stallion mounting mares. She was aware of what a man looked like, for she had often seen naked peasants play in the river during the warm summer months.

The mystery of the wedding bed! If coupling was as simple as it looked between animals, why did it bring so much misery among humans? Her parents were not happy. She could not think of anybody who was married and happy. And she kept thinking of Guillaume. I told Senda Tancred was different but even to me those words sounded hollow: had I not seen my own mother suffer because of coupling? How could Senda ever be happy when she longed for Guillaume to be in his father's place?

Guillaume sat with his eyes lowered during meals, and was constantly at his father's side during the day. He looked away when their eyes met. He was angry at Senda. Senda was desolate, she wanted to speak to him, tell him — what?

As I combed her hair I felt a sudden pain. Senda had changed: her laughter had not resounded in the hall since she was betrothed to Tancred, and something grave had entered her demeanor. She walked past Adeliza as if she weren't there. Perhaps, if Tancred were gentle, Guillaume would fade into a memory. Had Muriella, her predecessor, been happy?

"Senda, come! Your wedding dress is ready!" Mabille exclaimed. Senda opened her eyes and got up slowly, steam rising from her reddened body. I wrapped her in her blanket and slowly rubbed her dry. I helped her out of the tub and guided her to Lady Mathilda's bed. The red woolen tunic she was to wear had been kept in her mother's chest ever since she had come to Mauger's keep as a new bride. Mabille spread it on the bed and caressed the soft material, letting her rough finger trail over the silver embroidery and aquamarines that embellished the collar.

Senda stood looking open-mouthed at the tunic for the first time, but made no move to put it on. I had to take her blanket and slip a soft linen shift over her head. Then I helped her with the tunic. Senda had never worn such before — with a fitted bodice that laced in the center back and outlined her breasts in a way that made her blush.

The tunic, which reached below the knees, fit her perfectly. The sleeves were wide and the long wristbands were embroidered with the same silver thread. I arranged a small round red cap on her head, and pulled back her hair so it fell loosely below her waist. Lady Mathilda's slippers were a bit small, but after a few tries they fit.

When Senda was ready, Mabille and I stepped back to look at her. I caught my breath, for Senda looked so much like her mother, the bride who had seemed to me as a child to be as dazzling as the sun.

"Senda, you look beautiful, *beautiful!*" Mabille said in a wondering voice, as if Senda were someone new and important.

She brought Lady Mathilda's polished bronze mirror and held it in front of her. Senda looked for a long while. Her eyes were sparkling, her skin aglow, and her hair was a golden veil. Where was the pallid, plain girl we had known?

She turned toward me "Bernfrieda —" Her excitement faded as she saw her mother standing by me, holding a mantle. Lady Mathilda's face was white and expressionless as usual. Senda put the mirror on the bench next to her.

"You look well, Senda." She came closer and inspected her daughter carefully. "The tunic I wore at my wedding," she said pensively, touching it. "I hope it will bring you luck, child." She hesitated before handing her the mantle. "Tancred sends this to you. It was Muriella's. He would like you to wear it at the wedding."

Senda took Tancred's gift. The mantle was like new. It was a deep red velvet outside, soft white fur inside. I wondered if it too had remained in a chest for many years.

"Senda . . ." Lady Mathilda took the mirror that her daughter had hastily put on the bench. "Take it — I would like you to have it." Senda looked at her mother and then the mirror in disbelief. Such a precious gift! To be able to see herself anytime she chose? Overwhelmed, Senda stood there awkwardly, searching for the right words. She held the mirror to her breast.

"Thank you. Oh thank you, Mother!"

Lady Mathilda's smile was small and pallid, but a smile nonetheless.

"Father Raoul has arrived. They are waiting for you in the hall." Lady Mathilda turned away quickly, as if afraid to say more. "Pega," she called, "be sure to bring down my distaff for the ceremony."

The other women and I preceded Senda down to the hall and waited for her at the bottom of the stairs. As she came down, she put a hand over her heart and looked at Guillaume. I felt a heaviness in mine, which grew when I saw Tancred.

Admiring exclamations greeted the bride's entrance. Everyone who lived at Granville was present. Senda looked around the hall. Father and Tancred were standing side by side at the brazier. Guillaume stood next to his father, arms folded, staring past her. Father's eyes widened when he saw Senda, and he kept looking back at Lady Mathilda. Tancred gazed at his bride as if she were a vision.

A delighted smile spread on his face before he suddenly shut his lips. *His teeth!* I thought with surprise, *he is trying to look his best for Senda.* How lucky Senda was! I felt such a feeling of loss as I watched him. Part of me wished he would notice me, yearned for his hands to touch me, wondered what it would feel to be loved by him. Before he arrived at the keep I had shunned men. No one among Father's knights had ever made me wish to be loved. How easily they mated and discarded their women! But Tancred would love and be true to his wife. There would be no discarded mistresses in his house, no unwanted bastards.

He was wearing a new green tunic and brown leggings. He must have brought them with him from Hauteville, I thought, confident that Mauger would find him a bride. No man in the hall owned anything that would fit him. He strode to the trestle table covered with white linen where Father Raoul was waiting.

Lady Mathilda's heavy silver cross shone on the makeshift altar next to a platen with the freshly baked Host. In his white vestments the priest looked almost dignified. I had worked long summer hours with Lady Mathilda and her women weaving, sewing and embroidering them. The alb we had woven of white linen, and the cincture we had coiled from the best rope the keep could provide. Part of it could be seen through the side slits in the white chasuble, which had taken the longest to finish, edged as it was with an elaborate border of tiny embroidered Hosts. The stole around Father Raoul's neck and the white maniple on his left arm repeated the pattern.

Father took Senda's hand in his and led her to the altar. He faced Tancred. "I give you my daughter, Tancred. Honor and cherish her as your wife." His breath clouded in the cold room as he spoke. Tancred nodded and stood lost in the contemplation of his bride until Father reached across and nudged him. Fumbling, Tancred produced a heavy gold ring, took Senda's left hand, opened it and placed the ring on her palm. Now he is her new master, I thought suddenly. And mine.

Father Raoul celebrated Mass. He interrupted it at the Pater to give a special blessing and advice to the bride. At Communion Tancred and Senda shared the bread and the wine. Then Lady Mathilda turned to Pega, took the distaff from her and handed it to her daughter so she could demonstrate her spinning to the crowd. Senda was about to shake her head in refusal; but she took the distaff and stiffly spun a little wool. The crowd cheered and I joined them when they showered the couple with seeds, shouting the customary "Plenty! Plenty!"

Father led the newlyweds to the high table. Smiling, he relinquished his chair to Tancred while Senda took her mother's place.

Pale and unsmiling, Guillaume stood by the wedded couple, ready to serve his father. He did not avert his eyes when Senda looked at him this time. I could read plainly the despair on both their faces. Worried that someone else might notice, I left my bench and walked toward Guillaume.

Tancred was leaning toward Senda when he followed her gaze to Guillaume. He stood still for a moment and then picked up his cup, lifted it toward his son, and motioned for more wine. His face burning, Guillaume hurried to fill it. As if nothing had happened, Tancred turned his concentration to cutting a piece of meat for his bride.

Given the season and short notice, the cooks had done their best to create a wedding feast. Senda hardly touched the rich potage filled with meat and herbs and kept refusing the morsels Tancred gave her. Three kinds of roast venison and fowl and poached fish from the river were piled atop the tables. Tancred ate heartily and afterward enjoyed the honey cakes and baked apples that finished the meal.

Senda was exhausted by the time the meal was over three hours later. When Father and Tancred closeted themselves at one end of the hall while the servants cleared the tables, Senda followed her mother to her room to oversee the packing of her belongings, and to put away the wedding dress which, one day, would also serve Adeliza.

⚜ ⚜ ⚜

Senda trembled in her white linen shift as the women folded her wedding tunic. "Senda," I whispered, as I wrapped her new mantle over her shoulders, "Do not be afraid. It won't be so bad." She glanced at me mournfully and then stared at the floor.

The packing done, Lady Mathilda turned to Senda. "It is time to go down." She put her hand over Senda's shoulder. "Remember what Father Raoul said today. Obey your husband in all things, child, and he will treat you gently." She paused, for her daughter's pallor had acquired a greenish tinge.

"Bernfrieda!" Lady Mathilda hissed. I held Senda with one arm and pulled her hair back as she retched. Mabille found a basin and Senda bent over it, her whole body convulsing after each spasm. Afterward, I wiped her mouth and led her to her mother's bed. Her eyes closed, Senda's face was white as her linen shift. I held her hand while Mabille prepared mint tea to restore sweet breath.

"It won't last long," I whispered. But she shook her head and refused to speak to me.

The crowd was impatient downstairs. The priest walked to the makeshift bridal chamber to bless the bed. He waved the censor round it and then sprinkled it with holy water. The blessing over, Lady Mathilda led the procession to the bed, followed by Senda, who was leaning heavily on me. Senda squeezed my hand as she walked, her fingers icy. Her mother glanced at her with apprehension when we reached the bridal chamber, but did not speak. She motioned for Mabille to close the drapes, then pulled the covers away and gently slipped Senda's shift over her head, leaving her naked and shivering on the bed. I walked around the right side of the bed to Senda, pulled the covers up around her and waited there while Lady Mathilda called Tancred. Then she joined Father in the hall.

I pressed my hand on Senda's shoulder to steady her when Tancred entered the chamber. Accompanied by his son and two knights, he strode to the left side of the bed. He smiled at Senda. Guillaume unlaced his father's breeches and tunic, concentrating on the cloth as if it might escape if he didn't. When Tancred sat on the bed to take off his boots, Guillaume glanced at Senda over his father's shoulder, and his eyes filled with tears. A half-smile played on Adeliza's lips as she glanced at Guillaume and then Senda. Then she too walked out of the chamber.

Senda's teeth were chattering when I quickly bent to hug her before I left. As soon as Tancred was in bed with her, his knights opened the draperies again, letting the crowd file through the chamber, led by my father and Lady Mathilda. Since Guillaume was the only one related by blood to Tancred, he walked rigidly to his father and uncovered him while Mathilda lifted the covers off Senda so they both could be examined for hidden blemishes. I gazed at Tancred. His chest was covered with red curly hair and the thin white scar from a sword-stroke crossed his side. I glanced at his engorged manhood; the crowd around the bed laughed and shouted their approval. Senda sat with lowered head, hoping her long hair would shield her nakedness. But her mother pushed her hair behind her shoulders. Then the examination was over and the heavy draperies again divided them from the others.

The rest of the evening passed slowly, filled with more eating, drinking and ribald jokes. Lady Mathilda for once did not seem in a hurry to leave. Eventually, I forgot my usual caution and I left the hall. Outside I wrapped my mantle tightly around me, for the cold was intense.

The sun had set and it would soon be dark. Servants were still carrying food from the kitchen, which was located in a lean-to against the stone wall of the keep. Everyone else was inside celebrating the wedding. I picked up my skirt and made my way carefully over the frozen mud towards the bailey and the old cottage I used to share with my mother. The family that lived there now would be in the hall. I stood by the door; it opened easily when I pushed it. I moved slowly into the room: the hearth in the center, the four pallets still lining the wall, all was as I remembered. I knelt by my pallet and traced with my finger on its side the outline of the falcon my brother Henry had carved on the rough pine.

I thought of Tancred and Senda, their nakedness. *Would he be gentle?*

"Bernfrieda!" I heard a thick voice. I spun around. Alferio had appeared as if from nowhere. He must have followed me. Did my brothers notice? Could anyone hear me?

Alferio bared his two broken front teeth. "Five years I have waited for this, five years, Bernfrieda," he muttered. He pushed his mantle over one shoulder, unlaced the flap on his breeches and freed his manhood. I stared at his thick stubby organ. He squeezed my breasts so hard that I cried out. He pressed his manhood hard against my belly. I pushed at him. He let go of my breasts and pinned my hands to my sides.

"Leave me! My brothers!" I tried to shout but my voice cracked.

"Henry won't come this time, Bernfrieda," he said evenly. "Scream if you want, no one will hear you." I knew he was right. There were too many people in the hall; my brothers would not miss me.

Alferio freed one of my arms to fumble with my skirt. Suddenly furious, I pushed him with all my strength. He took a step backward but did not let go of me. He shoved me hard. I lost my balance and collapsed on my pallet. He fell on top of me and pulled my linen shift over my head, pinning it over my face with my own arms. I could hardly breathe. I could not move my hands for his were clamped on them at the wrists in a grip I could not break. He shifted his weight over my left leg. He found my opening and thrust inside. Pain seared my insides and I screamed. "Be quiet," he panted, "or I'll shove that cloth down your throat." The pain was deep and burning. I thrashed and writhed trying to get away. "Go on, move!" he muttered in my ear.

I lay still then.

When he finished he stood up and left. I sat on the pallet, sore all over. The sudden thought that he might come back acted as a spur, and I bolted to the keep. There was still some light outside and I realized that what had seemed like hours had only lasted a few minutes.

When I entered the hall I kept my mantle wrapped tightly around me. Lady Mathilda was still sitting in her chair. No one noticed me as I crept around the wall to the stairs. I dashed up to the empty antechamber and threw myself on my pallet. I began to sob.

Later I tore a piece of my shift and rubbed it over my opening, trying to staunch the flow of seed and blood. The smell of the oozy stickiness between my legs made me double up and vomit in the rushes. I hugged myself and shut my eyes tightly, but I kept seeing Alferio, his taunting laugh, his purplish engorged weapon. The image of my mother leaning over my pallet to kiss me goodnight flashed through my mind. He had violated me on my own bed.

❦ ❦ ❦

Lady Mathilda kissed Senda on the forehead the morning we left. Her face was pale and forbidding, and she glanced in my direction and nodded briefly without speaking. Even before we left the hall she had retired to her room to pray. Father saw us off in the bailey, his knights and Guillaume by his side. The wind flapped the long woolen mantles around their legs as they took turns embracing Tancred. Father kissed Senda. Guillaume came forward stiffly and brushed his lips against her cheek. I kept aside, tightly wrapped in my brown mantle. My brothers and a few of the women had bidden me farewell before we reached the bailey, but no one else. Senda and I climbed on the ox cart and crouched among her possessions. Tancred and his knights mounted their horses and prepared to go when Father took a step toward the cart. He looked at me for a moment and gave me his hand to kiss.

"Take care of yourself, Bernfrieda," he said. My heart filled with sadness; I barely touched his hand with my lips.

As the ox cart labored over the rough road to Hauteville, Senda told me about her night with Tancred. She said she had been aware of the unusual softness of the feather mattress even though she was stiff, waiting for Tancred to touch her. I was sitting on a grain sack, and changed my position, wishing it were a feather bed. I was still bleeding.

"Fredesenda." Tancred had used her full name and she turned her head toward him and felt his breath on her face. It was sour and she winced. She turned her face toward the wall.

"Do you know what is expected of us, Fredesenda?" Tancred's voice was soft, soothing, as if she were a child. She nodded, still staring at the wall.

Be quiet, or I'll shove that cloth down your throat —

"We must couple," Senda said with effort, "so that your seed may enter me. The sheets will be inspected tomorrow to make sure that I came to you with my maidenhead intact."

Tancred was silent for some time. Cautiously Senda turned toward him. He was resting on his elbow, watching her. She stared at the abundant red curly hair on his chest. When he spoke, his words were so soft that nobody in the hall could hear him. "Do not be afraid of me, Fredesenda," he pleaded. "You have come into my life late, but I treasure you already."

She could see his eyes in the semi-darkness. They were serious and sad. "I shall never hurt you, Fredesenda," he touched her arm.

"Go on, move !"

"He did not lie to me," Senda said. "But it was the worst ordeal I have ever had to endure, Bernfrieda. You have no idea."

I turned away, and stared out at the brown fields.

༚ ༚ ༚

I buried what Alferio did to me inside my mind, electing not to tell my brothers. I could have told them the morning I took my leave in the bailey with Senda. But what good could that accomplish? I did not want to leave them with knowledge that would endanger their own lives.

I told myself that night I would forget. I would never speak or think of it again. I did not even confess what I regarded then as my sin to the visiting priest at Hauteville. I began to believe that if I never thought of my violation, it would be as if it had never happened.

I never forgot. As I write each detail comes back to me, the rough texture of my shift in my mouth, Alferio's iron grip on my wrists, and the pain — O, the pain — helplessness, rage — how strange that the pain of more than forty years ago can still hurt.

I thought I had sinned because prudence dictated that I stay in the hall and instead I chose to leave. But that was a mistake, not a sin. It was Alferio who sinned, for I had no choice in what he did to me. Reliving my violation has allowed me to see clearly at last. The true sin was to bear such hatred inside all this time. Today I shall cleanse my soul in Confession, and then perhaps I shall truly forget.

I never told Senda. As we rode to her new home I sensed that she was too enveloped in her own misery to understand mine — *She is and has always been, insensitive to all that does not touch her directly. That morning I understood it clearly for the first time.*

But I too was insensitive. She loved Guillaume, not Tancred; and she was very young. Coupling under those circumstances, no matter how thoughtful her bridegroom was, must have been painful.

For labor and for pangs afterward: take 3 drachmas of the pods of cassia fistula, an ounce of savory, and another ounce of hyssop; powder all these together and give it to the woman in the juice of vervain warmed. And this potion when drunk causes her to be quickly delivered.

— transl. Beryl Rowland: *Medieval Woman's Guide to Health* (Middle English text from an earlier eleventh century text)

CAPUT VI

The Abbey of Santa Eufemia
On the eve of the Feast of St. John the Baptist (June 24)
In this year 1061 from the Incarnation of our Lord
The words of Bernfrieda

Hauteville, 1015

Dreaux, Onfroi! Come, meet your new mother." The two boys came sullenly forward. Senda tried to smile.

We had arrived at Hauteville in the late afternoon, after a long ox-ride, sharing the cart with many sacks of barley and wheat, and chickens in two wooden crates, the results of Tancred's negotiations.

The boys were the same height. Dreaux was twelve, two years older than Onfroi. Tancred had chosen to oversee their training himself instead of sending them to another lord's keep, as he had done with Serlon and Guillaume. The boys did not smile, but bowed in greeting. They were both dark of hair and skin, like Guillaume, though neither had his good looks. Dreaux seemed pleasant enough, but there was something disquieting about

Onfroi. Perhaps it was his narrow eyes, a shade of blue so pale it seemed transparent.

Tancred had gathered his household to greet us. Thirty men and women stood about the hall of his keep, regarding us silently. There was a drabness about them that reflected the neglect of the hall. I had not cared for the drunken laughter and merrymaking at Granville, the flamboyant colors worn by Father's knights. Though I had had no regrets about leaving, I felt suddenly homesick in that roomful of strangers. Five or six toddlers — as dirty and unkempt as the women beside them — were playing in the filthy rushes competing with dogs and cats for scraps of food. Filthy trestle tables without tablecloths — some in urgent need of repair — had been set up for supper.

I looked around the room. It was so different from Father's house. The ceiling was lower, the windows smaller. There was no dais and no private Lady-chamber. Dark woolen drapes separated the sleeping quarters. Tancred pushed them aside to show the room to Senda. He walked to the bed of oak timbers, big enough to sleep four, occupying a good portion of the right side of the room. Several pallets lined the rest of the walls. Tancred pulled the bed curtains aside. He smiled at Senda, but she turned away and walked around the room.

I often saw the smile fade on Tancred's face. Senda ran his household diligently, using her mother's advice, but she did it without enthusiasm. She was constantly busy at first, for the house had been long without a mistress and many things needed her attention. Some things were new to her, like supervising the care for baby Jeoffrey, the child who had cost Muriella her life.

"Make sure his nurse drinks plenty of milk, Bernfrieda," she would say, recalling the advice she had heard at Granville. "And that she eats her fill. And do not let her eat garlic, as I saw her do yesterday, for it is bad for the milk."

In the evenings, after the tables had been cleared, she sat quietly with Tancred and his knights, hardly speaking. I knew that her mind and her heart often wandered at those times, for she still thought of Guillaume. How could she prefer a mere boy to Tancred? How could she not see that Tancred loved her? Happiness such as her mother had never known was within her reach. There would be no bastards in this household, no concubines.

The longing on Tancred's face as he looked at Senda; the anxious darting of his eyes when she was late coming into the hall; the sudden frown that clouded his expression when someone spoke of Guillaume and she looked up from her sewing and followed every word — all told of Tancred's love for her.

Privacy did not exist at Tancred's house. Senda's bed was cocooned by curtains but her five women, baby Jeoffrey and his nurse, and I all slept in the same chamber on pallets. When it was very cold the nurse and the baby shared Senda's bed. Tancred rarely spent the whole night with Senda, preferring to sleep in the hall with his knights, as Father had.

But he visited her often. I lay wide awake in my pallet then, pretending to be asleep as he set the small candle on a stool by the bed. He would undress quickly, throwing his garments carelessly on the chest at the foot of the bed. Naked, he would lean over the candle, blow it out and open the bed curtain. I shivered at the scraping sound of the curtains against the wooden pole as he pulled them shut again.

I loved Tancred but tried to dismiss him from my mind when I thought of him. But my dreams spared me nothing. It was hard to be patient with Senda when she talked of Guillaume. She readily shared her feelings, but she left me alone when she saw that I had something on my mind. Had she loved her husband she would have recognized my love for him. But she lived her days indifferent to both his love and my pain.

🐦 🐦 🐦

Three months later, she realized that she was pregnant. When she told Tancred, his response surprised her.

"Are you sure?" he asked gravely.

"Yes my Lord. Bernfrieda says that is the reason for the dizziness I feel in the morning. And I have twice missed my flux."

"Senda." He took her hands. "Be careful. Do not tire yourself. Let Bernfrieda take charge of the house and the servants. I . . ."

"Are you displeased, my Lord?" Senda asked. He gazed at her silently.

When he spoke, his voice was unsteady. "You are more precious to me than any child you could give me."

Senda was bewildered.

"The children you give me, I shall love. But you are my most beloved, Senda. In my youth I may have felt otherwise, but . . ."

Later Senda tried to make sense of what Tancred had told her. The whole purpose of marriage is to have children, she said to me. Father Raoul had said it many times. Tancred already had five children, and she decided that was the reason for his lack of enthusiasm.

"Tancred loves you, Senda," I said coldly, irritated at her stupidity. I did not mention that he feared for her life because it would add to her worry about childbirth. Senda shrugged at my words. I opened my mouth to argue but then shut it. Things will change when the baby comes, I thought; it might not be long before even the memory of Guillaume faded away.

Spring came. Senda started a garden on the level spot at the south side of the house where Muriella had kept hers. Servants tilled the earth while she supervised them, telling them exactly how to lay the beds and mulch them with waste. The orchard house also took much of her time. She had servants cut the weeds and prune the apple and walnut trees. She became very fond of the orchard and garden because the place, with its high walls, afforded her a measure of privacy she had never had as a child or in the house.

❦ ❦ ❦

Senda grew big during the summer. Early that fall she was sitting in the hall mending when she suddenly stood up.

"Something is wrong, Bernfrieda," she whispered. "I think I am bleeding." I ran to her and as we turned to go the chamber, I saw a large watery stain on her tunic.

"You are not bleeding." I tried to sound calm. "The baby is coming." Her waters had broken. We had not expected it so soon.

The pains were mild and widely spaced at first, so I breathed a little easier. I sent a servant to the bailey to summon the midwife; another sped off on horseback to locate Tancred. Richvereda, who had been Muriella's handmaid, crossed herself furtively when the midwife arrived. Bent and emaciated, shrouded in a tattered black mantle, the old woman came in carrying a large cloth bag and the birthing chair. The midwife peered at Senda, bowed, and then put the bag on a stool and set the birthing chair next to the only window in the room. The chair was small, with a horseshoe-shaped seat and short tapered legs. Senda watched suspiciously; she had never seen a birth. The midwife carefully removed several small leather pouches from her bag, a sharp knife and a meat hook.

Senda recoiled when she saw the instruments, and I took her hand and held it tightly; I too was terrified.

"What else do you need, old woman?" I asked.

"More light," the woman mumbled. Though it was early afternoon, I motioned one of the women to fetch a torch.

"As for the rest, I came prepared." She grinned. Two broken, blackened upper teeth still clung to her discolored gums. She approached Senda, who shrank back. Her watery, red-rimmed eyes were now only inches from Senda's. Her fingers with their stained, broken fingernails, trailed over the swollen womb. A wave of pain overcame Senda and she cried out. The woman frowned.

"You must be strong, my Lady. You have lost the water already and this may go on for a long time." The voice was inflectionless, as if she were reciting an old chant.

The pains were soon stronger and closer together. Senda would walk the room when the pain abated, only to collapse on the chair in misery when it returned. The midwife did not speak again, but rubbed Senda's feet when the pain was most intense.

The candle went down a mark. The silence of the room was broken only by Senda's moans. She withdrew into herself as the time between pains grew shorter and shorter. During one such moment the midwife thrust her hand into her opening.

"The Lord be thanked. The child is in the right position," she grinned.

"How much longer?" I asked.

"The child is close. She'll deliver before the candle goes down another mark."

Richvereda crossed herself again. The other women spoke to each other all at the same time. I ordered sweet herbs to be thrown onto the brazier to overpower the stench the old hag had brought into the room. The contractions were very close now; Senda thrashed wildly each time they came. It took two women to restrain her and keep her on the chair. The candle burned another mark, yet nothing happened.

"What is the matter?" I grabbed the hag's thin arm. "You said she would have delivered by now!"

"She needs to push harder." The midwife shook her head. "The head of the baby is big."

"Be careful, old woman." I hissed. "Lord Tancred will have you flayed alive if anything happens to his Lady." As if summoned by those words, Tancred appeared on the threshold.

"How is she?" he asked, his face white.

Senda stared at him wild-eyed. "Go away!" she screamed. "Leave, leave!"

He walked in. I was stunned. A man had no place at his wife's lying-in! He motioned Richvereda and the other women to let go of Senda, and took their place. I did not dare speak. He put his arms around Senda in an embrace that became an iron grip when he needed to restrain her. Senda cried bitterly as wave after wave of pain sent her screaming against him.

"Old woman!" Tancred yelled. The midwife cowered. He lowered his voice until it was almost inaudible. "Do what you must, but beware. If my Lady dies, so do you. I'll have you cut into pieces with your own instruments."

The old woman's hands began to tremble. "I brought forth all of your sons, my Lord Tancred," she cried. "And all of them without blemish."

"Make sure my *wife* comes out of this alive," Tancred snarled.

"She needs to push harder." The midwife whined, her attention riveted on Senda. "Here," she handed me a small container. "Make her smell this." I watched as Senda inhaled the fine black powder. Her body convulsed. "Quick, stop her nostrils!" The midwife said to me. I did. Senda writhed and pushed, pushed and writhed, without relief.

Rivulets of sweat ran down Tancred's face and his voice was hoarse. "Why doesn't she give birth?"

"The baby's head — it is too big for her opening." The midwife wrung her hands.

"Don't let her die!" he commanded.

The midwife rummaged among the contents of her bag, picked up a container, hesitated, then put it down.

"There is something you can do for her, my Lord, before I resort to this," pointing at the bottle.

Tancred nodded. She asked for an egg and a basin of water. "Wash your hands in the basin, my Lord, so that she can drink of the water."

Tancred gently extricated himself and did what he was told. The midwife cracked the egg, discarded its content on the floor and filled half a shell with some of the water Tancred had used. Senda drank from the eggshell. Nothing happened, however, and new pain racked her body.

His face dark, Tancred opened his mouth to speak, but before he could, she picked up the small container and brought it to Senda's lips.

"Drink!" She said urgently. Senda obeyed.

"What did you give her?" Tancred asked hoarsely.

"Only juice of vervain, my Lord." We all waited to see what would happen. I mopped Senda's forehead with a clean linen.

The midwife took a small flask from her bag.

"Heat this on the brazier, quick! The juice will have effect very soon!" The midwife turned to Tancred. "It is thyme oil, my Lord," she explained. He was busy again holding Senda.

"I wish the Lord Tancred would go away," Richvereda whispered to me. "He will bring bad luck."

"I'll spread it over her opening," the midwife said, her voice shaking. "It should enlarge it. If this does not work, I'll have to use the knife."

Senda's face twisted anew as the hot oil was applied. I knelt by her and mopped her brow.

Later she said that everything seemed to happen slowly, and that voices seemed all to come from a great distance.

"Quick, don't let her faint, rub the soles of her feet with vinegar and use it on her palms too. She must push now. Push my Lady, push! . . . Look, the baby's head is coming!"

Everyone began speaking. Cries of praise and prayers of thanks were heard all at once.

Senda opened her eyes, revived by the pungent smells and the voices. Pain still clawed at her.

"It's coming, O it's coming!" the midwife yelled. "A male, my Lord; it is a male!"

"I can see that myself," Tancred snapped. He held Senda close to him. Then put his mouth by her ear and spoke softly. "Forgive me. I promised never to hurt you, and yet I caused you so much pain. Forgive me, my love." Senda did not respond. I felt like shaking her. Her eyes closed. Had she fainted again?

With great care, Tancred laid her on the bed, where fresh linens had been spread and took the baby from the wet-nurse. The child was big, its face red and puckered. Tancred smoothed the soft red fuzz on his scalp with his finger.

"Robert," he said, "his name shall be Robert, like our Duke. May you grow as daring and courageous as Robert The Magnificent!" Senda, who under my ministrations had opened her eyes, watched unsmiling.

He returned the baby to the wet-nurse, then sat on a stool at the foot of the bed until Senda fell asleep. After her breathing had calmed, he stood up. He caught my eye then. "She is fragile, Bernfrieda. We must take care of her." He put his hand on my shoulder. *What makes you think I am stronger? I am not what you think, neither is she. How can you be so blind? You can protect her all you want, not only does she not need it, but it will never make her love you.*

He left the room. I stayed by Senda. I wiped her face, changed the bloody linens, fed her some broth; stayed until she fell into exhausted sleep again.

During the next few weeks I made sure the servants knew what to do and that the food on the table was varied, and I fell into a pattern that was to continue for many years. Senda kept to her room, often taking her food there. One evening I went into her chamber to see how she was doing. She and the baby were asleep and I turned to go back to the hall when I saw Tancred. He was standing by the draperies that separated the chamber, looking at me, his arms folded.

"Why haven't you chosen among my knights, Bernfrieda?" He asked. "Any of them would be happy to marry you."

"I do not want to marry, my Lord. I am happy serving my half-sister."

"You could still serve her during the day, Bernfrieda. You could even sleep here, and visit your husband in his quarters if you chose."

I shook my head, feeling color rise to my cheeks. *It is you I want. Not Raymond who makes sport of snatching at any servant girl he can lay his hands on. Rodomer and Vukan can't speak more than a sentence at a time, and always stink of urine and ale. The others are nothing compared to you.*

I looked at him without smiling. For a long moment he considered me. Then he touched my cheek. "You are too pretty to become an old maid, Bernfrieda," he said quietly, and retreated into the hall.

*The first of his peers, their president and general, was
entitled Count of Apulia; and this dignity was conferred
on William [Guillaume] of the iron arm, who, in the
language of the age is styled a lion in battle, a lamb in
society, and an angel in council.*

— Edward Gibbon: *The Decline and Fall of the
Roman Empire*

CAPUT VII

The Abbey of Santa Eufemia
On the eve of the Feast of Saint Ulrich, Bishop (July 4)
In this year 1061 from the Incarnation of our Lord
The words of Bernfrieda

Hauteville, 1030

Fourteen years after Senda's wedding Father summoned Tancred to fight for their overlord, the Bishop of Coutances. Robert, who was now thirteen, rode with his grandfather and met Tancred in the city of Coutances. In the Bishop's house, they joined Serlon, Tancred's first-born by Muriella, his first wife, and Senda's brother, Mauger, who had also been raised there.

At Hauteville, with most of the able men gone, Senda and I enlisted field serfs to help with the house chores. Still, nothing was done right and we had to spend much time training the new servants. At least Senda was spared having to worry about small ones, for she had stopped having children. At Senda's request,

Tancred had not come to her bed since her youngest was born, a five-year-old girl named after her.

It was little Fredesenda who spotted the small group of knights in the distance. She alerted the household, and we all watched as they emerged from the thick woods that mantled the hill.

Senda and the three old knights Tancred had left hurried to the gate. I followed them. The group of men, twenty in all, reached the top of the hill and rode toward the clearing where Tancred's house stood. When they were close enough to be recognized, Senda put her hand over her heart.

Guillaume dismounted and walked in calm, measured steps to the gate. His short brown hair and eyes fringed by those long thick lashes were the same and yet he was different. *It is the way he holds up his chin that gives his face an assurance and strength only hinted at when he was fourteen. And he is so much taller than Senda now!* They looked at each other without smiling. Then he bowed deeply. *I wonder how she must seem to him after all these years. She too is so different from the thin, angular girl he left behind.*

It was Senda who spoke first, extending her hand as she greeted him. "Welcome Guillaume," she said, in a steady voice, "Your father is already in Coutances."

He took her hand with great care, as if it would break, and brought it to his lips, his eyes still on hers. His voice was deeper than I remembered when he answered her greeting.

In the hall he and his men were surrounded by the rest of the household. He sat down in his father's chair, and Senda ordered food and drink. He began to answer the stream of questions asked by Tancred's three knights and the women who begged him to tell them about Italy.

Senda picked up her sewing and seemed absorbed in it. Guillaume kept looking toward her as he retold the story messengers had told us so many times. He told an urgent, vivid tale. I could almost smell the scent of roses and jasmine that had greeted him and his Norman friends as they entered the palace of Salerno. They had stopped there at the invitation of the Lombard Prince Guaimar, Guillaume explained, on their way back to Normandy from the shrine of Saint Michael on Mount Gargano.

Guillaume put his wine cup on the trestle table next to him, and took off one of his tall leather boots. He held the boot high so everyone could see it. "Those who have sailed around Italy say that it is shaped like this. Here is Rome," he said, and pointed at a spot halfway between the top of the boot and the toe.

"Below it, here, is the south of Italy. Once this land belonged to the Emperor of Byzantium. Then the Lombards, a Germanic tribe which arrived in Italy soon after the fall of the Roman Empire, settled in the territory below Rome, here, on the coast." Guillaume ran his finger over the lower front of the boot. "Salerno is right here on the coast, almost straight across from the spur, where Mount Gargano and the Holy Shrine of Saint Michael are located. Twenty of us Normans who had just arrived in Italy were returning from that shrine when Guaimar invited us to Salerno. We thought we were in heaven. The sun was hot, yet the breeze from the sea kept us cool. Guaimar's palace was filled with treasures I had never seen before: enameled furniture, curtains made of the finest, most intricate lace, boxes inlaid with mother-of-pearl and ebony. The people were friendly, the food plentiful and superbly prepared.

"As we sat in Guaimar's hall we heard moans and cries coming from outside. People had filled the square that overlooked the sea right in front of Guaimar's palace. They carried sacks of food, wool, live animals and all the goods that one would see at a fair. But they were wailing and crying. When we asked Guaimar the reason for such sorrow, he pointed at the horizon. There, coming from the Sicilian coast, was a fleet of small white sails. Saracen ships." Guillaume traced an imaginary triangle straight across the toe of the boot. "They came from Sicily, the great island, which the Arabs wrested from the Byzantines two hundred years before." Guillaume stopped, took his cup and gulped some wine. He dried his mouth with the back of his hand before he continued.

"The heathen ships lined up along the horizon." Senda looked up from her embroidery and their eyes met. "We Normans

watched in amazement on that warm summer day as the citizens
of Salerno piled sacks of barley and wheat, bolts of silk, coins
and jewels onto the main square in front of the sea. Standing by
a large window on the first floor of his magnificent stucco palace
overlooking the square, Prince Guaimar told us it was the price
he had agreed to pay each year to prevent his coastal villages
from being pillaged. 'Let us fight for you, Guaimar!' We all
cried. And in the end we convinced him."

Guillaume looked at the faces around him. All were holding
their breath, waiting for him to go on. He took another swallow
of wine before he continued.

"That day, we threw the Saracens into the sea." The audience
cheered and Guillaume smiled. "Guaimar cried for joy and
promised lands and honors to any of the Norman knights who
would stay in Salerno. I did." Guillaume put down the boot and
leaned back in his chair, his eyes half-closed.

"I fought for Guaimar at first, and for his brother, Prince Guy
of Sorrento. I stayed in Aversa during that time, the city where
all Normans gathered when they were not fighting for the
Lombards."

Guillaume sat up and paused to drink again.

We had heard the story before, for Guillaume's messengers
came regularly to Hauteville. But it was different to hear it from
his lips. The flushed faces in the hall reflected their pleasure at
the tale. But Guillaume shook his head when asked for more and
let his knights do the talking. He took a leg of the cold roasted
pheasant a servant had set next to him and ate in silence, listening to the boasting. He looked up at Senda only once, when his
knights told how the Lombard Prince of Sorrento had offered
Guillaume his sister Yolanda in marriage.

After eating, Guillaume gave us the gifts he had brought from
Italy: for Lady Fredesenda a wrought silver chalice with enameled silver gilt mounts and a length of silvery silk. More silk,
deep green, for me. For Tancred, a sword of exquisite workman-
ship with a secret place in the hilt, a reliquary with a piece of the
finger of Saint Vito.

The women readied a bath for him. While his knights continued to boast, Senda listened in silence, her eyes on her sewing.
Guillaume came out of his bath with his hair wet, wearing a
clean linen tunic and chausses. Senda tried to concentrate on her
work, but her eyes kept going to him. Worried, I sat closer to her
and kept a close watch on Guillaume.

He lowered himself into Tancred's chair. His head slightly inclined to the right, he listened to his knights, answering a question now and then. The course of Senda's needle was uneven; she
held her breath when he spoke.

Later, as the sun set, Senda got up and walked toward the
door leading to her orchard. I rose to follow but she turned before she stepped out of the room and touched my arm, bidding
me stay. Unwilling to let her go, I took another step, but she was
firm. I sat back down and picked up her work. Guillaume followed her shortly afterward. She told me everything later, but
she had no need, for I could imagine all that happened between
them.

She opened the gate and walked toward a wooden bench under a walnut tree. The foliage was thick; the high walls that enclosed the orchard were scarcely visible. She tried to control her
inner turmoil. How many years had passed? That summer by the
river . . . She touched the brooch he had given her. She always
wore it inside her tunic, next to her breast.

*The gate opened. She looked up. Guillaume stood in front of her,
his arms folded, his face serious.*

"Were you not pleased to see me, Senda?"

"Of course I was pleased, Guillaume." Her voice betrayed her.
He knelt then, embracing her waist and burying his head in her
lap. "So many years," he said, his voice full of sadness, "so many
years."

*She kissed his wet hair and, when he raised his face to hers, his
lips. Slowly they stood up, still linked in their embrace, not wanting
to think, wanting to be children still. When he gently pushed her on
the grass, she felt his body, so close through the linen tunic, the thumping of his heart, and his desire for her.*

❦ ❦ ❦

"Come to Apulia, Senda," he said. "Come with me to Melfi."

She extricated herself from his embrace and adjusted her clothes. He too sat up.

"I am your father's wife, Guillaume,"

He shrugged. "Italy is a wild country, Senda. Nobody would dare interfere."

"But the Norman community is small. Dreaux, Onfroi — they would know. How could I live in sin with you?"

"They would not dare cross me. They owe everything to me."

She thought of waking by his side each morning, running his household, bearing his children. Children. She would have to leave little Fredesenda behind; never see her other half-grown children again.

"No," she said. "I can't leave."

"Come with me, Senda." He covered his eyes with one hand. "I could not stop thinking of you in my father's bed."

She wanted to kiss him; but if she did she would do as he wanted.

"I have borne Tancred six children." She looked at the grass in front of her feet. He stood, and pulled her up to him, taking her face in his hands and forcing her to look at him.

"I hated you for so long, because I could not erase you from my thoughts. Year after year I lived only to hear the scraps of news I could glean about you. I fought fiercely during those years. When I pierced an enemy's heart I was piercing yours. Fourteen years, Senda."

Abruptly he let her go, but still stood in front of her. "Tomorrow I'll leave. If you change your mind, I'll take you to Apulia; if you don't, I'll go to Coutances and never come back."

That night Senda lay awake by my side; as I had taken to sleeping with her. At dawn I saw her staring at the bed curtains. The next day, Guillaume left for Coutances.

❦ ❦ ❦

Early fall arrived, and so did Tancred, a month after
Guillaume left Hauteville. Senda knew something was wrong
the moment he dismounted; she immediately feared that he
might know about Guillaume's visit.

Tancred stood in the middle of the courtyard while his men
took care of the horses. He had aged. White streaked his
golden-red hair, but his back was still straight and he still looked
to me like the gallant knight who had ridden to Father's keep
fourteen years before.

Senda stood inside the entrance of the hall. When he saw her,
his face lit up, but he turned somber again in a matter of moments. He walked to her and took her in his arms.

"Welcome, my Lord," Senda whispered.

"Senda, I am sorry. Your father —" Immediately I understood
the reason for his demeanor. So did Senda. She searched his
face.

"Has something happened to my father, my Lord?"

"God knows I would have gladly died in his stead, my love.
Shortly after Guillaume arrived, your father was ambushed in a
major battle by a party of Belleme's. I did not realize he was
missing until after the battle was over."

"My Lord —" I took a step toward him. "Do you know what
happened to Armand and Henry?"

He shook his head dejectedly. "Your brothers too fell,
Bernfrieda. As did the knight Alferio — he tried to shield his
Lord with his body."

Henry and Armand were like Father's shadow, always behind
him, but if Alferio had tried to save Father's life, they must have
been cut down *before* him. I felt no gladness about Alferio's
death. Death equalized them all.

While Senda broke into tears and clutched me, my eyes could
not leave Tancred's compassionate face.

Later, I went with Senda into the orchard and we huddled on
the bench. I still felt no grief. I am glad, I kept thinking, that
God took Father and not Tancred.

"God is punishing me, Bernfrieda," Senda sobbed, her head
on my shoulder. "I know Father died because I sinned."

"No. Men sin like you did, all the time, and God does not punish them. Did He punish Guillaume? Men are killed by other men in battle, not by God."

That night in the hall after dinner I looked up and met Tancred's eyes. He was frowning as he toyed with his knife. Senda had left soon after the tables had been removed. She often retired early at night, preferring her bed to the long tales by the braziers. Tancred leaned toward me.

"I am sorry about your brothers, Bernfrieda," he said. "They died bravely."

"Thank you, my Lord."

"Did Guillaume stop here for long on the way to the battle-field?"

Had Guillaume betrayed Senda?

"He stayed one night."

"How — did Senda — seem to you?" He struggled to find the right words.

I can confirm his suspicions without saying a word. She betrayed him; she does not deserve him. Would he cast her from his house? If Senda falls will I fall with her? Could he keep me in his house if I betrayed the woman he loves? For he still loves her. I am still pleasant — my breasts are still firm — I already keep his house — I manage his servants — would that be enough for him to keep me?

"Senda was happy because she knew you would be, my Lord. She told me it was strange to see again one she had seen last as little more than a child. It reminded her of the times at Granville and made her realize how fortunate she has been all these years to be Lady of her own house." I lied without flinching.

He looked at me. His blue eyes were still searching.

To have betrayed him.

He nodded and looked at his knife. "Bring some ale!" He called. "Pour some for Bernfrieda, Raymond," he told the knight who had rushed to his side with a pitcherful.

That night Tancred came to her bed. He told Senda that Father had been buried in the chapel he had built after we left, in the bailey. She cried and told him she must pray on Father's grave. "Take me home," she pleaded.

"I'll take you to Granville before I go back into battle," he said.

They slept together that night.

Granville, 1030

I smelled the sea air even before we could see the coast. Then Father's weathered tower appeared, forlorn and dark. Senda and I sat in the empty cart; no sacks of grain to sit on this time. The oxen would not speed their pace. All seemed as we had left it: the livid waves battering the coast without pause, the seagulls swooping down on the water or resting on the rocky beach, oblivious to our small party. Even the old guard who opened the gate was the same. He waved at us, surprised, before he remembered to bow.

We ached all over when we finally climbed down from the cart. Senda and Tancred stood on the threshold of the great hall as a servant announced us. Her brother Mauger looked up from Father's chair, and stood up uncertainly, smiling when he recognized Tancred. Next to him sat a young woman who looked at us curiously.

"Welcome Tancred — and Fredesenda," Mauger was ill at ease.

"You look very different, Mauger," Senda said. "You were only five the last time I saw you."

Mauger took her hand. "I present my wife, Lady Alice of Conques."

Senda curtsied to the pallid young woman who sat in her mother's chair. Lady Alice bowed slightly. "Welcome," she echoed without enthusiasm.

Senda looked around, then turned to her brother. "Where is our mother, Mauger?"

He cleared his throat. "Take some food first, Fredesenda, and warm yourself by the brazier. Mother spends her days in the chapel. It is cold there, and you are chilled already from your journey."

Senda shook her head. "Later, Mauger; I want to see her."

He nodded. "Adeliza is here too. You remember her husband, Richard de Walchelin?"

The heavy young man sitting to the right of Lady Alice looked up when he heard his name and nodded in our direction. He turned toward a page and motioned for more wine. The child knelt to pour it and spilled some. Richard threw the contents of the cup in the child's face, continuing to survey us. The page hurried to refill the glass, red liquid trickling down his face. Richard de Walchelin had grown handsome, but his character had not improved. I wondered what Adeliza's life was like. We turned to follow a servant to the chapel.

We had not seen Adeliza since leaving Father's house; we had not even attended her wedding five years before. I remembered the frozen expression on Adeliza's face the morning of Senda's betrothal. I recalled the words Adeliza had spoken in our chamber shortly afterward.

You think you are going to be a great Lady, don't you?

The servant pushed the heavy wooden chapel door open and then stepped aside. Our eyes adjusted to the semi-darkness. Lady Mathilda was kneeling before the altar. Senda walked quickly to her.

"Mother!"

Lady Mathilda turned. "Adeliza?"

She rose from her knees, peering toward us. "Fredesenda?"

Lady Mathilda was wrapped in one of the dark tunics she favored, her face bony and white. Senda embraced her.

"How are you, Mother?"

Lady Mathilda shrugged. "Father Raoul is making arrangements for me to enter the nunnery in Coutances. Mauger and Alice will be glad. I sleep with the women now. Adeliza is making preparations. Have you seen her already?" Senda shook her head.

"She is not happy. Richard is cruel to her. She cannot bear him a live child."

Silence. Senda looked about her. "Is Father's grave here?" She asked softly.

Her mother turned and pointed to a slab in the floor a few feet from the altar. Senda knelt; slowly she traced her father's name with her finger.

Lady Mathilda stayed where she was. "May the Lord forgive him his sins," she said. "For they were many and grievous. I must pray for him constantly."

She spends her time praying but does not realize that she sinned as grievously. To deny love is the worst sin. She never loved him, or their children.

After a few more moments of prayer we rose from our father's tomb. Lady Mathilda looked at her daughter, a weak smile on her face. "I am glad Tancred is kind to you, Fredesenda." She kissed her daughter's cheek, then, dismissing her, knelt again to pray.

Senda stood by her mother's bent figure as if she wanted to speak. But in the end she turned around, her eyes full of tears, and I followed her outside.

In the hall, where Tancred and the men were eating by the brazier, she hesitated. Then she made up her mind and started upstairs. "Come, Bernfrieda," she commanded. We stopped a few moments in the antechamber, wondering who was sleeping on our pallet. I knocked on the closed door of the bed chamber.

"Come in!" Adeliza said imperiously. I opened the door and stood aside for Senda to enter. Adeliza was standing by her mother's open chest, holding a tunic. She was heavy with child, and I recalled her mother's words.

"Fredesenda — and Bernfrieda, of course!" There was no welcome in Adeliza's voice. She was thin, in spite of the advanced pregnancy; her face had lost its roundness and color. She studied Senda. "You look well," she said in the same cold tone she had used to greet her. "I saw your first-born. He looks like Tancred." She dropped the tunic she was holding. "Did you come to gloat over your good fortune? To compare your life to mine?"

Senda shook her head. "I came to pray on Father's grave; I did not know you were here. I never wished you ill."

"You married Tancred. You had his children — healthy, handsome children. I waited for Richard to reach manhood. And when he did, five years ago, I was *old*. Look!" She pointed at her belly. "This is the third time I carry his child. One I lost after scarcely three months; the other died at birth — and Richard wished I had died instead of the baby, so he could marry a young woman. He holds me dear only for the heir he requires." Tears were streaming down her face.

Senda stepped toward her. Adeliza stopped her with a gesture. "Go away, Fredesenda. I hope, O I really hope that someday you too will suffer as I suffer now."

Tancred did not argue that night when Senda asked him to take her home, even if it meant postponing his return to battle.

"A stranger in my father's house!" Senda cried, as the oxen plodded down the hill the next morning, leaving Father's keep behind. "Father is dead, my brother is a stranger. My mother too wrapped in sorrow to need me, and Adeliza —" Senda shuddered as she recalled the hatred in her sister's voice. "I do not want to ever come back. I shall carry Father in my heart and I'll pray for Mother . . . and Adeliza," she added after some hesitation. "But I'll never come back to Granville."

I had visited my mother's grave earlier that morning. I had found the place only because I knew she had been buried under a tall pine, which fortunately was still standing. The stones I had placed around her grave years before were gone, and brown brush covered the ground. I cleaned the grave as best I could and I brought the biggest stone I could carry to place over it. I dug a shallow hole for it with a stick, then I knelt to pray.

How different Father's burial had been. He lay inside a chapel; Father Raoul had celebrated Mass for him, and his friends had gathered to say goodbye at a stone tomb made to withstand the centuries. I remembered the cold windy morning I followed the two serfs who carried my mother's body, and that of her baby, wrapped in a coarse brown cloth. They dug the grave in silence, stopping every now and then to blow on their fingers. The wind had caught the brown cloth as they lifted the bodies off the ground to place them in the grave, and uncovered her face. It was as white as the moon on a cold winter night. Her long black hair danced wildly around her dead face, shrouding it in the end, even before the men caught the cloth and tucked it under her. They hastened to fill in her grave, and stomped over it when they were done. I had prayed there until I was so numb with cold I had fallen ill.

Senda searched for my hand as we rode back to Hauteville. I held it; but her sorrow was for Father. Mine was for the young woman whose neglected grave would soon disappear again. The tall pine would be cut down, or toppled by the fierce winds from the north. And then nothing would remain to mark the site. Why speak of her to Senda? I kept my gaze on the sea until it became a thin silver ribbon, then disappeared.

For he [Rogier] was a youth of great beauty, tall of stature and of elegant proportions . . . He remained ever friendly and cheerful. He was gifted also with great strength of body and courage in battle. And by these qualities he soon won the favour of all.

— Gaufredus Malaterra, transl. John Julius
Norwich: *Historia Sicula*

CAPUT VIII

The Abbey of Santa Eufemia
On the eve of the Feast of Saint Victor, Martyr (July 21)
In this year 1061 from the Incarnation of our Lord
The words of Bernfrieda

Hauteville, 1031

Rogier was born early the following spring. As with the other children, Tancred was present during the birth. He left soon after seeing the baby, though. Senda never knew Tancred's reaction. The birth had been long and troublesome because of the lapse in time between pregnancies, and she had fallen into exhausted sleep soon after giving birth.

Tancred held out his hands to receive the baby. He held the newborn at a distance, in order to see him better. He did not smile, but kept examining him. Dread enveloped me as I searched his face. The lines on his forehead were deep as he studied the baby. A Roman father about to command his newborn thrown from the Tarpea cliff could not have looked much different.

"He is a beautiful baby," I murmured. Tancred looked up at me. Without a word he handed me Rogier and walked out of the room. Troubled, I gave the baby to Richvereda and followed him.

Tancred sat in the hall all afternoon, drinking ale with his knights as they noisily celebrated the birth. As the hours passed he talked less and less and drank more. When the first shadows of night arrived, he stood up and walked outside.

I followed him. I waited while he relieved himself just steps from the entrance. As he staggered past me to reenter the hall, I caught his sleeve.

"I must speak to you, my Lord."

He gave me a searching look before nodding. I glanced around, looking for a place where I could speak to him alone. My intention was to reassure him that Rogier was his son. The bailey was deserted but it was still too cold to stay out long. I walked into a low rectangular building with a row of narrow slits for light in the back, where cows were kept. No one disturbed us. The stable boys had joined the celebration in the hall.

I closed only one side of the double doors in order to take advantage of the last light of the day. The smells of dung and straw permeated the small room. The cows looked calmly at us as we passed, and continued to chew.

As I led Tancred toward a stack of hay, I began to realize the foolhardiness of my plan. I would not be missed but Tancred would. He stumbled over a loose board and sprawled on the filthy floor. He waved away my attempt to help him and sat up, leaning heavily against a stack of hay. I stood awkwardly in front of him before I sat on the dirt facing him.

My desire to convince him that Rogier was his son was due to the certainty that he would see through my story. I had rehearsed my speech all afternoon. Now I could not say a word.

"She loves Guillaume," he mumbled. He looked at me, caught at my arm and pulled me toward him until my face was only inches from his. "True, isn't it?"

I struggled. He eyed me, surprised, and readily let go. All fear left me then. I stood up.

"She loves Guillaume. Always has." He put his face in his hands; sobbing or drunken laughter, I could not tell at first.

Some men cried when a friend died in battle, when they lost a parent or a child, when their sins were so great that nothing could atone them. But Tancred, weeping?

"My Lord." I touched his shoulder.

Great heart-rending sobs. I dropped to my knees and touched him. Then I pulled his face against my chest. Gradually his desolate crying stopped. I knew that I should run back to the hall. He pulled away from me and looked into my eyes. He raised his hand, pulled my wimple off and touched my hair.

"Your hair. So soft." He lifted a handful and held it against his cheek. "Beautiful Bernfrieda." He trailed a finger over my neck and then fumbled with my tunic. I unlaced it and helped him find my breast. I felt his lips on my nipple, his soft, prickly beard on my skin. I had loved him for so many years, dreaming of this moment, that I too wept now. He tasted my tears when he kissed me. I shut my eyes when I felt his manhood, braced myself for the pain, but he did not hurt. He held me in his lap and gently lowered me against him. Our closeness overwhelmed me, my face on his shoulder as I held him tight, wishing this to last.

"How different it could have been if Mauger had given you to me," he whispered, while we coupled.

Later he gently extricated himself from my embrace and we sat side by side, leaning back into the hay. We both gazed at the half-open door. Anyone could have seen us, and yet I did not care.

"This was not right," he said softly, after a short silence.

I love you. How can it not be right?

He was quiet for a long while. "I was not myself, Bernfrieda." He stood up and helped me off the floor. "Please." He smoothed his tunic with quick, nervous gestures. "I am glad it was not your first time," he said, without looking at me.

He hesitated, turned and walked toward the door.

I followed him — I wanted to tell him. "My Lord," I called.

He turned.

"I love you —" I said, before I could think. I should have held my peace. "— As I love my half-sister. I shall make penance for both of us."

He stepped into the bailey.

I willed myself to conceive his child. When my flux came, I grieved and blamed God for his cruelty. How foolish I was to think that He would reward my sin!

Tancred never acknowledged with words what had happened between us. Sometimes, during the following years, I caught him looking at me. He smiled his tight little smile when he met my eyes and looked away quickly. And I knew that he had not forgotten, that he was thinking of — of what could have been. That thought made my life bearable.

Tancred's behavior toward Rogier changed. He was a loving man and a forgiving one. Perhaps he saw the child Guillaume, who had left him so early, in Rogier. Perhaps he simply stopped tormenting himself and just accepted him. He grew attached to his youngest as he had never been to the other children. Handsome and affectionate, Rogier responded to love with love.

🌾 🌾 🌾

The visit to Father's house left a mark on Senda and she talked to me often of her mother's losses. After Father's death, Lady Mathilda had lost her status, her privileges and even her house. Senda became obsessed with what would happen after *her* husband died. She talked of Tancred as an old man. At sixty he was vigorous and gentle, but to Senda he had always been old. His first-born, Serlon, had married in Coutances just days after Rogier was born. He and his Lady Maud planned to come to Hauteville to live, so they could prepare for their future duties. When she learned of their plans, Senda wondered how long before she too would be forced to retire to a nunnery. I shrugged when she brought up this subject.

"Tancred is strong," I said. "He'll live many more years."

"But what about battles?" she argued. "Father was still young when he was killed."

"As he grows older, Tancred will send Serlon to fight in his stead," I told Senda.

"And Serlon's wife has yet to bear children. Lady Maud might even die as so many die with child. Why concern yourself about a woman you do not know? You may like her well enough when you meet."

The couple arrived in late fall. Senda was in the hall nursing Rogier, something she had never done with the other children. She had sent away the wet-nurse and put Rogier to her breast just hours after he was born.

The small pregnant woman who walked toward us could have been pretty, had it not been for the scowl etched on her plump face. Her travelling mantle was splattered with mud, but it was lined with fine fur, and the brooch that held it together was wrought gold. Before Senda could welcome her, Maud spoke. "Call your Lady, good woman!" she said haughtily. "Didn't anybody warn her of my arrival?"

Senda opened her mouth to tell her who she was, but Maud interrupted her. "And bring me something to eat. I am tired and hungry!"

Senda looked at her, speechless and angry. She handed baby Rogier to me and stood up. "*I am* Lady Fredesenda." she said. I pretended to nuzzle the baby's head to hide my amusement. Senda took a step and towered over Serlon's wife.

"And who are *you?*"

"I am — Lady Maud — Serlon's wife — forgive me Lady Fredesenda — I'd never seen a Lady nursing an infant before — I thought —" she fell silent and lowered her eyes.

Their first meeting had not been auspicious, and Senda's initial dislike was confirmed during the following weeks. Maud spent her days in idleness, claiming to be always too tired or too ill to help with household chores. Her family was grander than the Hautevilles, she pointed out to anyone who would listen, and she had married below her station. She avoided Senda, whom she feared. And thought peculiar.

On the other hand, I was fascinated watching my half-sister nursing her young. "Nursing gives me pleasure," Senda told me one day. The baby stopped suckling just then and turned to face us, and we laughed. Rogier must have been four or five months old then. He looked at us solemnly, his forehead wrinkling. Then he laid a small fist protectively over the breast and resumed his sucking.

"I wish I had done the same with the other children," Senda added with a sigh. "No one told me what a delight it could be — you have no idea, Bernfrieda. When Rogier sucks I feel something moving inside my womb. It is the strangest feeling, like being thirsty and knowing you are about to drink your fill. O Bernfrieda, I can't explain!"

I was envious. My flux still came regularly — perhaps I could still marry. Tancred's knights had all settled down with servant girls. Any of them would have married me if Tancred had asked. But these were fleeting thoughts. I would never share a man with another woman. *Not even Tancred?* I chased away that thought with determination.

Senda was too taken with Rogier to be concerned about Maud, and it was not my place to tell the future Lady of Hauteville what to do. Perhaps we gave Maud the wrong impression. Spring came and Senda sent the servants out to till the earth so that her garden could be planted. She stayed in the hall with her baby, delegating the supervising of the serfs to me. That fact alone demonstrated the extent of her love for Rogier; Senda was hitherto as passionate about her garden as her mother had been about her religion.

Maud joined me and watched in silence until the earth was ready to be planted.

"The lavender should be moved over there, against that fence!" Maud said suddenly. "You!" She called to the man closest to her.

"Move that bush over here." She pointed to the fence. I looked at her with disbelief, as did the servant. "Lady Fredesenda wants it here," he said, shuffling his bare feet in the dirt.

Maud reddened. "Do what I say or I'll have you flogged!"

The man looked at me.

"Lady Fredesenda was very clear this morning, Maud. She said to lay the garden exactly as it was last year." I spoke evenly.

"Your Lady is busy with more important things." Maud snorted. "Do not presume to tell me what should or should not be done!" She took a step and faced me. We were about the same height but she was so pregnant that her belly almost touched me. I backed up. She turned to the man.

"Do as I say!"

"No!" I told the servant. "Don't change anything, Alveredo!"

Maud turned to me and slapped my face. She raised her hand again and I raised my own trying to protect my face. Prudence prevented me from striking back. The future Lady of the house was close to giving birth. So I stepped back, provoking enraged cries from Maud as I evaded another assault from her.

Senda hurried from the hall, followed by Richvereda. Quickly she handed the baby to her and sprang toward us. She caught Maud's raised arm and twisted it behind her back. The girl cried out in pain.

"Do not ever touch Bernfrieda again," Senda hissed through her teeth. "Do you understand?"

"She would not follow my orders," Maud whimpered.

"She was following *mine!*" Senda said in the same tone, again wrenching Maud's arm so that she cried out again. "And you shall not interfere. She is responsible to me only." Senda pushed her away; I had to steady Maud or she would have fallen.

"If this happens again," Senda said, "I shall have you take care of the pigs."

Maud became a mouse after that. She did not dare tell Serlon what had happened, for she knew it would be useless. She had wit enough to realize that Tancred would support Senda in all she chose to do at Hauteville. Maud even managed to look more industrious and avoided me when she could. But she never forgave Senda.

વૈ̃ વૈ̃ વૈ̃

Unfortunately, Maud did not die in childbirth. Her son was born at the beginning of summer, exactly a year after Rogier. He was named Serlon, like his father, though we called him Serlo to distinguish between the two. As much as his mother hated Senda, Serlo loved Rogier. I often marvelled that Maud could produce such a son. He was a true Hauteville both in looks and strength, a brave little boy loyal to Rogier from his infancy.

The two boys grew up hearing of the Hauteville conquests in southern Italy. Rogier was a handsome child, and the messengers from Apulia who came with news of his stepbrothers' conquests indulged his breathless questions. When Rogier was ten, word came from Italy that Guillaume had fought the Saracens in Sicily. There were internal fights between the Saracen emirs in Sicily and their Sultan in Tunis. The Byzantines were eager to regain the island, so Maniakes, the Byzantine *Catapan* hired Guillaume and his Normans to fight the Saracens. There were just over five hundred Normans, and thousands of Arabs in Syracuse. "But they were no match for us," the messenger chuckled. "Hoping to take the Normans by surprise, the Emir of Syracuse himself exited his city with his men. When the surprise attack failed, there was an open battle and Guillaume *Bras-de-Fer* sought out the Emir, unhorsed him, and left him dead on the ground. Disheartened by their leader's death the Saracens gave up and the Normans won the day."

Rogier tormented the messenger for more information. He was pleased to retell the story at first, but Rogier's questions grew more pressing. What wood did the Normans use for their catapults? His narrow, darkly handsome face would contract in the effort to remember the smallest detail. How did Guillaume *Bras-de-Fer* build his war machines at Syracuse? Were the Arabs poor fighters or was he truly helped by Saint George when he killed so many? What exactly was Guillaume's reaction when he was denied his fair share of the booty by the wily Maniakes? How had he planned his revenge?

One winter day two years later, we received word that the Normans in Italy had conquered enough land to establish their own territory. The city of Melfi became their capital, and a separate house was allotted to each of the twelve men they elected to rule over them. Guillaume *Bras-de-Fer* was unanimously elected their leader and assumed the title of Count of Apulia.

"I hope my stepbrother Guillaume saves some land for me when I grow up," Rogier said when the messenger had finished his report. Everyone laughed — except for Tancred, who continued to eat. Senda's first-born, Robert, had just joined his stepbrothers in Apulia and Tancred missed him sorely.

Young Serlo cried that *he* too wanted some of Italy. It was his father's turn to frown. "No, Serlo, you must soon begin your preparations to become Lord of Hauteville. You must stay, as I did, to rule your domain."

"Let young Tancred do that!" Serlo cried passionately, pointing at his toddler brother. "Or my next brother," he said, for Maud was again pregnant. "I shall go with Rogier."

"These are wild thoughts!" the elder Tancred interrupted brusquely. "You both will be needed here when you are grown."

I looked up in surprise, as did Senda, for Tancred had always encouraged his sons to leave. His unwillingness to part with Rogier surfaced again months later when he had to decide where Rogier would train.

"If your father were alive," he told Senda, "I would send him Rogier — but he might as well stay here like Dreaux and Onfroi did before him and train at Hauteville. Serlon and I can teach him." Senda did not protest.

🐦 🐦 🐦

Shortly after Guillaume became Count of Apulia, a messenger from Melfi came to announce his marriage to Yolanda, the Lombard Princess of Sorrento. I followed Senda into her orchard that evening. She was sitting on her bench as usual, staring at the walnut leaves dancing in a little whirl of air on the ground. She pushed at them with her foot. The acrid smell of peasants' bonfires hung in the air. I waited.

"Did I make the right decision, Bernfrieda?" she whispered. I took her hand but she did not move.

"You do not know what it is like to be someone's mistress."

"Neither do you, Bernfrieda." She looked at me sharply.

"You don't remember my mother." I stood up. "If you had followed Guillaume to Apulia," I said, lowering my voice, "you would have been happy for a time, but how long would it have been before he decided that a marriage alliance would earn him more land? A rich bride is worth more to men than any love." I hesitated. "*Most* men."

"You speak as if you were a mistreated mistress yourself, Bernfrieda." Senda smiled, and pulled me back into my seat. "You have not known love."

"Love!" I snatched my hand away. "Father told Mother many times that he loved her, but when the time came, he brought a bride from Fleurs."

"Guillaume would not have forsaken me." I stood up again; took a moment to compose myself, lest I said something too injurious.

"You did right, Senda. Never regret it." *It was Senda who had not loved enough.*

"When I think of him now I'll think of this other woman, the one he'll call wife, the one who'll bear his children —" she buried her face in her hands and sobbed. I felt only irritation for her. She had borne his son! I had only those few moments in the cattle-byre to remember.

"Do not torture yourself with these thoughts of Guillaume."

"You do not know how much it hurts," she whimpered.

I watched the leaves dancing in the dirt, and did not speak again.

❧ ❧ ❧

Rogier grew up. His small frame became stronger, until he was tall and slender; his childish snub nose became thin and straight under a high, noble forehead. He and Serlon grew closer than brothers. They were always together, playing, hunting, practicing the sword with Tancred's men. Like Damon and Pitia they were fiercely loyal to each other. They liked the same food, the same friends, they even loved the same girl when the time came.

Rogier was fifteen when Goda, Senda's best weaver, had her son. Goda was sixteen when Jourdain was born, and while Rogier claimed him as his own, even Goda could not tell for sure if the baby was Rogier's or Serlo's.

When Rogier turned sixteen he was ready to go to Italy. When a request for men came from Apulia, Tancred refused to let Rogier go. That evening, Senda told me later, she found her son just outside the gate of the bailey, sitting on a lone boulder brooding over the green valley below.

"You must insist, Rogier," she said, putting a hand on his shoulder. "You must go." He shrugged.

"Not this time, Mother," he said.

"Dreaux and Onfroi were your age when they left."

"There will be other times."

"Are you staying to please your father, Rogier?"

He turned to face her. "Father is old. A few years will not make a difference in my life, but they will in his."

Senda argued no further with Rogier. But perhaps if she pointed out to Tancred the sacrifice he was unwittingly imposing on his son, he would change his mind.

She did talk to Tancred, but to no avail. Tancred could not understand why Rogier should rush to Italy when he was needed at Hauteville. More and more he relied on his youngest. In Senda's view, he had grown selfish, blind to Rogier's best interest. I said nothing to her but a few noncommittal remarks.

But I could understand why Tancred did not want to lose Rogier. Serlon, his first-born, was surly; the tension between Senda and Maud palpable, but Rogier was full of life. His laughter and enthusiasm were contagious. He was generous and quick-witted, the only person in the keep who openly displayed his affection for Tancred.

I too dreaded the time he would leave. He loved practical jokes. They were outrageous at times but always funny, like the time he substituted vinegar for the Mass wine. He had come forward immediately when the servant in charge of supplies was accused, and even the servant had to laugh. Knowing how much he wanted to join Robert in Italy, Rogier's patience surprised me and earned my respect.

"I wish Rogier could go to Apulia, Bernfrieda," Senda often sighed.

"He has nothing to his name here at Hauteville — what kind of life will he have if he waits much longer? He should go to Guillaume — what if Tancred lives to be seventy?"

There was something else on her mind. If Rogier went to Apulia she felt sure Guillaume would recognize his son. In all those years she had never heard directly from him. All messages were directed to Tancred, although formal greetings to Lady Fredesenda were always included. Rogier was the only link she had with him.

But Rogier never met his father. Late that same summer news came from Apulia that Guillaume had died.

Undoubtably the lot of the serfs was very hard. Behind the bare texts, we must envisage a crude and primitive world with its moments of tragedy . . . the Lord was apt to lay claim, even in defiance of custom, to the exercise of an arbitrary authority.

— Marc Bloch, transl. L. A. Manyon: *Feudal Society*

CAPUT IX

The Abbey of Santa Eufemia
On the eve of the Feast of Saint Lawrence, Martyr (August 10)
In this year 1061 from the Incarnation of our Lord
The words of Bernfrieda

Hauteville, 1047

Tancred turned ashen when the messenger from Apulia brought news of Guillaume's death from an old wound that had never properly healed. He had left no heir. His widow, Yolanda of Sorrento, returned to her brother's house. The Norman barons of Apulia voted Dreaux to succeed his brother, and he took possession of the keep in Melfi.

Tancred sat by the brazier in the hall, refusing all food and drink, leaving all duties to Serlon. Maud ministered to Tancred, convinced she would soon be Lady of Hauteville. He remained by the brazier for two days; then Rogier pointed out that we should ask the grey monks at Saint Evroult to pray for Guillaume's soul. Once Tancred realized that he could still do something for his son, he wanted to leave immediately.

Senda went into her orchard after hearing the news. I found her crouched by the bench under the walnut, head buried into her knees. She was startled when I appeared; she looked up, her eyes full of tears. I sat by her side.

"Release him, Senda," I said softly. "It is time you let Guillaume go."

"I stayed when I could have gone with him," Senda said. "I thought it was the right thing to do — for my children — I stayed for them — and now? Where are they? The boys in Apulia, the girls married off — only Rogier is left. And I was carrying him inside me at the time. If I had left, Tancred could not have taken him from me."

"You know it was the right thing to do, Senda. You were not free to follow your heart. Guillaume is dead now. Dead!" I repeated. My words were cruel, but she had to hear them. "But you are alive! Let him go, think of him now and then if you must, but start living again! Go with Tancred to Saint Evroult, ask forgiveness for Guillaume's soul — and for your own."

🌱 🌱 🌱

We left Hauteville at dawn the next day, for Saint Evroult was a full four day's ride from our house. We stopped at midday to eat the cold mutton and hard wheaten bread servants had packed in the morning. Even when a summer downpour caught us early in the afternoon, we continued to ride. We pulled the hoods of our mantles over our heads and continued at a slower pace. The rain stopped later in the day, and the sun appeared, chasing the light mist that had settled over the bright green fields, which were dotted with sheep and edged with thick bushes of heather and broom.

That night we took shelter in a peasant's hut. The owners of the place huddled with their sheep at one end of the shack, leaving the open hearth to us. The place stank but we were grateful, as the steady rain resumed at dusk. The following days were a repeat of the first. On the fourth day the border of the forest of Saint Evroult appeared in the distance, and Tancred judged that it would take three hours to reach the Abbey. I inhaled deeply the fresh earthy scent that rose from the ground as it dried, but shivered in my damp mantle, wishing Tancred would stop and give me a chance to shake the excess water from it.

"Are you tired, Mother?" Rogier asked Senda, who had been riding quietly by my side. He cocked his head to the right in a gesture characteristic of his mother.

"No, Rogier," Senda replied, though I knew her heart and mind were in turmoil. "See to your father."

Rogier nodded, spurred his mount and joined Tancred in the lead. They trotted side by side as far as the edge of the forest, then stopped to wait for us.

Tancred's eyes were red-rimmed, his white hair and beard bedraggled from the rain.

"Hurry, lest nightfall find us still on the road." He turned his mount and headed toward the forest.

"Mother." Rogier touched Senda's arm and she glanced at him. His resemblance to Guillaume normally brought joy to her, but today she could not bear it.

"Mother, Abbot Thierry will help him." He believed that she was worried about Tancred.

༖ ༖ ༖

In the forest, we had stepped into another world, dark and mysterious, different from all I knew. The sunlight filtered through the thick leafy oaks that soared upward, taller than any tree I had ever seen. At first all looked brown, in stark contrast with the bright pastures we had just crossed. Brown was the ground, covered with damp leaves and brown was the bark on the trees. Even the redolence of the forest I pictured as dark, a strange musty mixture of decay and sweet scents. The soft, steady murmur of the river Orne had followed us for much of the ride and seemed louder in the trees. It was growing dark, and I judged that we were close to the Abbey.

I grieved for Guillaume, and I worried about Maud. If Tancred died of a broken heart, Rogier would join his brothers in Apulia, but what would happen to Senda? And me?

Mathilda had died in the nunnery in Coutances shortly after Rogier was born, and Adeliza had died in childbirth the same year. Her brother, Mauger, was a stranger to her — if Senda returned to his house, she would be little more than a servant.

Tancred stopped in sight of an ancient stone footbridge dotted with dark moss, and waited for us. He led us across the river at a shallow ford he knew. The sun shone briefly over the water, but was hidden again by thick foliage as soon as we reached the other side. The ground dipped, and I felt suddenly chilled. I shivered and I spurred my mule toward the gentle hill ahead.

When we entered a large clearing in the forest, I looked up and saw a dark mass against the setting sun. All weariness left me. I glanced at Senda and saw that she too seemed revived by our proximity to the Abbey. Here Tancred would be consoled by Abbot Thierry and by the Masses the monks would offer for Guillaume's soul. Perhaps she too would find peace.

Straight ahead, the upper floor of the guest house loomed over the Abbey walls. Narrow arched windows peered at us in the advancing darkness. The dark stone walls, evenly cut and tightly joined, gave visitors a sense of symmetry and smoothness. Tancred rang the bell next to the great oaken gate until a thin young monk opened the door and stood uncertainly in front of us.

"I am Tancred of Hauteville," Tancred said wearily. "We came to see Abbot Thierry."

The young monk stepped aside and let us enter the courtyard. He helped Senda dismount. "But — Abbot Thierry died while travelling to the Holy Land, my Lord. Prior Robert just became the new Abbot."

"Robert de Grantmesnil?" Senda spoke for the first time.

"Yes, my Lady." The young monk said in his high-pitched voice.

Tancred winced. Abbot Thierry had been the one who had turned Tancred from a dissipated youth into the man he was. I

knew Tancred had looked forward to Abbot Thierry's words;
even his mere presence would have eased his sorrow.

The monk led us to the guest house while Tancred and Rogier
took care of the horses. Here we were met by the Brother
Hospitalier who greeted us and led us up the wooden stairs of
the massive grey building to a small dining hall at the top. This
hall divided the long narrow dormitory that occupied the upper
floor into two sections, one for men and one for women. The
Brother proudly pointed out that there were separate latrines at
each end of the dormitories which emptied directly into the
river. In spite of this luxury our dormitory resembled an over-
sized monk's cell: two rows of pallets lined the walls, each with a
wooden crucifix over it; no hangings on the walls, no chests or
tables. We had to set our sacks of belongings on the floor.

We joined the men in the small dining hall. There were no
other guests at Evroult, and the Brother Hospitalier brought us
generous portions of cold roasted fowl, a jug of wine and white
bread. We ate in silence, too weary to speak. Afterward we went
to our separate lodgings. Senda and I chose the pallets closest to
the dining hall, under a window that overlooked the gatehouse
and the forest, well away from the latrines. The Brother brought
us blankets and a candle for the night before bidding us
goodnight and disappearing down the stairs.

Our pallets were hard, and the straw mattresses thin. But I
was grateful for the dry blankets. We took our tunics off and
settled down for the night. Senda tossed and turned on her pallet, and I knew that it was not just the hard mattress that kept
her awake. I felt sorry for her; but my heart went to Tancred.

Hours later, in the middle of the night, I heard the bell call
the brothers to Matins and then fade in small waves of sound.
But silence never returned. The bell of the gatehouse rang
loudly, followed by knocks and a fainter sound like weeping.
Senda sat up as the noise continued. The bell rang again and the
knocking became frantic. Cautiously, we both walked to the
window that overlooked the entrance. I undid the peg that held
the shutters together and we looked outside.

The moon was high and the night clear. Two people were standing by the gate — a tall thin man and a small woman who leaned against him. The man kept looking around like a hunted animal. He looked up. He had just a stubble of blond beard and was wrapped in the coarse brown mantle of a serf. I did not see the woman's face, for she kept it lowered, but I could see that her mantle was finer than his. The braid that had kept her hair in place was still intact only at the nape of her neck. The rest, like a black mantle, covered her shoulders and the lower part of her back.

The barking of dogs and thumping of hooves came from a distance. When the gate finally opened, a strip of light pierced the darkness. The young man began shouting.

"For the love of God, let us in, Brother; our lives are in danger!"

"What do you want? Who are you? Honest people do not come in the middle of the night!"

"Please, we need sanctuary — we *must* see the Abbot."

"I won't disturb him at this time. Come back tomorrow." But the peasant forced his way in. The light shone again and faded as the door was shut. Minutes later, several men rode to the gate and pulled the bell. But the gatekeeper had left his post, and the anger of the men was reflected in the furious tolling of the bell.

I began to worry that the men outside would break the door down. They wore leather jerkins and mail coats and those who were not holding flaming torches had their long swords, axes and lances ready in their hands as if preparing for an attack. I pointed to the pennons on their lances. "Look Senda, they are from Walchelin — they are *Richard's* men!"

We had seen Senda's brother-in-law as an adult at Granville shortly after Father's death, but my most vivid memory was of young Richard methodically tearing a small fox apart.

Senda squinted. "I don't see Richard. But then he may look quite different now."

Over the years, we had heard about Richard's rising star in Caen, and his friendship with Duke Guillaume *le Batard* (The Bastard). Like the Duke, he was arrogant and cruel. He had accumulated a fortune through the death of his first two wives and the murder of his young neighbor, Sarulo De Maistre, who was found beaten to death one evening. No one had openly accused Richard of this murder, but the assassins were never found. Tancred, who had praised Richard's bravery on the battlefield, had little doubt that Richard was involved in Sarulo's death. A year later, when Sarulo's father died heirless, Duke Guillaume locked up the widow in a convent and bestowed De Maistre's large estates on Richard.

Whatever Richard's intent it is bound to be no good. What could he want with these two?

The strip of light shone again as the gate was opened at last. We quickly wrapped ourselves in our mantles, and went down. Tancred and Rogier had preceded us; they were standing behind Robert de Grantmesnil.

The new Abbot wore a black mantle over a long white gold-trimmed tunic and the triangular Abbot's cap. He had come straight from Matins in the chapel.

"Welcome," he addressed the newcomers. "Though it is a late hour for a visit."

The young couple was standing to the Abbot's right. The woman's head leaned heavily against the man's shoulder, her white face still, her eyes closed, her hair completely undone. The light wind in the courtyard danced with the long black strands, lifting and pushing them over her pale face. Wearily the woman lifted a work-roughened hand to her face and pushed her hair aside.

Mother's coarse fingers, as they touched my cheek.

The woman's hands were assurance enough that she could not have done anything wrong.

"We come from Walchelin, my Lord," the captain said, still on his horse. The young Abbot's lips turned downward but he did not speak. "We have been running after those two." He pointed at the pair.

What has Richard done to them that they had to flee?

"They forced their way in, my Lord," the gatekeeper said in his high-pitched voice. He pointed at the young man. "I told them to come back, but he shoved his way in."

The Abbot studied the couple.

"Who are you?" he asked kindly.

"Evisand, my Lord," the young man said. "And this is my betrothed, Hirtrude. We belong to the de Maistre estate —"

"Lord Richard is expecting us to bring them back, my Lord," the captain interrupted.

A few minutes passed before the Abbot replied. His face was unsmiling and he seemed absorbed in thought. I could see him thinking. *How dangerous would it be to cross a favorite of the Duke? Duke Guillaume was overly sensitive to any infringement of his power by the Church.*

At last the Abbot spoke. "Tell Richard de Walchelin that these peasants have asked for sanctuary and are now under my protection."

"But — my Lord!" The captain was agitated. "They are fugitives, they have broken the law — they belong to Lord Richard — he will be furious."

"No temporal authority, however great, has jurisdiction inside these walls. If you are tired, you can rest, and leave tomorrow. But these peasants will stay."

"No, my Lord, we must return." The captain pulled back on the reins of his mount. "Do not think this is the end," he shouted at the pair. "Lord Richard will come for you." In a few moments he and his men disappeared down the hill.

"Come!" the Abbot said to the two peasants. "You have much to explain."

The small crowd dispersed and I followed Senda upstairs. But sleep, what little we had, was marred by nightmares. Senda woke up crying and whispering Guillaume's name. I comforted her until she fell asleep again. In my dreams, the face of the fugitive girl kept changing into my mother's.

ⵣ ⵣ ⵣ

Abbot Robert received us shortly after Prime the next morning. Brother Gaufredus, his secretary, came to fetch us. The Brother's attention was riveted on Tancred and Rogier. He bowed formally to Senda and barely glanced in my direction, pompous and full of self-importance. He led us quickly down the stairs of the guest house and onto the cloister walk.

Scents of lavender and thyme from the garden filled the cloister. Several young apple trees graced a corner of the garden. The corridor was paved with small red bricks set in a herringbone pattern. The brick wall that faced the garden and rose to meet the massive rafters of the ceiling turned into a series of graceful arcades which rested on slender pillars. These were crowned by carved fluted capitals and rested on a short brick wall, giving the effect of many arched windows surrounding the courtyard. Climbing red roses graced this short wall, reaching almost to the tops of the arcades in places.

The cubicles of the *scriptorium* lined the corridor ahead. When we passed by them, Tancred glanced in their direction. As if taking a cue, Brother Gaufredus stopped and motioned us to follow him into the first booth. He stood over a young monk who was working on an illumination. We crowded around the young scribe, awed at his beautiful work on the parchment; but Brother Gaufredus tapped his foot impatiently.

"No!" he said, taking the quill from the young monk. "You are doing this all wrong, Anselmo!" He leaned over, and with a few strokes drew a small kneeling figure. "There, that is the way to do it."

He studied the rest of the page. "Your penmanship is good, very good," he murmered, and returned the quill to the young scribe.

Brother Gaufredus was so openly delighted with his correction and so generous with his praise that I began to like him just a little. We stepped out of the cubicle and onto the cloister walk. Brother Gaufredus hesitated.

"If you are interested, my Lord," he told Tancred. "I could show you Queen Emma's Missal."

"Perhaps on the way back, Brother Gaufredus."

"You have the Missal of a queen?" Senda said with awe.

"The Missal belonged to Lady Judith, the Abbot's stepsister," Brother Gaufredus said, like a peacock ready to fan his tail.

"She inherited it from her father, the late Count of Evreux, who in turn received it from his. Lady Judith's grandfather was the Bishop of Evreux and brother to Queen Emma." Brother Gaufredus cleared his throat. "The Queen gave him the Missal as a gift after she married King Ethelred of England." He paused. "More than three hundred skins from unborn lambs were used to make the book."

Tancred's eyes met mine. He turned to Brother Gaufredus. "Perhaps you could show it to us," he said.

Gaufredus bowed and turned again toward the *scriptorium*, sliding one hand over the other inside his sleeves.

Brother Gaufredus stood in front of the desk where the book lay open. He closed it, picked it up and reluctantly handed it to Senda, who admired the soft leather binding of the book, the aquamarines and rubies that studded it. She touched its small lock and key, delicately wrought in pure gold. But she disregarded the treasure inside. She ignored the thick rows of writing as she turned the pages to the brilliantly colored illuminations. I instead was entranced by the writing. "Wait, Senda!" I touched her hand as she was about to turn the page and pointed with my chin at the monk. "I want to hear the words!"

She shrugged and handed the book back to Brother Gaufredus. He took it with both hands, held it against his chest for a moment, then brought it close to his eyes. His voice was deep and slightly quivering. *He is reading words that are a thousand years old! If one knew how to trace them — those mysterious symbols could preserve one's impressions forever!* Awed, I spoke my thought aloud. Senda grinned at my words. "And what thoughts do you have that are worth preserving, Bernfrieda?" Senda had asked. I looked up at Tancred, who stood against the wall with his eyes closed.

"You should not think lightly of the written word," Gaufredus snapped. "It is a tool given us by God to write about his greatness. That is how it is best used." I lowered my eyes, mortified, and determined to say nothing more on the subject to Senda or anyone else. Afterward, as we stepped into the shady corridor, Senda pulled his sleeve.

"Did Lady Judith take vows, that she gave something so precious to the Abbey?" Senda asked.

"Oh no, my Lady! Lady Judith gave the Missal to Saint Evroult simply to please her half-brother, the Abbot. She and the new Abbot's brother, young Arnold, came to live here two years ago, when their mother died."

"How old is she?" Senda asked curiously.

"Lady Judith is twelve, my Lady, though her maturity and beauty are well beyond her years. The Abbot is besieged by the many offers for her hand . . ."

Hardly surprising. Even if Lady Judith were homely, her money would make her irresistible.

We reached the doorway leading to the Abbot's quarters. One by one, for the stairs were narrow, we climbed to a small antechamber and then a stone doorway. A monk opened the door. Brother Gaufredus led us into the chamber before withdrawing discreetly to the side.

Abbot de Grantmesnil stood up from behind the oak table where a young girl in a blue tunic was seated beside a youth of about the same age as Rogier. At first I thought that they were the two we had seen the night before, but their clothes were too fine. The girl's tunic had an embroidered gold band around the neckline and sleeves, and her shift was of the finest, softest linen. Her features were delicate and her thick golden-brown braid hung down her back, partially hidden by a long gauze veil kept in place by a thin gold circlet studded with aquamarines.

Tall and dignified in his grey Benedictine robe, Robert de Grantmesnil looked much different in daylight, and years from the youth we had met fifteen years before. I knew he was exactly the age of Senda's first-born, Robert Guiscard, for they had met at Saint Evroult shortly after they had sworn fealty to their respective Lords at nineteen. They had gone to the Abbey to purify themselves with a week of prayer and fasting — de

Grantmesnil before returning to the Duke's court in Caen; Guiscard before leaving for Italy.

Robert de Grantmesnil had no intention of becoming a monk until ten years later, when he surprised everyone by leaving the court of Duke Robert the Magnificent in Caen. He asked Abbot Thierry of Saint Evroult to receive him and train him in the Benedictine Rule. Because of his noble origins and connections, everyone knew that some day he would take Abbot's Thierry's place. When, Abbot Thierry, in his nineties, decided to go on a pilgrimage to the Holy Land and died before reaching his destination, the monks of Saint Evroult duly chose de Grantmesnil as their new Abbot.

Rogier bowed briefly over his ring, but his eyes went to the girl at the table. The Abbot introduced his half-sister, Judith of Evreux, and his brother Arnold. The young couple stood up; he bowed and she curtsied gracefully.

After Tancred explained the reason for our visit and requested Masses for Guillaume, the Abbot asked about our Robert and the Normans in southern Italy.

Oblivious to the discussion, Rogier gazed at Judith. She glanced at him and blushed. Arnold's blond eyebrows went up and he moved closer to his half-sister.

Senda also noticed Rogier's interest in the girl. She bit her lower lip, turned to Judith and asked her if she had seen the peasants who had arrived at the Abbey. Judith nodded.

"My brother will marry them this morning," she said, looking at her hands.

Abbot Robert turned to us when he heard Judith refer to him. He told us the peasants' story.

Hirtrude and Evisand had been promised to each other since childhood. Just before they were to be married, when Hirtrude was thirteen, the girl had caught Richard's eye and he had summoned her to the keep. She served Richard's second wife, Lady Busilla, for three years, sharing Richard's bed whenever he pleased. He had tired of her even before Lady Busilla died. A few months later, just prior to Richard's marriage to Lady Constance of Belleme, Evisand asked his master's permission to

marry Hirtrude. Richard refused; he had other plans for the girl.
A friend in Caen had offered to pay Richard handsomely for her
services. That night, Evisand and Hirtrude had fled Walchelin
for Saint Evroult, where they hoped to marry and receive sanctuary.

Tancred grimaced. "Fugitive serfs are a serious matter —"

"I granted them sanctuary," the Abbot said calmly. "They will
stay and serve the Abbey."

"It'll be a sizeable loss to Walchelin. Is the man skilled?"

Abbot Robert nodded.

"A carpenter. The loss will be to the de Maistre estate, where
they are originally from. I knew their young master, Sarulo, years
ago, before Richard de Walchelin took possession of his estates."

"But Church law rules this Abbey. Richard de Walchelin must
surely accept that."

I detected a certain satisfaction in the Abbot's voice. "Lady
Judith has Hirtrude in her care now," he said. "If you, Lady
Senda, would like to join her, I am sure Judith will be delighted."

"Oh yes, Lady Senda, please come help me choose a dress for
Hirtrude; there are so many things to do! My women washed
her hair but I still must have her combed and bathed, and a garland made, and we must provide a proper wedding feast —"
Judith's eyes were luminous with excitement. She enjoyed preparing Hirtrude for her wedding; she liked the idea of playing
benefactress and treated the peasant as a child to be indulged.

Lady Judith's quarters were down the hall from the Abbot's.
Sunlight streamed from a large arched window over the rushes
on the brick floor. Several large oaken chests lined the walls and
a large bed draped in red damask took up almost the whole
width of a wall.

The peasant was huddled in a corner when we entered the
room.

"Hirtrude, get up!" Judith called joyously. "You are to be married this morning and you must get dressed!"

Judith walked to a chest and opened it. She pulled out several
tunics, more than I had ever seen owned by one woman, and
piled them up over the arms of her four women till she found a

suitable one. "Here," she said. "Do you approve, Lady Fredesenda?" Senda trailed her hand over the soft red wool and nodded. Judith turned to one of her women. "She'll wear this!"

She ordered one of her women to bring water to wash the grime from the peasant's face and another to lay out a long linen shift. With Senda's assent, she sent me with one of her women to gather red roses from the cloister garden. Judith insisted on making the garland herself.

As the women were washing and dressing the bride, it became clear why Hirtrude had caught Richard's eye. She was about my height, but much more slender. The resemblance to my mother that had seemed so close the night before was only in her long black hair. Her skin was unblemished and her eyes dark blue. When Judith placed the rose garland on the bride's head, she took a step back and clapped happily at her creation. But Hirtrude was in tears.

Judith gasped in dismay when she noticed. "Why the tears?" she asked. "He can't hurt you now. The Abbot will see to your protection — and you are to be married!"

Lady Judith has no idea of what Hirtrude must have gone through. How could she, pampered and cherished as she had been all her life? She believes that all will be put aright now that the peasants are under her brother's protection.

"No! Lord Richard — you don't know what he is like —"

"Richard de Walchelin will not dare defy my brother!" Judith proclaimed proudly.

Hirtrude lowered her head and hugged herself. Her tears ceased while we walked to the church, though her face was still puffy.

At the church door Evisand stood awkwardly beside the Abbot, his short blond hair combed. He started when he saw her, then looked at the Abbot.

Hirtrude brightened, and Evisand responded. We accompanied the bride up the steps then stood to the side in a loose circle around the young couple and Abbot Robert. Hirtrude took Evisand's hand. Their heads bowed, they stole a glance at each other while they listened to the words that bound them.

"Quod Deo coniunxit, homo non separet," the Abbot said gravely.

As the newlyweds bent to receive the blessing, Hirtrude gave a small cry. The garland of roses had slipped on her clean hair, and a small thorn had pierced her skin. The drop of blood that formed on her forehead matched the color of her tunic. Quickly Judith stepped to her side and adjusted the garland.

We were walking down the steps toward the refectory and the wedding feast Judith had promised when the young gatekeeper came running toward us, pursued by mounted soldiers.

"They are back, my Lord! They forced their way in —" Several men on horseback overtook him and Richard de Walchelin was towering over us, fat, with the doughy complexion of a man not often in the saddle.

"I am here to claim my serfs," he said. Abbot Robert folded his arms.

"Why did you force your way into the Abbey?" he asked with contained anger.

"Forced? Why, the good Brother here opened the gates — I am pleased to see you again, my Lord de Grantmesnil. You are sorely missed in Caen." The sarcastic greeting echoed unpleasantly in the courtyard.

"I don't miss Caen, Lord Richard. Nor the company I kept there."

"A pity for us." Richard looked around. "Ah, here they are!"

He pursed his lips as he surveyed the couple. "What is the meaning of this?" he asked, pointing at Hirtrude.

"I have just joined this young couple in matrimony."

"I'll take them now." Richard's voice quivered with anger.

"I granted them sanctuary. They will stay here and serve the Abbey. They may leave only of their own free will."

"Are you refusing to return them to me?" Richard snarled.

"Church law is clear, Lord Richard. They may leave only of their own free will."

To our surprise, Richard smiled. "They are valuable serfs. I need Evisand's skills; and I have found a position for Hirtrude in

Caen." *A most unpleasant smile.* "I'll compensate the Abbey well. Name your terms."

They are but chattel. Their lives have meaning only as long as they are useful to their masters. Rebels like these two are hunted down like animals. Even Tancred thought of Evisand only in terms of his skill as a carpenter.

"These young people are married now. They cannot be separated." The Abbot's voice was firm.

"If that is your condition, then I give you my word that they will not be," Richard said.

Abbot Robert was taken aback; a lord's word is not lightly given. He turned to the couple.

"Do not return them to him, brother!" Judith stepped forward before Robert could address the pair. Richard stared at her, his eyes wide in appreciation. Arnold, who saw this, flushed angrily.

Does Lady Judith really care for Hirtrude? Or is she angry because Richard was spoiling her pleasure?

Richard turned his attention to Judith. "Why not, my Lady?" he purred. "I will forgive all fines, and I will pay them two gold coins if they come back of their own free will." He gestured toward Evisand. "And they will not be separated."

Evisand turned to Hirtrude. *He was tempted. The de Maistre estate was all he knew; his family, friends, everything important to him was there. Now his Lord was giving him a chance to return with his bride, without punishing him for his disobedience.*

"No!" Hirtrude cried suddenly, and buried her face on Evisand's chest. Gently, her husband took the garland off her head. His finger lingered over the scratch on her forehead. He did not look at his Lord, but shook his head in refusal.

The Abbot turned back to Richard. "Their answer is clear, Lord Richard, and so is Church law."

"According to the temporal law, de Grantmesnil, these are my serfs. My property."

"The spiritual supercedes the temporal," Abbot Robert replied evenly.

"Duke Guillaume will be *certain* to resent your invocation of the Church in this," Richard spat.

"If the Duke objects, I shall answer to him."

Is the Abbot willing to defy the Duke to protect them? Is he moved by their plight? Or are they merely pawns — a means of chastening Richard? Or perhaps, a way to prove the "spiritual" might of the Church over even the mightiest "temporal" power?

Richard, feigning submission, turned toward his men. Then he nodded to them imperceptibly and suddenly four of his soldiers led their horses up the steps and surrounded us. With the broad of his sword, one of them stunned Evisand and lifted him onto his saddle. Another bent over Hirtrude as she screamed and hit her across the mouth with his open mailed hand, before pulling her across his horse.

The action took but a few moments. As the soldiers cantered through the gate, Richard shouted, "I'll keep my word, de Grantmesnil! They will not be separated!"

He spurred his horse and was gone.

Judith, Senda and I ran to the gate and then up the wooden stairs that led to the walkway around the walls. Below us the Abbot was shouting for horses. Richard and his men rode down the hill and into the clearing. Alerted by a monk, Tancred, who had been resting in the guest house during the wedding, ran out to join the Abbot, with his sword drawn.

"That horrible man!" Judith said through tears. "O, Lady Fredesenda!"

Six soldiers had dismounted and were standing by a large pit in the clearing. *He intended to kill them from the very beginning, their value meant nothing to him. Torturing them will give him much more pleasure than torturing a fox.*

The soldier carrying Evisand threw him off the horse; he fell halfway into the hole. As he tried to rise, a dismounted soldier swung a large iron-edged wooden shovel and knocked him on the head. He fell into the grave, and they threw his bride after him. Her arms flailed; then Richard shouted. The soldier swung the shovel, and her arms disappeared. Quickly the soldiers began to fill the pit.

By the time the contingent from the Abbey reached the clearing, Richard and his soldiers were gone. The Abbot and his men dismounted and dug furiously until they extracted the bodies and laid them on the dirt, side by side.

Abbot Robert kept clenching and unclenching his hands as he watched. A monk knelt by Evisand to close his eyes. His shout pierced the silent clearing. "He is still alive! My Lord he is still alive!"

The rest rushed down the wooden stairs to meet the Abbot and his party inside the gates. I stayed behind. They crowded round Evisand when they brought him in, rejoicing when he regained his senses.

Why didn't they let him die? He will spend his life consumed by impotent hatred. He will have no recourse, no revenge, only sorrow, only memories. Being alive will be the worst torture, as it was for my mother.

Someone had thrown a kerchief over Hirtrude's face. Strands of her dirty hair were blown softly by the light summer airs. I turned again to the darkening forest.

That night I dreamt not of what I had witnessed hours before, but of my mother's face by the river's edge, blood trickling from her mouth; death ready to claw at her.

🌱 🌱 🌱

Abbot Robert wrote a complaint against Richard de Walchelin to Duke Guillaume. He heard nothing for weeks. Then he received a reply. Richard, knowing how sensitive Duke Guillaume was to any infringement of his rights by the Church, claimed that the peasants had not actually entered the Abbey when his men arrived, and that Abbot Robert willfully prevented his soldiers from taking the peasants back.

Tancred rode to Caen to testify on behalf of the Abbot, but he was just an old country knight and his testimony did not carry much weight. Richard's connections were too powerful. Duke Guillaume wrote to Abbot Robert that he had chosen not to pursue the matter. After all, Lord Walchelin told him it had been resolved satisfactorily. The Duke reprimanded Abbot Robert and warned him sternly not to overstep his authority in the future.

Rogier, the youngest of the brothers, whom youth and filial devotion had heretofore kept at home, now followed his brothers to Apulia; and the Guiscard rejoiced greatly at his coming and received him with the honour which was his due.

— Gaufredus Malaterra, transl. John Julius
Norwich: *Historia Sicula*

CAPUT X

The Abbey of Santa Eufemia
On the eve of the Feast of Saint Augustine (August 28)
In this year 1061 from the Incarnation of our Lord
The words of Bernfrieda

Hauteville, 1057

Tancred never fully recovered from the death of Guillaume. And then, only six years after Guillaume's death, word came that Dreaux had been murdered. Onfroi took his brother's place in Melfi. Almost immediately, we began to receive news of the ongoing quarrels between Onfroi and Robert. Once, a messenger told Tancred that Onfroi had thrown Robert in a dungeon in Melfi after yet another quarrel. Tancred sent a fiery message to Onfroi, and Robert was eventually released. But their disagreements continued and Tancred soon realized that he was powerless to prevent them. He withdrew into himself, spending hours in the hall. He rarely joined his knights on the hunt, and delegated duties to his first-born, Serlon. He lost interest in Senda, though he continued to treat her as the Lady of the house. But he did not follow her with his eyes anymore; he did not wait expectantly for her to come to the dinner table. Now all his affections were transferred to Rogier. I wished during those years for things to go back to the time before Guillaume and Dreaux had died.

Rogier, who was twenty-six, postponed his yearly trip to Saint Evroult because Tancred was sick again.

Tancred had been relatively at peace since Onfroi died the year before. Robert Guiscard had taken his place in Melfi, and there had been no more quarrels. During the three years Onfroi had been Count of Apulia, Robert had sent message after message describing the abuse he took from his jealous half-brother. He had implored Tancred to intercede on his behalf. But the effect of Tancred's messages only lasted a short time. Tancred had often roared throughout the house, tormented over his powerlessness.

Robert, now Duke of Apulia, invited Rogier to join him in Italy with as many men as he could recruit. He was afraid that the same Norman barons who had rebelled and caused Dreaux's death would rise against him once more.

"But we have no men left to send Robert," old Serlon had protested. "We can hardly defend ourselves in case of an attack."

Tancred nodded. "Robert needs ten times the number we could send him. Rogier and young Serlo should go recruiting. Fulk de Bonneval is going to give his young son, Thierry, to Saint Evroult next month. All de Bonneval's retinue will go to the Oblation — a good occasion for recruiting."

"Are you going to Apulia this time, Rogier?" old Serlon asked. "You have waited longer than any of your brothers."

"No." Rogier answered. "But I'll go to Saint Evroult to recruit."

"It is settled then." Tancred, ill, his breathing labored, rose from his chair. His health had been declining for a long time. Later Senda sought out Rogier, and found him at his favorite spot, outside the wooden palisade that surrounded the bailey.

Unlike Guillaume, and most of the other Hautevilles, Rogier could compromise. She felt a wave of pride. *He is the best of them all*, she thought. She put a hand on his shoulder, and sat next to him on the rock.

"You must go, Rogier, you know you must go. You are twenty-six already and you have nothing."

"Not while Father is ailing."

"He is not going to improve. But he could live many years still."

"What about you, Mother? Maud is a vulture! Who would protect you if I left? Father is getting weaker, and Serlon pays no heed. Robert can fight his own battles a little longer. I'll find him some men."

"I have Maud's measure; I always have. You must think of yourself . . . and Judith."

Senda knew that she had touched a sore spot. Rogier was in love with Judith of Evreux. On each anniversary of Guillaume, Dreaux and Onfroi's death, Tancred led us to Saint Evroult to have special Masses told. Since Rogier also went to the Abbey each Lent, he had seen Judith and Arnold on many occasions. Over the years he had developed a deep affection for Arnold and the attraction he had felt for Judith during that fateful stay at Saint Evroult had changed into love.

Judith was twenty-two the last time I had seen her at Saint Evroult the year before on the anniversary of Guillaume's death. She was tall and fair-skinned, and had inherited her mother's looks. Hawise of Giroie had been known throughout Normandy for her pearly teeth and flawless skin before she married the Lord de Grantmesnil, the Abbot's father. Even when she was widowed after twenty years of marriage, her teeth were still strong and white and she was able to capture the heart of the Count of Evreux, who was ten years her junior. She had three grown sons by then and the youngest, Arnold, was just four. When I had last seen Judith at the special mass for Guillaume, her braided hair swung heavily down her shoulders. Her clear blue eyes were bright with the excitement of love and the certainty that no obstacle was too great.

She too loved Rogier. Indulged by the Abbot, Judith had refused all offers for her hand and remained true to Rogier. Yet

Rogier was a cadet son, rich only in dreams of conquests. Since Judith was heiress of Evreux, and second cousin to Duke Guillaume of Normandy through her father, she could aspire to a much higher match. Rogier knew that his only hope to win Abbot Robert's consent was to go to Italy and carve his own fortune.

"Judith will wait, Mother," Rogier said curtly.

Tancred did not linger for years. Two weeks later, just a week before Rogier was to go to Saint Evroult for the Thierry de Bonneval Oblation ceremony, Tancred died.

He was sitting in his chair in the hall, staring at the coals. Senda was in her chamber with the other women. I was in the hall, near Tancred, supervising the setting of the tables for the evening meal.

"Robert — like Onfroi — Rogier —" Tancred said suddenly, and I turned to look at him, surprised.

He looked up at me, his eyes bleary and red-rimmed. "I am tired," he sighed, and tried to get up. He fell back gasping, and I rushed to his side. I tried to help him up but he gripped my arm to prevent me. I looked around wildly for a servant but he gave my arm a little shake and mouthed, "No."

"Tancred!" I cried out. His breathing rattled in and out painfully.

"Rogier —" His pained breathing stopped and he slumped forward against me. I do not know how long I held him, unable to think or move. Maud came out of the bed chamber and frowned. She climbed on the dais and reached to touch him but I stopped her with my hand. Shocked, she let her hand fall.

Her scream rang loudly through the hall: "He is dead, dead, Tancred is dead!"

Senda and her women rushed out of the chamber. They surrounded us. Someone gently extricated me. Servants picked him up and took him into the bed chamber. Senda stood, hands clasped against her chest, bewildered.

When her women were finished preparing Tancred's body for the vigil, we went in. Senda stood by the side of the bed. Tancred's hair and beard had been trimmed; his face was unearthly white. The women had put a linen cloth dipped in wax over his face to make a mask of his features.

"What will happen now, Bernfrieda? What will happen now?" I could only hold Senda and murmur soothing words. The choices for both of us were grim. The monastery in Coutances, where her mother had died, was probably a better solution than staying at Hauteville where Maud would be mistress, or going back to her brother's house where she would be no better than a stranger. But in the Coutances monastery she would be alone, away from her children, most of whom were now in Apulia. Even young Fredesenda was in Italy, married to a Norman ally of Robert.

"I sent for the priest," old Serlon spoke evenly. "We'll bury him on the hill, next to my mother."

Two days later, at the simple ceremony by the grave, I stood at Senda's side without tears. I told myself that I had been expecting Tancred's death for so long that it was no surprise. Rogier took his mother to the house; I followed them slowly. I let the crowd pass me and I reached the stables alone. Surely now I would feel something. I closed my eyes, willing my mind to go back to that afternoon. Tancred was healthy and strong then, and I had held him in my arms. I shut my eyes and remembered the prickly feeling of his beard on my face, the warmth of his mouth on my breast, the feeling of closeness when he had entered me.

I had felt those things once, but those precious moments were lost forever. Now they were merely an abstract memory. And I wept, finally, at that great loss.

That evening, Serlon took Tancred's place at the table. Senda went to sit next to him when Maud stopped her, saying, "That is my place now." Serlon was studying his trencher. As Senda turned to walk away, Rogier spoke.

"This is my mother's last night at Hauteville, Maud. Let her sit in her own chair."

"Have you decided to leave, Senda?" Serlon asked, and added a trifle apprehensively, "You know you are welcome to stay."

"Mother will come to Saint Evroult with me for young Thierry de Bonneval's Oblation. We will leave from there for Apulia."

"I too shall go with you, Rogier!" young Serlo cried out.

Maud raised her hand. "No!" she cried, but there was mayhem in the hall. Everyone was speaking at once, and her son did not hear her.

Maud sat down on the bench in her usual place and Senda sat in her chair. Dinner was served. The young men's enthusiasm was contagious; but Maud hardly touched her food that night.

Old Serlon and the remaining few old knights came to bid us farewell the next day. Rogier, Senda and Serlo left on horseback; Jourdain and I drove in the ox-drawn cart that held our possessions. Four young men who had been recruited for Apulia followed the cart on foot.

Maud took leave of her son in her new chamber. As the cart turned behind a grove of willows near the river, I realized that I would never see her again; I would never again see Hauteville. I felt a moment's apprehension. What awaited us in Apulia? What could be worse than what we were leaving behind? I looked into the whispering willows, then over the lumbering backs of the oxen, as the soothing rhythm of the cart wheels carried us forward.

Fulk himself, mindful of the life to come, gave his son Thierry, whom Abbot Thierry had baptized, to God as a monk in the monastery of Saint Evroult . . . and the gift was witnessed by Robert, Abbot of Saint Evroult . . . Tancred of Hauteville's son Rogier was present then on his way to Italy.

— Orderic Vitalis, transl. Marjorie Chibnall: *The Ecclesiastical History*

CAPUT XI

The Abbey of Santa Eufemia
On the eve of the Feast of Saint Giles, Abbot (September 1)
In this year 1061 from the Incarnation of our Lord
The words of Bernfrieda

Saint Evroult, 1057

The Abbey of Saint Evroult looked more like a keep preparing for a siege than a place of worship preparing for an Oblation ceremony. A small garrison of soldiers inspected our small party at the gate.

"Orders from the Abbot," their captain told us when we asked. At the guest house, Bonneval's relatives and friends mingled with an unusual number of armed soldiers. Serfs were stacking rocks under the walls as if preparing for an attack.

Early the next day we went to Mass. As we stepped down into the cloister, Judith of Evreux and her maid almost ran into us. When Judith saw Rogier, her serious expression turned into one of pure joy. She greeted us but her worried eyes never left Rogier. "I am to leave right after the Oblation. Go to a nunnery," she said. Her maid nudged her. Judith nodded and followed her quickly.

We soon found out that the Abbey was on alert because of a possible attack by Richard de Walchelin. That evening, at supper, Rogier sought out Brother Gaufredus — who was Abbot Robert's secretary at the time. Flattered by Rogier's interest, Gaufredus told us readily all that had happened.

Two weeks before, the Abbot had received an order from Duke Guillaume that Lady Judith was to be given in marriage to Richard, widowed for the third time. Duke Guillaume also asked for an account of all Judith's possessions and inheritances which he expected the Abbot to turn over to Walchelin immediately after the marriage. Abbot Robert had a long private conversation with his half-sister. Afterward he dictated a reply to Duke Guillaume.

"Walchelin rode to Saint Evroult shortly before young Thierry de Bonneval's Oblation, for which we have been making preparations for months." Gaufredus said, "It will be a splendid affair. The Abbot wants to encourage other noblemen to give their children to the Abbey — oblations are becoming rare, and how is an Abbey supposed to survive without the rents and holdings pledged to it by the families of the boys who would become monks?"

"What about Walchelin?" Rogier interjected.

"I was coming to it," Brother Gaufredus said in an injured tone. "I ushered him into the Abbot's study, and I'll never forget their conversation":

'My Lord de Grantmesnil,' Richard de Walchelin said, smiling. He might have been greeting a long-lost friend. His smile faded when he saw that the Abbot had made no motion to greet him. 'Did you receive Duke Guillaume's message?' he asked.

The Abbot nodded. Richard stood in front of him, his legs apart, his right hand on the hilt of his sword. 'I have had no luck in my marriages, my Lord Abbot. Not one of my wives could give me a son. This should please you, for your sister's son will be my heir.'

The Abbot raised his hand to stop him. 'My sister and I thank you for your offer,' he said gravely, 'which we must decline.'

The fat folds on Walchelin's neck trembled when he spoke. 'You do not understand, de Grantmesnil. Have you really forgotten how things go in Caen? The Duke's request is his command!'

'I would be the first to comply if I could,' the Abbot said calmly. 'Judith was once promised to young Sarulo de Maistre. She never wanted to marry after he was murdered, and has recently expressed a desire to take vows as a nun. Surely Duke Guillaume will understand.'

'This insult you'll pay for, de Grantmesnil. Duke Guillaume will not be as understanding as you may expect. I will tell him you have forced your sister to take the veil rather than comply with his order.' Then he turned and strode from the room.

Brother Gaufredus paused to sip from his cup of cider. *The Abbot is sending Judith to a nunnery to put her out of Richard's grasp.*

Brother Gaufredus gazed sadly at the bottom of his cup. He took the cinnamon stick he had used to flavor his cider and sucked on it for a moment, then put it back into the cup, to use again later.

Evisand was in the cloister garden tending the apple trees when Walchelin left. That peasant must have waited for me for hours, for he sought me out as soon as I stepped into the cloister to go to church! He asked me what had brought Lord Walchelin to the Abbey. He was upset and I did not want to talk to him at first, for I thought that nothing good would come of our conversation. But he held tight to the sleeve of my habit, twisting the fabric as he spoke — and he spoke with such intensity — I tried to get away, say that I was busy, but he kept mauling my sleeve. 'When is he coming back?' Evisand kept asking, 'When is Lord Richard coming back?' I told him I did not know, I tore away from his clutches and almost ran into the church.

Brother Gaufredus shook his head. "After all these years, and all our ministrations, Evisand has not yet found his peace. He has resumed his old trade and works in the orchard now and then, but he never remarried and keeps to himself most of the time." *How could he ever be the same? Richard destroyed his life as surely as if he had killed him that day in the forest.*

The following day Senda and I too saw Evisand. He was sitting on the step of the church side door on the cloister walk. He was looking straight ahead, lost in thought. I pointed him out to Senda. She stopped when we reached him and called his name. He looked up in surprise, he hurried to rise and bowed deeply. "Lady Fredesenda."

He was now much sturdier and looked taller. A short beard framed his narrow long face, as fine and light as his hair.

Senda nodded. "I am glad to see that you are well, Evisand," she said. He was surprised she used his name though, after all, Hirtrude's terrible murder had made its impression. It was strange, however, that he remembered her. She had been merely a bystander at his wedding.

Senda climbed the steps to the church door, then stopped and turned toward him. "My son Rogier is recruiting men for his brother, the Count of Apulia. Would you like to go to Italy, Evisand? I could ask the Abbot to release you."

Evisand shifted his weight. "Thank you, my Lady. I still have work to do here."

⚜ ⚜ ⚜

Fulk de Bonneval walked toward the altar leading five-year-old Thierry by the hand. Several knights followed him to act as witnesses, Rogier among them. They stood in a semicircle in front of the altar. Fulk produced the petition drawn up on Thierry's behalf which gave his son and a large donation to the Abbey of Saint Evroult. Fulk wrapped Thierry's small hand into a small altar cloth, and presented him to Abbot Robert. Before accepting the gifts, the Abbot asked the faithful to pray. He also prayed silently. Then with one hand he took the parchment, and with the other the small wrapped hand and accepted the boy into the Abbey's confraternity. A monk came forward and gently took the little boy away from his father, symbolically dividing him from his family.

Fulk and the witnesses returned to their seats. The little boy, finally understanding that he would not be permitted to rejoin his family, began to wail. Elizabeth de Bonneval stepped toward her son, and was immediately checked by her husband.

ๆ๊ ๆ๊ ๆ๊

Later, in the refectory, Abbot Robert introduced Rogier to the crowd and gave him a chance to recruit some men. The crowd listened to Rogier's promise of glory, riches and land in Apulia. By the end of the meal, five knights had pledged themselves with their thirty foot soldiers.

I was back at the guest house packing for the long journey ahead before the meeting in the refectory was over. Clouds had chased the sun away and the shadows of evening were not far away. As I repacked Senda's chest I came across her mirror. On impulse I took it out and walked to the window. I opened the shutters and held it in front of my face. For a few moments I studied my reflection. In the metal's golden glow, my image looked softer and younger. Still, I studied with dismay the loosened contours of my face, the deep line across my forehead and the two streaks of white hair on either side of my face.

The gate bell tolled. I put the mirror on the sill and looked down. The gate was not opened. After we had arrived, the Abbot had given specific orders not to let anyone into the Abbey without his permission. His fears were about to be realized, for Richard was waiting with a small army in front of the gate. The Abbot hurried to the walls, followed by Fulk de Bonneval and the other guests. On the sentrywalk he was flanked by Rogier, Serlo and Jourdain. Rogier whispered something to Serlo when he saw Walchelin.

Senda and Lady Judith were also on the sentrywalk a short distance from the Abbot. I thought about joining them, but I decided that my view was probably better. Someone else must have thought the same, for I heard a noise to my left, from a window on the men's side. All were closed except the one closest to the guest's dining room and the stairs. I did not think much of that, as my attention was all for the drama unfolding below.

"I'm here as Duke Guillaume's representative to claim Lady Judith of Evreux as my wife. Open the door!" Richard shouted. He looked up at Abbot Robert, whose arms were folded on his chest in his characteristic obstinate posture.

Rogier leaned on the walls with both hands.

"I come in peace. Are you *still* refusing me entrance?" Richard called, turning his head as he spoke so all could hear.

"If you come in peace, lay down your weapons —"

A sudden flash. Something flew straight in front of me. It struck Richard in the throat while the Abbot was speaking. An arrow. Walchelin brought his hands up. Blood was gushing from his wound; he fell heavily onto his horse's neck.

My heart was pounding. The assassin must be inside the guest house! A man's shadow moved behind the open window, making for the stairs. He let drop the homemade bow when he saw me, and stood there wide-eyed. Evisand had exacted his revenge.

I ran to him. "Hide that bow! Here, give it to me!" I picked up the bow and arrow, looking round for a hiding place. Quickly I buried it under the tunics and mantles in Senda's chest.

Evisand regained some composure. "Death came too quickly for him," he said softly. "May God have mercy —"

"Go! Hurry!" I pushed him toward the stairs. "There is mayhem down there and no one will notice if you melt into the crowd now. If anyone questions you, say you came to see Rogier about going to Italy. Do you understand? And you must indeed come with us now, Evisand! As for me, I have seen nothing."

Outside, Richard's captain was howling treachery. He rushed to his Lord and prevented a fall. "They have murdered Lord Richard!"

"The Angel of Death! I saw him!" a man shouted in a shrill voice. "You all saw the flash? The Angel of Death, I tell you!"

Now everyone was calling and shouting at once, terrified, clustered in knots for mutual protection.

"True! A flash of light! I too saw it!" someone cried out, soon echoed by others.

I picked up the mirror on the sill, with my fingertips, careful to remain hidden.

Two soldiers dismounted, eased Walchelin from his saddle and laid him on the ground. Blood gushed from Richard's throat with every movement of his body.

All grew silent while they watched Richard die. Then swords were drawn and shouts went up with the rattle and clang of metal.

"The Angel of Death? A wooden arrow with an iron tip — this killed my Lord!" The captain held the arrow over his head for all to see.

Fulk de Bonneval appeared on the wall and stood by the Abbot.

"Calm your men, captain," he said loudly. "I am Fulk de Bonneval. The Abbot did not give the order to kill your Lord. The one responsible will be found and punished."

"A miracle, a miracle!" People murmered among themselves as if the captain had not spoken.

"The Angel of Death struck him down as he struck the first-born of the Egyptians! God have mercy!"

Evisand climbed up the sentrywalk to stare at his victim.

The Abbot was very pale; yet his authority was unyielding in the face of calamity. "Lay down your weapons, soldiers," he called to the men around Walchelin's corpse, "so you can enter the Abbey. Your Lord Richard needs our prayers."

"No!" the captain shouted. "No one touches my Lord! We take him back to Walchelin."

The soldiers wrapped Walchelin in his mantle, slung him across his saddle and tied him securely to his horse.

"Duke Guillaume will raze this Abbey to the ground if justice is not carried out!" The captain shook his mailed fist at the walls. "You may say that God struck down my Lord Richard, but you all must know who killed him! Duke Guillaume will torture the truth out of you, monk!"

A menacing sound rose from the crowd at the threat. Someone threw a rock at the captain, narrowly missing him. He turned then and left at a gallop, followed by the other men.

"I will leave for Caen at once, Lord Abbot," Fulk said, "and reach Duke Guillaume before —" he pointed at the cloud of dust down the hill. He turned to the crowd on the walkway. "Did anyone see who killed Lord Richard?" he shouted.

Nobody answered de Bonneval's question. He and his men left soon after, making straight for Caen. Judith left for the convent. That evening, Evisand came to see Rogier; Senda secured his release from the Abbot, and the next morning he left with us for Apulia, the bow and mirror safe in Senda's chest.

THE ABBEY OF SANTA EUFEMIA
1062

According to Malaterra it is clear that by granting large fiefs to Rogier, [Robert] Guiscard was afraid of creating a power that would counterbalance his own, and that he therefore preferred to compensate his brother with money rather than land.

— Ferdinand Chalandon: *Histoire de la Domination Normande en Italie et en Sicilie*

CAPUT XII

The Abbey of Santa Eufemia
On the eve of the Feast of Saint Adalhard (January 3rd)
In this year 1062 from the Incarnation of our Lord
The words of Bernfrieda

The fragrance of the orange peel Senda has thrown on the hot coals in the brass brazier at our feet pervades her room. It is heavenly to sit at this desk again, feel the warmth of the midday sun on my back, hold a newly sharpened quill in my hand.

I feel a new sense of urgency. In just a short while the sun will lose its warmth and the grey shadows of the evening will prevail. Now that the days are short I shall have to work quickly. The weeks of fever last fall left me exhausted; I am aware that time is not without limits.

I have filled the ink horn. The empty reddish page is ready. The scraping knife and the goat tooth are in my pocket. I touch them once in a while, aware of their slight weight. I have used them far too often over the course of the fall.

When I first set out to write, I thought I would finish my labor by Christmas. I sat eagerly at my desk each morning after the daily walk with Senda. Words flowed easily on the new soft parchment until I had finished eleven chapters of my work.

I kept going to the *scriptorium* each afternoon, copying the life of Saint Agatha as usual. Brother Gaufredus heard that Senda had purchased many sheets of fine parchment — as I said, nothing escapes him — but he never suspected that she had bought it for me. When he inquired, I hinted that the vellum was a gift for one of her sons.

I had to tell Senda. She noticed that I was not copying from a manuscript. And I began to realize how fickle memory is — how difficult to tell the past so that those who know nothing about it may understand what happened. Senda's eyes danced when I told her.

"So this time Amatus of Monte Cassino inspired you, Bernfrieda! You should consort less with the good brothers. Why do you want to use the quill to tell my story? You are already telling it with the needle. And you are more accomplished at that." She pointed at the tapestry.

Senda was jovial late last spring. Her sons were allies again. They were fighting the Saracens near Messina in the island whose great mountain spits fire.

Today she is so preoccupied that she barely notices what happens around her. Gone are the easy smile and bantering of those days. Horrible events have taken place since then, events that have finally spurred me back to my desk after an absence of months.

Writing became a mighty labor after I wrote about the death of Richard de Walchelin. Day after day I sat at my desk in the early hours of the day, before it became too hot to work, staring at the parchment in front of me. I had to use the scraper and goat's tooth so much on that first page that I could almost see through it. Afraid to waste precious parchment, I decided not to write another word until all that I wanted to say was clear in my mind. Still, when I set about writing it, words were stilted and sentences awkward.

I spent September laboring each morning and undoing my work each afternoon, like Penelope. But the queen of Ithaca had a purpose: to preserve her house and herself for Odysseus. I labored in vain. Soon it became painful even to sit at the desk and I began to avoid it. Perhaps that is why I fell sick, though the same fever had already plagued me once since we came to Santa Eufemia. There are marshes not far from the Abbey and many sicken with the fever; older people often die of it. I too resigned myself to die without finishing my chronicle. The memory of Senda's sons would survive, but nothing of ours.

Why did You spare my life? I do not want to live. What new torture do You have in store for me? You never listened before — but now look: I pray to You — let me die — there is nothing for me here.

Although too weak to even feed myself, I felt keenly that I would survive. I don't remember much of those days. Morning and evening, Brother Aldric insisted that I drink an infusion of absinthe and cinnamon to keep the fever at bay. I spent hours in the infirmary of the Abbey looking up at the rafters, some as big around as a man. They soared upward to a central ridgepole, creating a design like an upended flower. Senda stayed away, afraid of catching the fever.

Brother Gaufredus came regularly instead, though he rarely stayed long. Once I was awakened by his pungent smell — sweat, cinnamon and vinegar.

"She opened her eyes, Brother Aldric! Here, let me help!" Someone lifted my shoulders and forced a few drops of a foul-tasting potion into my mouth. Gaufredus's face loomed large, his small eyes dark as he peered at me.

"Take your draught, Bernfrieda," he said. "You have wasted enough time already, and I need you in the *scriptorium*."

I closed my eyes and when I reopened them he was gone.

Slowly, as I searched for ways to continue my chronicle, events began to fall into place. By late autumn, I was partially recovered, and I knew how I should continue my story. I began to talk more to God, as I used to when I was very young. I spent the warmest part of the fall day in the garden. When the sun came out and the walls inside the Abbey were sweating, it was warmer outside. Wrapped in furs, I often dozed in the midday warmth, soaking up the sun like the flat Calabrian lizards on the brick walls of the garden. I relived the events that had been obscured by time, feeling again anger, humiliation, unbearable sadness, envy and joy. After my sunning I walked back to Senda's room to eat with her. A bit of boiled meat, the broth in which it was cooked, and a piece of dark bread were all that I could eat during my sickness. After I returned from the infirmary, Senda often tried to entice me with morsels that came directly from the Abbot's cook: *blanc-manger* made with local almonds and tender ground chicken, a piece of lamb roasted in sage and mint, accompanied by the ruby wine produced on the hills surrounding the Abbey; a baked apple drizzled with honey and fragrant with cinnamon. Still I could eat very little.

When Rogier took Lady Judith, Abbot Robert's stepsister, as his bride on the last day of November, I stayed at Santa Eufemia while Senda, the Abbot, and most of the Norman brothers rode to Mileto, in the hills south of Santa Eufemia, for the ceremony. By the time they returned two weeks later, the joy of the long-awaited event had been shattered by a new fight between Robert and Rogier. When I began this chronicle, I meant to record the past. But I cannot ignore what is happening now. It will determine Senda's future — and that of all Normans in Italy. I must record this while each detail is fresh in my mind. Later I will finish the tale of the past. I shall work faster — now that I see the way.

⚜ ⚜ ⚜

"It was heavenly in Mileto. You can't imagine the music we made, Bernfrieda." Brother Gaufredus put his quill down and leaned back on his chair. I looked up briefly before I dipped my quill in the ink horn and traced a new letter. *He wants to know what Senda thinks of the wedding of Rogier to Judith. He always starts in that roundabout way when he wants to extract some information.* It was the morning after they had all returned from the wedding, and we were sitting in Brother Gaufredus's cubicle inside the *scriptorium*. The screens had been taken down from around the cloister walk outside and rebuilt inside for the winter. I shivered as I wrapped my woolen cloak tightly around my middle.

"We sang as if we were back at Saint Evroult in Normandy. Brother Aubrey intoned the chant at the Introit. The choir, all the brothers from Saint Evroult, chanted the Antiphon. It was the wedding Psalm, the 46th, and Brother Aubrey sang each verse between our repetition of the Antiphon. With my eyes closed I could imagine I was back in Normandy."

Brother Gaufredus sighed. "One has to be careful when dealing with powerful people. I know something about it, Bernfrieda. Here I am a long way from civilization, all because I sided with my Lord Abbot when he angered Duke Guillaume *le Batard*!" He picked up the quill again, dipped its point into the ink horn and cleaned the excess ink on the rim. "And if Robert Guiscard had not offered Santa Eufemia to my Lord Abbot, we would still be wandering, like the biblical Jews." He wrapped an inky finger around a curl in his beard.

"How unfortunate you could not come to the wedding," he said, returning to the subject that interested him. "What a wedding feast it was, Bernfrieda!" He beamed at the memory. "It began soon after the ceremony at noon. Tables laden with food, roasted peacocks studded with their own feathers, mounds of roast meats, poached Calabrian fish, fruit, vegetables, sweetmeats — the feast we had at Saint Evroult when Robert de Grantmesnil became Abbot was nothing in comparison!"

I looked up, anxious to divert his attention. "You miss Saint Evroult?"

Brother Gaufredus sighed. "Nothing compares to Saint Evroult."

"But winters are warmer here," I said quickly, lest he return to the subject of the wedding. Brother Gaufredus shrugged.

"A small advantage, in such a savage country. But the weather *was* glorious the day of the wedding. Lady Judith was a most beautiful bride in her red tunic bordered with ermine. A gold circlet studded with rubies held her hair in place. A true

Norman Princess. Duke Guillaume's bride herself could not have outshone her."

Brother Gaufredus's face was animated and his small eyes were bright as he spoke. I looked down at the parchment, suppressing a smile at his enthusiastic description of Judith. *He won't be deterred from the subject of the wedding! — What enthusiasm when he speaks of Judith! — His disdain for worldly beauty is not as sincere as he would have me believe.*

"Your Lady Senda seemed aloof during the wedding." Brother Gaufredus continued, glancing at me. I did not react to his bait. "She seemed nervous. And she rarely smiled the whole three days she was there. I did watch her carefully." He scratched his hairy chin with the quill. "I was worried she too might have caught the fever that kept you here."

I'd wager you did worry, but I doubt you were worried about her having the fever.

"You are very quiet, Bernfrieda. Has your Lady's mood rubbed off on you or are you still ailing?" Brother Gaufredus turned his chair toward me and stared openly so that I could not ignore him.

"My Lady was probably just tired." I looked briefly at him. "The climb to Mileto is not easy."

"Well, it is not strange that she would be upset," my teacher said primly, ignoring my comment. "The rumors we heard just prior to the wedding about Lady Judith having taken the veil back in Normandy were upsetting. Those of us who followed my Lord Abbot to Italy knew there was no truth to that story. There was never any talk of Lady Judith taking vows. My Lord Abbot made it clear to the Abbess he only wanted his stepsister kept out of Duke Guillaume *le Batard's* grasp. Who could have spread such slander?"

I bit my lip and reached for the scraper. His chatter had distracted me and caused me to scrawl. I concentrated on scraping, hoping that brother Gaufredus would quit talking. *Like dripped grease from a roasting capon, the fight between Robert and Rogier will explode soon. Until then, Brother Gaufredus, you must wait to find out about Senda's homecoming from the wedding.*

❧ ❧ ❧

Senda was desolate when she returned from Mileto. She took her mantle off, handed it to me, then threw herself on her bed, ignoring the basin of warm water ready for her. She lay staring at the bed curtains, the skin under her eyes purplish and swollen in her pale thin face. I dipped a linen cloth in the water and gently cleansed the dirt and sweat from her face. Her eyes closed and she bore my ministrations without protest. I knew she was troubled and that I would have to wait to learn why, so I let her be. I took a new marked candle from the chest, lit it to measure the passing of the hours, fetched the embroidery and sat by her.

Earlier I had neatly folded the long tapestry into a small square. I opened it with care and searched for the spot I had been working on. I came across the early scenes at Hauteville that Senda had insisted on embroidering herself. I had embroidered the first one but she had not liked the way I had portrayed Rogier.

"He was not *that* small, Bernfrieda!" She unraveled my work as I watched resentfully. I had spent much time choosing just the right gradation of colors to embroider Rogier and I knew she would not be as careful. "Don't you remember? He was the tallest of my children. And the most handsome."

I said nothing. Robert, not Rogier, was the tallest, and sturdiest. Her love for Rogier blinds her at times, even if Rogier deserves that affection. Ten years he longed to join his stepbrothers and then Robert in what seemed to him adventures worthy of Charlemagne. Ten years he spent in his father's house after reaching manhood. Ten years of long winter nights warmed more by the arguments on strategy with Tancred's men than by the burning braziers around which they huddled.

And no one could have stopped Rogier once he finally left Hauteville to join Robert in Apulia five years ago. He became his brother's most loyal ally, and Robert was delighted at first. Then they drew swords against each other three years ago because Robert insisted on paying for Rogier's help with gold rather than land. Since then they have alternately been allies and enemies. Even when they join forces against a common enemy and become invincible, everyone knows each victory over the Byzantines or the Saracens will be followed by a new struggle over the spoils: what stocks of food belong to whom, what prisoners to sell as slaves, and, above all, how to divide the conquered land they both covet.

I finally found the spot on the tapestry where I had left off: the scene of our arrival in Melfi from Hauteville. The new colored woolen yarns Alberada had gifted to Senda lay in a heap in the flat round basket in which they had arrived. I admired their rare hues. Alberada often sent unusual gifts, even though she is now a former daughter-in-law. Of course the main reason they keep in touch is to spite Gaita. Robert knows of Senda's messages to Alberada: nothing that happens at the Abbey goes unreported to him. He can hardly forbid them from communicating, since after the annulment, he trumpeted all over southern Italy that his first wife was as dear to him as a sister.

This time Alberada had sent some gold yarn and a brilliant blue, very rare because the dye is made with ground *lapis lazuli*. It is the color we needed in the scene we were embroidering.

Alberada wore a tunic just that shade of blue when we first met her the day we arrived in Melfi. We were all weary from weeks of traveling. While I slouched beside Senda on the linen chest in the oxen cart, the smell of cooking roasts, and the colors and bustle of people filled the bailey of Robert's keep. Followed by Alberada, Robert appeared in the arched doorway of the stone tower to greet us, and I forgot everything else. The likeness of the only man I have ever loved walked briskly toward us. I was so tired that for a moment I thought it was Tancred himself, striding toward us, as vital and powerful as he was when he first came to Hauteville.

"Welcome, Mother! And you too, Rogier!" Robert said with warmth. His voice was pleasing, though not as deep and resonant as his father Tancred's had been. He helped his mother off the cart and then turned to the young girl behind him. "The Lady Alberada, my wife." Robert took the girl by the hand and led her to Senda. She looked thirteen, fourteen at the most.

Alberada flushed as she curtsied, and her narrow black eyes darted from Robert to us before she lowered them. Robert studied Rogier for a moment before hugging him hard. Rogier was flushed when Robert let him go. *His childhood hero, the brother he has impersonated so many times in his games at Hauteville.*

Senda stood very still before she gave her hand to her firstborn and her gaze followed him constantly during the visit — this forty-two-year old warrior who had left Hauteville as a youth — could it have been twenty-three years before?

Robert sat and stroked his short, golden-red beard as he surveyed us washing in basins of warm water. We must have seemed a sorry lot to him, as we were covered in dirt and wearing our drab travel cloaks. Yet the warmth in his voice seemed genuine. He was glad for the thirty soldiers and five knights Rogier had brought with him. And I realized as he began to tell us about all he had acquired in Apulia that we were a prized audience. Who more than his family could appreciate how high he had risen in the world?

He was happy to see Senda. He kept her by his side and shared his trencher with her. It appealed to him, I understood later, that his mother was brave and had dared travel so far to see him. I stared at him constantly. Tancred had been the same age when he first came to Hauteville — the small lines around the eyes — but never those deep lines between Robert's brows which gave him an expression of discontent. Robert's beard set him apart from the clean-shaven Normans in the hall and added to his likeness to Tancred; but I sensed that the resemblance was only skin deep. There was a gentleness in Tancred that his son lacked. Senda mentioned this later in the privacy of our chamber. She surprised me, for I had not realized that she had noticed it in her husband.

🐦 🐦 🐦

I was still embroidering the scene in Melfi when Senda called my name. She turned toward me as if that small movement cost her much pain. "This time one of them will die, Bernfrieda," she whispered. "Rogier's eyes when he looked at Robert were those of a hawk ready to dismember its prey. O, I know one of them will die this time."

"You come from a wedding and you talk of dying!" I masked my worry. *I always fight off Senda's dragons. She relies on me for that. Yet I am helpless against the sorrow her children inflict on her.* "Rogier has been fighting alongside Robert prior to this wedding. Do not be so obsessed with their quarrels, Senda. They fight and they make peace."

"Robert was jovial at the wedding." Her blue-green eyes turned dark. "He was affable with Judith and her stepbrother Arnold — who fetched her from the convent — as if it was not he who had spread the rumor about Judith taking vows in Normandy. For his part, Abbot Robert was so incensed at such an ugly rumor about her that he travelled to Rome to convince Pope Nicholas that she had never been a nun." Senda shook her head. "Rogier behaved as if nothing happened, but I saw the anger in his eyes when he looked at Robert."

"You can't prove Robert spread those rumors, Senda."

"I do not need proof, and neither does Rogier." She retorted, propping herself up on her elbow. "As if this is the worst Robert has done!"

I got up and fetched wine from a clay jug by the chest. Carefully I poured out a cup. "Drink," I said. "You are still very pale." She took the cup and drank thirstily, then handed it back to me. "It was such a great day for Rogier and Judith," she continued after a moment. "They have been true to each other for so very long and they are so handsome together."

I nodded. Before coming to Italy, Rogier had no hopes of marrying Judith. But five years later the situation reversed itself. Even while we were still at Saint Evroult that Christmas, the Abbot angered Duke Guillaume and had to flee that Abbey shortly afterward.

After only five years in Italy, Rogier's fortune was second only to his brother's; the exiled Abbot had no objections when Rogier asked for Judith. Secretly, Abbot Robert de Grantmesnil sent his brother Arnold to Fleuri to fetch Judith from the convent where she had spent years in hiding.

Rogier was with Robert, fighting the Saracens in Sicily, when he heard that his bride was coming. Leaving catapults and wooden towers behind, he set off to fulfill the dream that had warmed his long nights on the battlefield for so many years. He met her at San Martino d'Agri, a small village in Calabria, and brought her to Mileto, his capital. With splendid colorful pageantry, he took her hand at the entrance of his unfinished cathedral.

I can imagine what a regal couple they made! Of all Senda's children, Rogier is the most handsome, the one who looks most like our father Mauger. His thin nose, slightly hooked at the end, and high forehead give his countenance a refinement that Robert and the other children lack.

Senda darkened. "You don't understand." She got up and paced the room. "Robert broke the understanding he had with Rogier, who needs his rightful share of land as he must give Judith her morning gift."

"Stop pacing up and down, Senda," I said. "That will not stop the fighting." *But this battle could be fiercer than all others! The Lombard custom of the morning gift has been adopted by all Normans in Italy. Robert gave Gaita a great amount of land. How can Rogier give any less to his bride?*

Senda stopped in front of me. "You know that Rogier will not rest until Robert gives him the land!"

We were both silent. Senda fingered the yarns in the basket on the desk by my side. "There will be no truce this time. Rogier told me so on the day of his wedding. Everyone noticed the tension between Robert and Rogier when they spoke to each other during the wedding feast. Toward early afternoon Rogier got up and left the table. I decided to speak to him. Robert frowned when he saw me get up. But he went on eating."

Senda closed her eyes and stroked her forehead. I could imagine the scene at Mileto. The air, filled with the aroma of roasts still on the spits in the open kitchens, the warmth of the early afternoon sun, the bustle of hundreds of guests who had converged on Mileto.

"I caught up with Rogier." Senda continued. "He seemed surprised to see me but did not speak. The guard jumped to attention when he recognized his master and hurried to open the portcullis. We walked to the short wall to the right of the keep; you remember, Bernfrieda — where the hill drops sharply? Rogier put his foot on the stacked rocks, leaned forward, and looked at the country below. Brown fields bordered by chestnut woods, not the heather-edged green fields and oak forests of Normandy. Yet there was something familiar about the feeling of space and power that comes with being perched high on a hill.

"'Look, you can see my borders just beyond Robert's tents.' Rogier pointed in the distance to Robert's white tents dotting the hill. 'Robert owns land all around me.' Rogier picked up a rock and threw it down the valley. 'Land *I* conquered. How can I gift it to Judith, when I have so little of it?'

"I tried to soothe him, Bernfrieda. I told him that Judith would not care about land; God knows she is happy just being his wife. But Rogier would not listen. He picked up a handful of small rocks and began to throw one after the other right in front of us. Each throw was shorter and more intense than the preceding one, so that the last one ricocheted and almost hit my mantle. 'Have you talked to Robert since he arrived?' I asked him as we stood in front of the keep. 'Have you impressed upon him how important it is that he gives you land for a morning gift?'

"Rogier picked up another rock and threw it. 'Even last night I approached Robert, Mother,' he said.

"You should have heard him, Bernfrieda." Senda let the blue yarn slip through her fingers. "The way Rogier described the scene with his brother — I felt as if I had been right there with him. I was soon as angry as he was." Senda picked up a tangled mass of blue yarn and sat on a stool facing me. She found one end and began wrapping the yarn around my hands.

"Rogier went to Robert's tent after dark." Senda said, as she quickly twirled the wool around my palms. "Jeoffrey Rudel boasted at dinner that Robert had given him the lands Rogier had conquered around Messina. He could not bear the thought that Robert had given freely to a mere ally what his own brother had begged him for just a few days before. He stormed to Robert's tent even though he knew he would find him asleep."

She stopped to unravel another tangle before she continued. I was tired and I did not want to hear about another fight. "Senda . . ." I began; but she paid no attention.

"He asked him why he'd given Jeoffrey land he'd asked for. There was a great chart on the floor — he almost tripped on the rock that held it open. Robert told him it was his land, and it was none of Rogier's concern."

My hands began to feel heavy as Senda continued to wrap. A lot of thread lay in the basket. But the real heaviness I felt was inside. I braced against the familiar feelings of helplessness and anger washing over me.

Senda shook her head and stopped wrapping yarn for a moment. I lay my hands in my lap, but she motioned for me to lift them again. She pulled on the thread and resumed.

"Rogier was appalled." Senda told me. "He didn't covet Robert's land — all he wanted was a chance to earn his own. Like Rogier, Robert too was landless when he came to Italy. He too sought the help of his older stepbrothers. Had it not been for Guillaume *Bras-de-Fer*, Dreaux, and Onfroi he would not be Duke of Apulia today. But according to Rogier, Robert believes Dreaux and Onfroi hampered him in every way they could. Guillaume would have been blamed also, had he not died. After he married Alberada, though, Robert had plenty of money and men, so he feels he owes nothing to the others . . . all Rogier wants is a fair share of the land he conquered. He needs it now; if Robert does not give it to him there will be no peace. Rogier may need Robert's protection, but his services may be more necessary to Robert for the campaign in Sicily. They are quarrelling about Messina and the lands around Reggio. I fear Rogier will try to take them with the sword if Robert doesn't keep his promises."

Senda was finally finished wrapping wool. She took the end of the blue thread with shaking fingers and began to twine it around her own hand, forming it into a ball. She looked as exhausted as I felt.

"Forty days, Bernfrieda. Do you understand? Forty days to hand him over the land or fight." Senda shook her head. "After Rogier finished telling me all this, I was in hell. I don't even remember walking back with him to the hall. Robert was lifting a cup to his lips when we walked in. I saw the looks he and Rogier exchanged. Yet Robert continued to drink as if he were heartily enjoying himself. Rogier, of course, was silently furious the rest of the evening.

"I left the morning after for Santa Eufemia with the Abbot. Arnold escorted us back to the Abbey. He is a very nice young man — almost annoying in his eagerness to please." She smiled briefly. "Of course I am unaccustomed to that from *my* sons — the Abbot is very fond of his younger brother and has great hopes for him."

Such a handsome young man, Arnold. He looks more like Judith than his full blood brother. And like Judith he laughs easily, though hints of sadness often pass on his face — and he is loyal. He is close to Abbot Robert, who raised him at Saint Evroult after their mother's death. And he is fiercely attached to Judith. The Abbot told us that he had almost drowned once, trying to save Judith's puppy when it fell in the river below the Abbey. Arnold threw himself into the swift current trying to reach it. He never did, but he earned his sister's complete devotion. The Abbot considers there is nothing they would not do for each other.

"Time will not help." Senda said. She slid her fingers from the brilliant blue ball in her hand and threw it in the basket. She pulled out another handful of yarn she had tangled earlier and placed it in my lap. "You may untangle this, Bernfrieda," she said.

⳩ ⳩ ⳩

Brother Gaufredus watched me in silence, his small eyes alert and curious. "Do not scrape so hard, Bernfrieda. Why are you so restless?"

"How can I not be restless, Brother Gaufredus?" I said. "My Lady grieves; her sons may fight to the death over the morning gift for Judith." I slammed my scraper down on the table. Gaufredus looked like a surprised rat. Then he looked up at the ceiling. "Isn't it interesting," he said, "that if one looks closely enough, one can always find a woman as the source of all strife."

"But it was not Judith's fault! Rogier has no land for her morning gift. How is it her fault that Robert never keeps his word? That, Brother Gaufredus, is the true reason for their fight, and none other!" Gaufredus was leaning forward, his eyes glittering.

He had tricked me into saying more than I ever intended. I covered my parchment and took my leave for the day.

When Count Rogier heard that this youth — whom he loved no less than the Countess his wife — had died, he was overtaken by great sorrow and anger and that day he killed many in battle.

— Gaufredus Malaterra, transl. John Julius
   Norwich: *Historia Sicula*

CAPUT XIII

The Abbey of Santa Eufemia
On the eve of the Feast of St. Angelbert (February 18)
In this year 1062 from the Incarnation of our Lord
The words of Bernfrieda

The days are still short and cold. Senda gets up late these days. After the wedding, I forsook my pallet in the antechamber, for she asked that I sleep with her. She has a recurring nightmare; only I, it seems, can keep her monsters at bay.

In her dream last night she was alone on the wooden sentrywalk on the walls of the Abbey, waiting for a messenger to bring her news of yet another battle between her sons. Cloaked in her red mantle, her hands tightly clasped to her chest, she watched a column approach. Black-cloaked and hooded, the messenger was surrounded by foot soldiers and knights in full battle array. The knights' mail coats were dull, the blues, reds and yellows of their shields stained. Senda strained to guess the colors of the pennants on their lances. They were black.

Drums drowned all other noise. She rushed down the wooden stairs. When the men entered the courtyard, she stood in front of the church door, directly across from them. The messenger's voice resonated in the empty courtyard, echoing off the red brick wall of the cloister to her right, and the yellow-white stone arcades in front of her, then ebbing into the livid grey sky. But still she could not discern whose name he called. Hundreds of soldiers watched her greedily. *Which of your sons would you rather see dead? The cunning Duke of Apulia or the impetuous Count of Mileto? Speak, Lady Fredesenda!*

She awakened trembling and drenched in sweat. I pulled the fur-lined coverlet over her and held her close, as when we were young. She curled up against me, and I stroked her hair. My hand rested lightly over her eyelids, to chase her nightmare away.

"God is punishing me, Bernfrieda," Senda whispered, "but how can I atone for my sin when I feel no remorse?"

"Sleep, sleep. It is not God who is punishing you."

⳥ ⳥ ⳥

I leave a candle burning all night, which is a luxury we never had at Hauteville. I keep the braziers going too. Brother Ambrose refills the baskets each day and brings us more candles when I ask him. It is a strange feeling to know that there is a limitless supply.

Sometimes I push the heavy pelt aside and open one of the wooden shutters that keeps the cold and the light outside. Senda sleeps deeply, wrapped in her fur coverlets. I can work only for a little while before the cold numbs my hand. The pale gray light is so much better than the dim glow of the candle on my desk that I hardly notice.

There is so much to write! I even stopped going to the *scriptorium* last week in order to have more time.

"I thought you were serious about your work!" Brother Gaufredus put his quill down and gave me his full attention, for once. "How can you forsake it because of a bit of chilly weather?"

"It is not a bit of chilly weather. My fingers get numb and I can scarcely write. I don't understand why the *scriptorium* is not heated in winter."

"It benefits the soul greatly to suffer the cold, Bernfrieda. Remember Saint Pardoux? He rejected all heat, save that from the sun's rays. It is a way to ennoble the spirit, like not changing one's shirt from Christmas to Christmas."

He didn't need to remind me of the smell of his unwashed shirt that time when I had the fever.

"I'll come back from time to time, Brother Gaufredus. But I am not as young as you are and I must take care of myself." *He had not forsaken me when I needed him.*

He sighed. "I won't let anyone touch the life of Saint Agatha until you return. The scribes here are much too careless."

⚜ ⚜ ⚜

When I sit down like this to continue my chronicle, I look over what I have already written. I vowed long ago not to use the scraper until I finish each chapter. I know I must keep writing, for if I stop, as I did last summer, I may never pick up my quill again; though my sentences say so little of what I intend.

In January's second week Lady Judith sent a letter to Senda, who asked me to break the seal and read it. "Put to some use all that time you spent in the *scriptorium*, Bernfrieda!" she said grimly. I hurried to do her bidding. I scanned the parchment. The penmanship was poor. Judith's scribe had taken no pride in his letters. Even the margins were uneven. I pointed that out to Senda but she waved her hand, got up in her lion-head chair and leaned forward. "Tell me what she *says!*"

Lady Judith begged her to plead with Robert, for she had been unable to convince Rogier to take Robert's gold within the forty days Rogier had given Robert. Rogier had pledged the lands around Reggio and Messina to her as a morning gift and had vowed to deliver them before the end of the summer. He had taken his soldiers, abandoned Robert's army in Sicily and then declared war on his brother. Word had just reached Judith that Robert had left Melfi and was riding south toward Mileto to fight Rogier.

As I read I could almost see Judith's pretty face crumpling, close to tears. It did not surprise me that she would try to drag Senda into this new quarrel. The need for reassurance was strong in Judith, who rarely saw beyond herself. Still, it disgusted me that she had disregarded the effect her letter would have on her mother-in-law.

"What does Judith think I can do?" Senda grabbed the lion hand-rests till her knuckles were white. "They have never listened to me before."

❦ ❦ ❦

The last day of January, after Mass, Senda and I walked toward the gate for our morning stroll on the beach. I passed the villains and servants who had also attended Prime at the Abbey church. Senda trudged behind me without enthusiasm. It was just after dawn, and the air was damp from the night's rain. Violet hills crowded around us as if a more leisurely distance among them would not protect the Abbey. The smell of wet hay hung in the air. Servants had spread it in front of the church to make the muddy courtyard viable. Guards walked atop the narrow wooden platform built on the white stone walls that encircled the buildings of Santa Eufemia. The thick walls prevented us from gazing at the sea just beyond them, but I could smell the salt in the air. Acrid, familiar, so like my early years on the Cotentin and yet so different. Even in winter there is a sweetness here, mingled with the pungency that reflects the gentleness of this sea. Grey waters invade the beach, leaving soft semicircles on the sand as they withdraw. They carry algae, shells, a dead fish. The waves never lash the beach with wild fury here as they did against the rocky promontory under Father's keep. In a way they reflect the change in my life and Senda's, from the turmoil of our early and middle life to the quiet we found at the Abbey. Yet what real peace can there be for Senda as long as her sons are fighting?

We picked up the hems of our tunics and mantles as we crossed the muddy courtyard, careful to step on the hay. The Abbey formed a square, as at Saint Evroult. The church took most of the northwest side of the square, with the cloister running parallel to it; on our right, large, graceful arches in the white native stone disguised the entrance to the storehouses.

As we approached the gate, a sentry on the walls shouted that a large group of people was approaching from the south, from the direction of Mileto. Though they were still too far away for him to identify their colors, Senda stopped and looked at me, the color the morning air had brought to her cheeks suddenly gone. "It's Rogier, Bernfrieda!"

Her nightmare!

She ran toward the gate. Soon the sentries shouted that the banners were crimson and silver, Rogier's colors. Gathering her tunic and mantle in big handfuls, Senda ran to the wooden stairs that led to the walls and nimbly climbed to the top, leaving me well behind. When I reached her, she was leaning over the stone wall, unmindful of the rain that had begun to fall. When she turned, her eyes were dark against the pallor of her face.

"It's a funeral procession, Bernfrieda. Look!"

Black-robed monks led the somber column plodding through the mud toward the Abbey. Their chanting and the lugubrious sound of drums could be heard in the distance. In their midst was a black-draped litter carried by eight men, two on each pole. On it lay a corpse, wrapped in grey cloth and securely tied to the sides of the litter at the neck, chest, abdomen and legs. Foot soldiers in brown leather jerkins followed. Twenty knights flanked the column and closed it, reining in their horses to keep pace. With their colored mantles and the red-and-blue lance pennants and their shields decorated with heraldic devices, they were like peacocks in a brown flock of grouse. The steel of their short mail coats glinted in the pallid morning sun. All wore conical leather helmets, reinforced and decorated in triangular sections with metal strips over a mailed hood. Senda stared, her eyes wide, her lips slightly apart like the stone figures on the corner pillars of the cloister. She looked ready to faint.

I grasped her with both arms. "Senda, it can't be Rogier. They would not bring him to Santa Eufemia — they would lay him in

Mileto." At first it was as if I had not spoken. Then she turned, and she began to tremble against my shoulder.

The chanting grew nearer. Dread enveloped me in spite of my words. *Those huge war horses, their manes twisted into strands, the painted scabbards and battle axes hanging from their sides — they are right from her dream!* "Senda! Listen! It is not Rogier!" I repeated. I held her tightly against me, as when she was hurt as a child. We watched in silence as the procession wound down the hill, the chanting and drumming very close now.

Suddenly Senda leaned from the wall and pointed at a knight who had moved ahead. "Bernfrieda, look!"

There was no mistaking Rogier's short brown hair — he wore no helmet — nor the proud tilt of the chin. The small silver lion gleamed on the right side of the red woolen mantle we ourselves had woven.

"Come," Senda said, as she turned and stepped down the stairs, her pace again as light as that of a young girl. "We must get ready for him." I followed Senda down the stairs and then to her apartment. When she said, "I wonder who died," her tone was almost gay. I hoped she would not seem so lighthearted when the funeral party arrived.

"We'll know soon enough." I said.

When Rogier was announced, everything was ready for him. He bent slightly when he entered the room, as if he were coming into a tent.

As he used to do when he came back from the hunt at Hauteville, he discarded his red mantle on the floor as he entered. I picked it up and hung it on the pole high on the wall with Senda's clothes, just as I had hung it before. Rogier hesitated, then saw his mother in the alcove and rushed to her.

Senda clung to Rogier; he rested his cheek on her smooth linen wimple. His dark looks were more like mine than Senda's, his tall slender figure was so much like Father's. Afterwards Rogier turned to me and took my hand. "You do not age, Bernfrieda."

He's known how to charm from the time he was a baby.

"Sit here, Rogier." Senda led him to her chair and then sat on the stone bench next to him. Gratefully he sank into it and closed his eyes for a moment. She took his left hand in hers. "You look pale, my son."

Rogier was not just pale, he looked haggard. Unshaven and splattered with mud, he stank of old sweat and blood.

He put his free hand over his eyes. "I have not slept much lately," he said. "I — brought back Arnold's body. He was killed two days ago."

"What happened?"

"He was killed only minutes after our first attack. His horse was felled by an arrow and crushed him. That horse was a gift from Judith." Rogier ran a hand through his hair.

There is nothing they would not do for each other, the Abbot had said. Until now the quarrel was between the two brothers. This changed everything. I thought of Judith's lovely face; how vengeful was she?

"O Rogier! And Judith?" Senda wailed.

"Judith cannot be consoled. She has not touched food since Arnold died. She weeps constantly. Robert agreed to a truce so we could take his body to Santa Eufemia. He will pay for this — I swore it to Judith!"

"Let me speak to Robert!" Senda pleaded.

"You cannot solve this problem for me, Mother." Rogier pulled Senda to him and kissed her forehead. "This is between Robert and myself."

⽵ ⽵ ⽵

Arnold's body lay below the altar on a high trestle table draped in black . The monks had washed him and dressed him in his mail coat and green tunic and had left his head uncovered. His face was grey, his blond hair dull on the black pillow. His long green mantle had been draped around the lower part of his body; his hands were joined over a crucifix. His helmet, sword, and shield lay at his feet. There was no apparent wound or disfiguration on him. I knelt by Senda and Rogier during the vigil. *Will Judith insist on revenge? How much power does she have over Rogier? Will he listen to her? O Senda, this is the onset of your nightmare.*

Senda and I left the church at sunset. Rogier, Abbot Robert, and the monks prayed by Arnold all night and most of the next day. As I left, I caught a glimpse of the Abbot's face; he stared rigidly ahead, his beak nose thinner under the hollows of his eyes. Later that week, clad only in a long white linen tunic, Arnold was buried under the church floor near a side altar. His mailed coat, helmet, shield, and sword the Abbot gifted to Rogier.

☙ ☙ ☙

Nothing happened for almost a week after Rogier went back to Mileto. Senda was listless for days after her son left. She kept to her room, and took her meals there. Then just two days ago her mood changed. She seemed excited, almost feverish. "Bernfrieda, ask the Abbot if I may see him today. And get my saffron tunic when you come back."

As Senda expected, the Abbot invited her to eat the midday meal with him in his private quarters. I took her fine saffron tunic from where it hung and helped her put it on. She asked for the red velvet mantle lined with fur that Tancred had given her on their wedding day. I caressed the soft fabric as I took it out of the oaken chest where it had lain since we had left Melfi. The mantle smelled of the lavender bunches I had placed over it and of the aromatic wood with which the chest was lined.

I placed it on Senda's shoulders. "The gold brooch!" Senda ordered, and I went back to the chest and took the brooch Robert had given her when she first arrived in Melfi. Senda carefully took off her worn silver one and watched suspiciously as I placed it on the desk.

We walked quickly, in silence, to the other end of the dark corridor that separated Senda's rooms from the Abbot's. I knocked on the heavy chestnut door.

A young monk led us into the antechamber, then disappeared through another door and came back moments later to show us into the Abbot's dining room.

The room was rectangular; a large arched window afforded a view of the hills. A long table covered with heavy white linen cloth was set up in the center of the room.

Robert de Grantmesnil, Abbot of Santa Eufemia and previous Abbot of Saint Evroult, was standing by the window. He turned when he heard us and crossed to meet my half-sister.

What a toll Arnold's death has taken on him! He looks so pinched and thin — and he looks unkempt even though he has recently been shaven. And his hair has white in it! I never noticed that before.

Weeks after we had settled in Melfi, word came that the Abbot had to leave Saint Evroult and was in Rome pleading with the Pope to intervene in the quarrel with Duke Guillaume. But even the Pope could not appease the enraged Duke, who proclaimed that he would hang Robert de Grantmesnil from the nearest oak in Normandy if he ever tried to return. After that, Abbot Robert and the monks who had followed him into exile began to wander from court to court looking for sustenance and protection. Senda interceded with her son to help. She reminded him of their friendship in their youth and of the help and kindness Abbot de Grantmesnil had shown to Tancred. So when the Abbot arrived in Melfi, Robert received him warmly. He soon made him Abbot of Santa Eufemia, the new Abbey he was building on the southern border of his lands.

We knelt as the Abbot approached. *Though she is his benefactor's mother she feels as awed as if she were still a minor knight's wife and he still the Abbot of the greatest Abbey in Normandy.* He took her hands, raised her to her feet and greeted her warmly. She kissed his ring.

"It is good that you join us again, Lady Fredesenda." The Abbot spoke gravely. "I was worried about you."

Senda nodded, "I need to speak to you, my Lord Abbot."

"I am at your service my Lady, but it would please me if you partook of some food first."

Abbot Robert motioned for the wine to be poured. It was an exquisite red wine, produced at the Abbey especially for the Abbot and his guests. The meal began with fish balls made with a mixture of spinach and white fish immersed in juice of pomegranate. The taste was quite delicate; I took advantage of the fact that the serving monk, who shared my trencher, was too preoccupied to eat much. The serving monk next fetched dishes of roasted hare, boiled leeks and pickled lampreys. Senda took very little, but I ate well.

"I grieve for you, my Lord," Senda began. "I am mindful that it was an arrow from my son's soldiers that killed your brother Arnold."

I glanced at Abbot de Grantmesnil with apprehension. He shook his head. "Life is cruel, my Lady. And complicated. There are no enemies I can rage against. Your son Robert rescued me at a time when everyone else had forsaken me. His quarrel is not with me. I know he grieved when he heard of my loss."

How can he forgive so soon? Is he a saint? Or a shrewd politician?

Senda frowned. "You are generous, my Lord Abbot. And you are right. Robert has no quarrel with you. It is his own brother he wishes dead."

"My Lady!" the Abbot said sternly. "Robert Guiscard and Rogier are similar in many ways. I know that in their hearts they do not wish each other's death. But they are proud. Each is fearful to yield to the other — perhaps Arnold's death will shake them into seeing what a tragic waste their quarrel is."

"Or make each more determined to prevail over the other," Senda said. "I doubt that this death, however painful, will make them end this war." She paused.

"I need a messenger, Lord Abbot. A man who can write and relay faithfully my words, and is strong enough to travel to Melfi — perhaps even farther."

"You will try to plead with Robert Guiscard, my Lady?"

"Yes, I must try." Senda said, almost in a whisper.

The Abbot was silent for a while. "Brother Gaufredus," he said finally. "He is a gifted scholar and a fine diplomat — and young enough to withstand long journeys."

The mother of Robert Guiscard must receive letters on the most important events of our time. Brother Gaufredus will love to be so close to power. How often he has tried to extract information from me!

"Brother Gaufredus then. With your leave I shall send Bernfrieda to fetch him this afternoon, to give him my message."

The Abbot nodded.

"Thank you, my Lord." Abbot de Grantmesnil accompanied her to the door. As I put away her finery, I waited in vain for her to tell me how she planned to plead with Robert. *Why should Robert listen to her when he can defeat Rogier and silence him once and for all?* But Senda seemed so determined that I kept my peace.

Brother Gaufredus gaped at me that afternoon when I told him Senda wanted to see him. Knowing what the Abbot had said about him, I looked at my teacher with renewed interest. His face was pallid and delicate, half-hidden by a short brown beard, straight on his cheeks but curly on his chin. He was slight but — unusual among thin men — clumsy. When he stood up, he stepped on the hem of his robe. He followed me through the dark hallway to Senda's chambers. *A fine diplomat who steps on his robe? He does not look at all like the Byzantine diplomats I saw at Robert's court. They were old, dignified, and had full, important beards. Gaufredus is too young — not yet five-and-thirty I'd wager — and his beard is too thin, and he pulls it so much.* In spite of his avid curiosity, he had not asked the reason for the summons.

The Abbot had given Senda the best rooms in his house, as was fitting for the mother of Robert Guiscard. Yet the corridor leading to her chamber was narrow and full of shadows, the only light coming from a small arched window high on the wall.

I pushed the oaken door open to let in Brother Gaufredus. Awed, he hesitated on the threshold. I snapped my fingers to show him the way. Senda was standing by her chair, facing the sea, but turned when she heard us come in.

She is holding Tancred's sword!

Brother Gaufredus gasped. I stood still for a moment and felt the blood drain from my face. I left Gaufredus and I took my

place on the stone bench next to the window, where I had left
the unfinished tapestry.

Senda studied Brother Gaufredus. *Brother Gaufredus, a gifted*
scholar? A fine diplomat? Most suited as a messenger? She wishes his
outward appearance could match the Abbot's description. He looks so
slight in his black robe. He keeps shuffling his feet . . .

"I called you to be not only my messenger, Brother Gaufredus,
but also my witness. Are you willing to be both?"

He glanced around, looking for an escape route. Then he met
Senda's stare and stood still. He nodded.

"Swear," she said. She held the sword high in front of him,
pushed a jewel on the side of the hilt, which opened a small reliquary in the handle. She pointed to the shrivelled relic inside.
"Swear on the holy finger of Saint Vito that you will not repeat a
word of what I say unless I give you leave." Brother Gaufredus
shifted his weight, blinked, and did as he was told.

She motioned him to sit at the desk. Quickly he picked up
the quill in front of him and dipped it in the ink.

She is still undecided! She keeps running her finger over that worn
silver brooch. The lion and the deer have almost disappeared.

"You must help me stop Robert, Brother Gaufredus," she said,
breaking the long silence. Gaufredus's relief turned into panic.
He gasped, quill in midair.

"My Lady —"

"One has to be careful when dealing with powerful people,
Bernfrieda . . ."

"Otherwise Robert will destroy Rogier." Senda's blue-green
eyes were relentless. He found it hard to meet her stare. Carefully he put the quill down. He realized full well the danger of
her request. Angering a Duke had already cost his Abbey a great
price.

"My Lady," he said hesitantly, "your sons have not always been
enemies. They are both headstrong, impetuous — disagreements
are inevitable."

"This latest disagreement has cost the Abbot's brother his
life!"

Suddenly she closed her eyes and swayed. I rushed to her side and put my arms over her shoulders to lead her to her chair. She sank down into it. I spoke to her as firmly as I would an unruly child. "Enough, Senda. I'll fetch you some wine."

"Stop hovering over me," she said. "Fetch some wine for Brother Gaufredus!" She did not drink.

I brought Gaufredus his wine. He looked at me over the cup's rim. *He is surprised at the familiarity with which I treat Senda.* Then he cautiously put the cup on the desk. *It is a fine wine, much finer than he is accustomed to; he wants it to last.* He mopped his brow with the sleeve of his robe.

"How can I help, my Lady?" he said finally.

"The first message is to Robert," she said. "Don't write it down — *tell* him that I must see him as soon as possible. Tell him I know something that may affect the validity of his second marriage."

I almost dropped the wine decanter. I sat down on the bench. *Why had Senda not confided in me? Blackmailing Robert! He will be absolutely furious. He dotes on Gaita. And he depends on the marriage to bring him Salerno!*

Brother Gaufredus looked confused. *Why had she not spoken up two years ago, when the Pope scrutinized Robert's first marriage under Canon Law?*

Senda stood up leaning against the desk. Gaufredus picked up the quill again. Their eyes met. "The next message is for Pope Nicholas," she said in a flat voice. He began to write.

"You must write to him that Robert Guiscard is not Tancred's son. He is the son of Guillaume *Bras-de-Fer.* Therefore he is related to Lady Alberada only within the eighth degree and his first marriage is valid." Senda seemed perfectly calm.

She is mad. The war between her sons has driven her mad. Would Robert kill his mother if she stood in his way? He has killed others for much less. Would he spare her?

And what will Robert do to me? He knows Senda confides in me, and I mean very little to him. Why does Senda have to ruin our life here? We are finally at peace. And my chronicle . . .

Brother Gaufredus finished and put the quill down. He seemed to have trouble breathing.

"You swore on the Holy relic," Senda reminded, holding the sword in front of him. "Never to speak to anyone without my permission. Do not forget, Brother Gaufredus."

He nodded, the white of his beady eyes showing.

Senda put the sword on the desk, took the manuscript from him, rolled the parchment, sealed it, and placed it inside the chest. I refilled Gaufredus's cup but my hand shook and a few drops spilled on his robe. He watched the red liquid sink into his sleeve, and I knew he was thinking of blood.

"Thank you, Brother Gaufredus. You must go to Robert in Melfi. You must leave immediately. I have already spoken to the Abbot." Senda was rummaging inside the opened chest, but her voice was still strong and clear.

"But — the message to the Pope?" Brother Gaufredus said with great effort.

Senda walked to him and handed him two gold solidi.

"Forget you ever wrote that message," she said. "You must never tell anyone, Brother Gaufredus, unless I need you to witness."

She touched her worn silver brooch, hesitated, and then went back to the chest. She took the gold brooch and handed it to Brother Gaufredus. "Show this when you arrive. Robert will see you right away."

After that she sat down and stared at the sea again as if he had already left. I took him to the door and almost had to push him outside. "Wait for me in the *scriptorium*," I whispered as I shut the door behind him.

I turned to Senda. "Have you lost your mind? Robert will never forgive you! Why didn't you tell me what you were scheming?" I was suddenly aware her lack of confidence in me was the true reason for my anger.

Her eyes were bright in the pallor of her face. "I had no choice. I must save Rogier. Leave me alone now, Bernfrieda." She spoke to me as if I were a servant. I turned and left.

In the *scriptorium*, Gaufredus was holding the brooch in one hand and the two gold pieces in the other. He looked at me and sighed. We sat in silence for a while.

"The Lord shield me from the wrath of the powerful. This is my punishment for coveting what I had no right to. Why didn't she call for Brother Odo?"

"You have nothing to fear, Brother Gaufredus. All you have to do is relay a message."

Senda and I are the ones who are in danger. I picked up a quill and stroked it against the desk.

"But Duke Robert will be furious when he finds out I wrote the message to the Pope! Oh, I wish she had never called for me!" He put the brooch and the coins on the desk and stared at them, his head in his hands.

"Forget you ever wrote that message — you need not tell Robert." *The message to Pope Nicholas is her safeguard. She never intended to send it to him.* "If Duke Robert ends the war with his brother, they'll resume their alliance and wrest Sicily from the heathen Saracens. Think about it, Brother Gaufredus. You can help shape history!"

He began to smooth his beard. I told him how both Robert and Rogier would be grateful to him in the end. After a while he picked up the brooch and the coins from the desk.

"I wonder if the Abbot will let me take the white mule," he said, and smiled a tight-lipped little smile.

🐦 🐦 🐦

I stayed much longer than usual at the *scriptorium* that afternoon. After the candle that kept time went down two marks, I returned to the chamber. Senda stepped toward me from the window when she heard me enter. Without a word, I walked past her into the alcove, picked up the tapestry from the floor and sat on my bench.

"I *am* sorry, Bernfrieda," she said. I tried to thread my needle but my hands kept shaking and I had to give up.

"Had I told you what I planned to do, you would have discouraged me, you know you would have."

"And what if I had?" The tapestry slid to the floor. "Do I have such power over you, Senda, that you fear my words?"

"It is not that — O, Bernfrieda, I can't stand you being angry at me." She tried to take my hand but I snatched it away. She slumped into her chair.

"You do not understand," she sighed. "You have no children."

"I have no children," I repeated, trying to control the trembling in my voice. *Who raised you — and your children?*

I picked up the tapestry. It still took me several tries to thread the needle with the brown wool I had chosen.

"Why are you so angry at me? I told you I am sorry." She tapped her fingers on the lion armrest.

"What if Robert decides to kill you?" I asked. "And me?"

"Robert? Have you lost your senses?"

Had she not even considered the idea?

"If you keep holding that cloth so tightly you will end up soiling it. Stop worrying about this. I took precautions."

I looked at the embroidery. *Thread and cloth cannot do justice to the expression in Robert's eyes, or the way he carries himself. Will Senda's precautions be enough?* As unconcerned as Saint Peter in Brother Gaufredus's illumination, Robert stared back at me.

*It was generally agreed and some actually said that Robert
[Guiscard] was an exceptional leader, quick-witted, of fine
appearance, courteous, a clever conversationalist, with a
loud voice, accessible, of gigantic stature, with hair
invariably of the right length and a thick beard . . . he had
the physique of a true leader; he treated with respect all his
subjects, especially those who were more than usually
devoted to him. On the other hand, he was niggardly and
grasping in the extreme, a very good businessman, most
covetous and full of ambition.*

 — Anna Comnena (1083-1153) daughter of
  Byzantine emperor Alexius Comnenus, great
  enemy of Robert Guiscard, transl. E.R.A. Sewter:
  The Alexiad

CAPUT XIV

The Abbey of Santa Eufemia
On the eve of the Feast of Saint Patrick (March 17)
In this year 1062 from the Incarnation of our Lord
The words of Bernfrieda

W hy did you summon me in such a hurry, Mother? I was about to leave for Mileto when the monk arrived." Robert stormed into the chamber unannounced, and strode toward the lion-head chair where his mother was sitting. Senda sat up straight and did not extend her hand or show any sign of greeting. Pushing his mantle aside, Robert rested his hands in his belt, waiting for her to speak.

Robert's broad, regular features were like Tancred's, the full lips, wide cheekbones, straight nose. And so was his coloring. But Tancred had never looked at Senda with such dislike. He barely glanced in my direction when he came in, yet I knew he was as aware of me as I was of him. I set my embroidery down on the stone bench.

Senda leaned forward in the great chair, and put her hands over the lion heads. "You were about to leave for Mileto," Senda repeated slowly, "to lay siege to Rogier's capital. Leave Rogier alone, Robert — end this madness! And give your brother the land he needs."

Robert glared. "You asked me to ride from Melfi to tell me this?"

"Robert, you must end this quarrel with Rogier!" Senda said.

"You have summoned the wrong son, Mother." He crossed his arms. "It is Rogier who burns my land, steals my cattle, slaughters my serfs. Do you expect me to hand him Apulia?"

She rose from her chair. "Enough, Robert. I did not call you here to argue, but to insist you cease this war with Rogier."

"Insist?" Robert arched his right eyebrow. "I am thirsty," he said, glancing in my direction. "Fetch some wine, Bernfrieda."

I hurried to the wine cabinet, filled one of the long-stemmed silver cups Alberada had given Senda, then handed it to him.

Robert took it and gulped the wine down before motioning me for more. He held the cup as I refilled it.

"You are unreasonable, Mother." Robert wiped his mouth with the back of his hand. "I have no intention of harming Rogier."

"I know you will not. If you do you'll have to put Gaita away, and take Alberada back to your bed," Senda said quietly.

Robert raised his eyebrows, and laughed.

Gaita was not just a young wife who pleased Robert greatly; she also gave him a rightful claim to Salerno and its rich territory. Her brother Gisulf would soon make yet another bad alliance, giving Robert the excuse to take the city on her behalf. Then he could unite the bits and pieces of Italy he had conquered or inherited, and form a great kingdom to rival even Normandy.

"Why didn't you come forward two years ago when I married Gaita, if you knew of an impediment?"

She did not answer immediately. "I had more reason to be silent then. I did not want to thwart your plans. I still don't; but your argument with Rogier has become vicious. Stop it — stop it now."

Robert gripped the stem of the cup with such force that it bent. "What is it, Mother? Do you know of an impediment?"

"Tancred was not your father."

Robert gave her a long, unbelieving stare. He walked to the desk, set the twisted cup on it, and turned his back to her.

"Who, then?"

He seems so indifferent, so detached. Does he not care? Does it not make any difference to him?

"Guillaume *Bras-de-Fer*," Senda said,

He turned and faced her, amazed. "My half-brother?" Senda nodded.

He began pacing the floor. The implication would be immediately clear to him. He was too careful and scheming to miss it. The fact that he was a bastard would not hurt him. Wasn't Duke Guillaume of Normandy a bastard too? Italy was a wild country; normal conventions did not apply. But he needed the support of the Pope to lend legitimacy to his conquests. And how could Pope Nicholas support him if he openly defied Church law? He would be eight generations removed from Alberada, and not seven, as he had proven to the Church. He would have to take Alberada back, lose Gaita *and* his claim to Salerno. Even the Pope would not be able to help him if his own mother spoke out.

"Who else knows of this? Besides Bernfrieda and the monk?"

"No one."

Robert stopped and stared at her. My stomach clenched.

"There is a letter from me to Pope Nicholas," Senda continued, looking at him steadily, "that will be delivered if you do not stop fighting Rogier. Or if anything happens to me."

"Will you give me the letter if I make peace with Rogier?"

"No. It will be kept where it is. Unopened."

"How can I be sure someone will not open it?"

"You can't. Nor can I know that you will not hurt your brother. But if you keep your word and reach an agreement with Rogier and respect it, I'll keep mine. Otherwise I will have to stop you."

Robert looked at the rushes for a few moments, rubbing the scar on his eyebrow. "I'll send you a messenger as soon as I speak to Rogier," he said finally.

"Not one of your men, Robert. Take Brother Gaufredus with you."

Robert began to speak, then changed his mind and spat, narrowly missing the hem of her shift. Abruptly he turned and left the room.

⚜ ⚜ ⚜

That evening, Senda motioned me to open the shutters so she could watch the sun sink into the sea. She sat on the stone bench in the alcove under the window ledge, rested her chin on her hand and stared at the thousand small suns reflected in the sea. As usual at this time of the day, I fetched the polished bronze mirror from the chest and handed it to her. I removed her wimple, unbraided her hair, and began to comb it. When I finished, she looked in the mirror, slowly tilting her head backwards until her hair reached the floor and the skin under her chin stretched. I glanced in the mirror, about to beg her to speak to me. Bathed in the cold winter sun, her reflection was soft, the contours of her face blurred, the lines around her mouth and eyes gone. She looked like her mother. *Helplessness and sorrow are not all I feel. When Senda first told me to go away, her voice was like her mother's. It could have been Lady Mathilda sitting there. Nothing will ever be as before, and Senda will never know.*

⚜ ⚜ ⚜

Yesterday, around midmorning, Brother Gaufredus returned from Mileto. He came straight to Senda's room, his beard and habit still splattered with mud.

My teacher walked into the chamber with new assurance. He nodded in my direction and then bowed deeply to Senda.

"You are back sooner than I expected, Brother Gaufredus," Senda said.

Gaufredus nodded. "Yes, my Lady. I spent more time on my mule than on solid ground these past few days."

"What happened?" Senda sat down in her chair, forgetting to ask Gaufredus to sit.

I brought a stool for him and some wine. Then I busied myself with my embroidery.

"Duke Robert tried to talk to his brother as soon as he arrived in Mileto. But the gates remained closed for him, and Count Rogier refused all negotiations. He appeared on the walls and shouted to Duke Robert to save his breath, for he had heard enough lies."

Senda paled and clutched her brooch.

Gaufredus shook his head. "The Duke camped outside Mileto for two whole days, sending messenger after messenger to his brother. All in vain, for Count Rogier refused to receive them." Brother Gaufredus sipped from his goblet, swallowed, and sighed deeply. "Lady Gaita, who had followed the Duke, also tried to send a messenger, with the same results. Then on the third night Duke Robert's sentries saw some movement just outside the walls and went to investigate. They reported that Count Rogier and several of his men had slipped out of Mileto. When the two men who followed them returned the next day, they said that Count Rogier went into Gerace, a small village in the hills, three hours south of Mileto, to gather reinforcements. Duke Robert was enraged. He had an understanding with the citizens of Gerace and did not expect them to change sides. But they are Byzantines." Brother Gaufredus shrugged. "One can't expect a Greek to be true to his word."

Senda turned toward the window and looked outside. "*Robert* has gone back on his word many times," she said.

She seemed immersed in thought. Brother Gaufredus waited until he was sure she could not see him, then looked at me and turned his cup upside down. I smiled, in spite of the uneasiness I felt over his news, and I refilled it.

"Duke Robert left immediately for Gerace, my Lady," Brother Gaufredus said, after taking a long drink. "He was convinced that if he could see his brother he could reassure him of his sincerity. He said to tell you that he would enter Gerace in disguise, that he had a few friends he could trust there. He ordered me to come back and tell you all that happened."

Senda stood up and began pacing the room.

"Yes," she said speaking more to herself than to Brother Gaufredus. "If Robert speaks to Rogier he will convince him. Perhaps he already has. But why is Rogier so stubborn? It must be because of Judith. She is brokenhearted over Arnold's death; what if he does not forgive Robert?"

Brother Gaufredus mopped his brow with his sleeve. Senda looked at his grimy face as if seeing him for the first time.

"You must be very tired, Brother."

My teacher nodded. "I —" he began, but she interrupted him. "Go and rest then. Tomorrow you'll lead me to Mileto."

Gaufredus opened his mouth, but thought better of it and bowed deeply. He bowed again before leaving, though Senda had turned away. He walked out of the room as if all the weariness of the journey had caught up with him at once.

Senda was still looking out the window when I returned.

"I must talk to Judith," she said, crossing her arms.

༚ ༚ ༚

Gaufredus was in the courtyard that afternoon as I returned from the kitchen with some of the foods especially cooked for Senda to take on her journey. He was sitting on the short wall that enclosed the cloister by the *scriptorium*, his shoulders slumped forward.

"Are you all right, Brother Gaufredus?" I stopped, and set the basket of food next to him.

"I am all sore," he moaned. "Your Lady wants me dead."

"Nonsense," I replied. "It is because my Lady trusts you that she wants you to accompany us."

Brother Gaufredus shrugged. "It'll be useless anyway. Count Rogier won't listen to her. He wants blood."

"Have you taken Count Rogier's confession?" I said sharply. "You know his mind so well." I picked up my basket.

He put a hand on my arm. "Did she tell the truth, Bernfrieda? Is Duke Robert the son of Guillaume *Bras-de-Fer*?" I hid a smile as I turned away; I had been waiting for that question from the day Senda had first spoken.

"Aren't you ashamed, Brother? You swore never to talk about what my Lady told you."

"But you know the truth, Bernfrieda, you were in the room with us —"

"Still you swore," I said. Like a child caught in mischief, he lowered his eyes.

It was not Robert who was Guillaume's son.

There is a story that Robert's wife Gaita, who used to accompany him on campaign, like another Pallas, if not a second Athena, seeing the runaways [Robert's retreating soldiers] and glaring fiercely at them, shouted in a very loud voice: How far will you run? Halt! Be men! — not quite in those Homeric words, but something very like them in her own dialect. As they continued to run, she grasped a long spear and charged at full gallop against them. It brought them to their senses and they went back to fight.

— Anna Comnena, transl. E.R.A. Sewter:
  The Alexiad

CAPUT XV

Mileto
On the eve of the Feast of Saint Anicetus (April 19)
In this year 1062 from the Incarnation of our Lord
The words of Bernfrieda

As soon as it was light we left the Abbey with an escort and provisions to last us two days. We rode until midmorning, following the shore of the Gulf of Santa Eufemia. Then we turned inland and reached the banks of the stream at the base of the hill where Mileto was perched. The stream is seasonal. During the summer months only the whiteness of its empty bed can be seen, but at this time of the year it was full, its waters running swiftly. The wooden bridge which Rogier's men had built over the stream had been damaged sometime in the last week, for Brother Gaufredus had used it just days ago. It needed to be reinforced before we could cross, so Senda ordered our tents raised while our escort made repairs.

Just before dawn our tents were folded, our belongings packed again, and we rode in silence as the morning sun slowly climbed in the sky. The uphill path narrowed in places, making the climb

dangerous, and I thanked God for my mule, who seemed unaware of the steep slope to its right. The brief watering stops
were the only relief to our misery. The wide-hipped clay jugs
slung on the flanks of the mules kept the water cool. Just before
midday we saw Mileto in the distance. Eager to arrive, Senda
urged us to go on, though it was high time for a rest.

The tall cathedral and the square stone tower looked grayish
in the trembling air, dwarfing the stone walls that encircled
them. Below the walls Robert's tents, hundreds of them, looked
like a swarm of ants encircling a morsel.

We hurried downhill and then up again for the final climb. As
we approached Robert's camp, our escort unfurled the white
banner with the silver cross of Santa Eufemia. Under its warrant,
we reached the large tent in the center.

Even before we dismounted, Gaita opened the flap and
stepped outside. Tall, as tall as any of the handful of Norman
soldiers that instantly surrounded her, Robert's wife took a few
steps and stood in front of Senda. Gaita was a big woman, but
pleasingly proportioned. She wore a short linen tunic over a mail
coat that reached to her knees, split in the middle to allow her to
ride. Mail leggings and a huge sword completed her attire. Her
braided blond hair, her one concession to her womanhood, hung
well past her waist in a thick rope. Otherwise she could have
been a soldier. *Marriage has not changed her taste in clothes!*

I liked Gaita. She was brave, and not just in a warrior's sense.
She was blunt to the point of rudeness, but all knew where they
stood with her.

"Welcome, Lady Fredesenda," Gaita said loudly, but her welcome was not reflected on her face.

Senda nodded and then dismounted, her face equally stern.
We followed Gaita into her tent, leaving our escort just outside.

Nothing inside betrayed the presence of a woman. The tent
was sparsely furnished with light cane stools and chests. Battle
gear lay in an untidy heap in a corner next to an unmade pallet.

Gaita sat on one of the stools and motioned us to do the
same.

"Robert told me," she said flatly. "That is the reason I came here. I hoped Rogier might listen to me."

"Robert has gone back on his word too many times," Senda remarked.

Gaita flushed. "It is clear where your allegiance lies, Lady Fredesenda. It would have made more sense to me had Robert told me that you were not also *his* mother!"

"That would not have stopped him." Senda's voice was cold.

"You lied, didn't you? This is only a ploy to make him stop fighting Rogier. You lied, but the Pope would believe you — and you would continue to lie, even if it cost you your soul, wouldn't you?"

Senda shrugged. "Believe what you want. My aim is to stop Robert from destroying Rogier."

"But now it is Robert's life that is in danger!" Gaita's grip tightened, her knuckles white around the sword hilt.

Senda stared at her.

"When Rogier came out of Gerace his spies told him that Robert had followed him inside. Rogier ordered the city surrounded and now Robert is trapped in the city."

Senda looked like a statue.

She never thought that Rogier could outwit Robert . . . now all she has done is useless; she has no power over Rogier!

"I want my sons to be at peace. What good does it do for us to argue, Gaita? We are wasting precious time — I would have gone directly to Gerace, but I need Judith's help."

"She has refused to see me. I doubt she'll listen to you. All she does is mourn for her brother — she wants revenge, not peace."

"You of all people should be able to understand that, Gaita." Senda said.

"Arnold's life was lost in battle," she said in a low voice. "My own father was betrayed and murdered. Had Guaimar's life been lost on the battlefield I would not have demanded revenge."

Guaimar had been murdered by his brothers-in-law years before. Robert had captured and executed his murderers. For that reason alone he had earned Gaita's complete devotion.

Gaita held Senda's gaze.

"I will do anything to have Robert released."

"Judith will not refuse to see me," Senda said as she walked to the entrance. "I'll go to her. Get new mounts ready, Gaita — perhaps we can reach Gerace by nightfall if we leave within the hour."

🦐 🦐 🦐

We rode to the massive portcullis that guarded the entrance to Mileto. "Perhaps I misjudged Gaita. She is a good match for Robert," Senda offered. I nodded. *Only your resentment has prevented you from seeing that from the start.*

Judith of Evreux was on the stone wall over the gate of Mileto, peering in our direction.

Senda stopped a few feet from the wall. "Judith!" she called, "open the gate to your mother!"

Judith disappeared, and a deafening noise of clanging chains accompanied the raising of the portcullis.

"Welcome, Mother!" Judith said in a loud voice as she hurried toward Senda. She fiddled with the gold braid that graced the neck of her light blue tunic as she spoke. A white, gauzy veil held by a gold circlet fluttered about her delicate features and braided brown hair. *No matter how serious the situation, Lady Judith always manages to look her best. She could preside at court, in Caen or over a fine banquet right now. Gaita looks as if she slept in her clothes, and so do we.*

After they embraced, Judith mounted her mare and led us to the tower. We crossed the bailey. Mounds of round stones lay in heaps by wooden catapults, ready to rain on Robert's camp. Huge pans sat lined by the kitchen fires filled with oil, ready to be heated and thrown over the first who dared to attempt an assault on the walls.

Large wide steps led to Rogier's hall. We mounted them on horseback, dismounting just in front of the hall. I admired the massive square tower made of local grey stone. Judith preceded us into the great hall. Here we left Brother Gaufredus and the other men, and followed Judith up a wooden staircase on the left. Upstairs a small hall divided two large chambers; one was for Lady Judith and her women, the other for Rogier and his knights.

More stairs led to the top of the tower, much like Father's house, and to a wooden sentrywalk around the roof.

I felt hot and uncomfortable walking inside the arched portal of the hall. It was early afternoon and my brown tunic was soaked with sweat and coated with dust. As we climbed the wooden staircase it was much cooler, but the rushes on the wooden floor in her chamber were not fresh, and the two women sitting around their looms looked idle. They hurried down, however, when Judith asked them to bring stools and refreshments. Judith led Senda to her own high-backed chair. After Senda sat down she leaned toward her daughter-in-law.

"I need your help, Judith," Senda spent no time on pleasantries. "I am here to see that this conflict ends. I know Rogier will not forgive his brother unless you do."

Judith complained, her voice high-pitched. She was near to tears. "Why should I stop Rogier now that he has the upper hand? It is only a question of time before Robert is captured in Gerace. Why should Arnold have died in vain?"

Her sorrow was real, but I felt like shaking her.

Senda reached over and took Judith's hand. "You are right," she said evenly. "Robert is to blame. But he came back here from Santa Eufemia ready to ask forgiveness and sue for peace with Rogier. He is sincere this time. Oh Judith! Even the Abbot forgave him and bears him no ill will. It was because of Arnold's death that Robert agreed to stop this war. Think of how they will cherish and honor Arnold's memory if they make lasting peace because of him."

Robert got his gift for persuasion from Senda, not from Tancred or Mauger. Judith regarded her mother-in-law in silence, then nodded weakly. Tancred may have taught his sons to kill boars, but Senda had taught them how to win other battles. Brother Gaufredus would hear of this triumph of Senda's; I would see to that.

"Judith, think, if Rogier kills Robert, would he ever forgive himself? And you? Then you would both be left only with the sorrow of having lost a brother. Forgive Robert for Rogier's sake!" After a long silence, Judith asked, "My brother the Abbot forgave him?" Senda reassured her anew.

"If he forgave Robert, I must do the same. What do you wish me to do, Mother?"

"Come with me and Gaita to Gerace. We must leave immediately, while we still have several hours of light; we might reach Gerace by nightfall."

Judith looked doubtful. "Gaita is coming also? They say her father Guaimar trained her on the battlefield, that she is a better soldier than her own brother Gisulf."

Senda nodded. "Gaita fights as a man, but she joins in this for Robert. You are coming for Rogier; do not ride by her side if you do not wish to."

In the end Judith agreed.

They are so different, the Norman Princess and the Lombard one. One raised at Saint Evroult, surrounded by monks, the other trained on the battlefield, surrounded by enemies. Delicate as a sage flower this one; fierce as mint the other.

Refreshments were brought in; Senda and I drank avidly and splashed our hands and faces in cool water. Senda leaned back on the chair with a sigh and closed her eyes. Her skin was sallow and her mouth tight, as if she were trying to master pain. She looked exhausted. *Lord help her! Strange how these words come so naturally! My truce with God is so recent and before then, prayer meant nothing to me. I lived without God for so long. As a young girl I shut Him out because He did not care for my suffering or my mother's. How could I accept the words of Father Raoul, when he condemned my mother? And why did He let Alferio violate me on my pallet and not strike him dead with one of His bolts? And how could I love a God who prohibited me from loving Tancred?*

I always attended the services of the travelling priest. I took Communion regularly without ever revealing in Confession that I thought it an empty ritual. It never occurred to me to do otherwise. I did not want to be an outcast, as Mother had been.

When I moved to Santa Eufemia I went to church, often twice a day, with Senda. She took great comfort from her visits. I often watched as she prayed by my side, her head bowed, her eyes closed. I mimicked her motions but I felt nothing.

It is only recently that something changed. Nothing extraordinary. As I began to rethink the past and write my chronicle, I also began to realize that I had survived! For the first time I talked to God as if he listened. I never recite the prayers I was taught in my youth. They still mean nothing to me. But I have learned to tell God what is on my mind.

God help Senda. And speak to Robert and Rogier tonight.

Basil, who had invited the Duke [Guiscard] to his house, took shelter in a church but was stabbed to death with his own knife. His wife was taken, impaled and thus died with great suffering.

— Gaufredus Malaterra, transl. John Julius
   Norwich: *Historia Sicula*

CAPUT XVI

Gerace
On the eve of the Feast of Saint Paschasius Radbertus (April 26)
In this year 1062 from the Incarnation of our Lord
The words of Bernfrieda

We left Mileto at dawn the next day. The captain of our escort pointed out to Senda that the light would not last enough to take us to Gerace. The climb was long and steep, he said, and the hours of light too few. Senda raised her eyebrows and her mouth hardened as he spoke, but she took his advice.

Judith and Gaita acknowledged each other politely when they met, but they chose to ride apart, Judith on her litter in the middle of the column, Gaita on horseback in the lead.

We rode in silence on the hilly path to Gerace, stopping to rest in the shade of olive trees when the sun became too hot.

Toward late afternoon we started again, and rode until a violent summer storm caught us on the road. We took shelter in a peasant's hut while the soldiers raised tents. The owners of the place huddled with their goats at one end of the shack, leaving the open hearth to Senda and Judith; Gaita remained with her soldiers outside.

The powerful stink inside made me choose a cane stool just outside the door, under the crude overhang made of branches and twigs where Brother Gaufredus was sitting.

My teacher looked bone-weary as he dried his dripping beard with the sleeve of his robe. *The memory of this trip will last him a lifetime.*

"Why do you smile, Bernfrieda?" Gaufredus dropped his sleeve. "What is there to smile about?"

I looked at my feet. It would not do to share my thoughts with him, for I had long known that his sense of humor never included himself.

"Would it please you if I weep instead? Using a bush as garderobe and a stinking bench for a pallet is truly enough for tears. But I smiled because I was thinking of Count Rogier and Lady Judith. What a handsome couple they make." The lie came easily to my lips.

Brother Gaufredus sighed. "Only a woman could think of something so silly."

"Did you see Evisand when you went to Mileto, last week?"

"A leech could not keep closer to Count Rogier. He should have been drawn and quartered, but Count Rogier treats him as if he were a knight's son."

"Count Rogier might never have married Lady Judith had it not been for Evisand,"

Brother Gaufredus nodded. He kept moving around on his stool as if tormented by lice. "It was as clear as a summer day to me that Lady Judith was Count Rogier's from the moment he set eyes on her. And how could it be otherwise? Her breath smells of cinnamon, her figure is full and straight like a ripe ear of wheat, her hair is as golden as the reflection of the sun on a quiet mountain lake." He leaned back against the hut and sighed.

Why, Brother Gaufredus can match the chronicler Amatus in flattery! I wonder what will happen when Rogier realizes the extent of that gift?

"I was the Abbot's secretary at the time," Brother Gaufredus continued. *Why does he always have to remind me of the obvious? He knows I was at Saint Evroult then; does he think my years are making me forget?* "I saw how often the young man came to visit. After a while even Abbot Robert understood that it was not piety that brought Rogier back to the Abbey so frequently, and he stopped inviting him to his quarters. He liked the youth but knew that he was no match for Lady Judith.

"But the young Hauteville would not give up. He tried to see Lady Judith in church — no man was more devout than he during that time." Brother Gaufredus chuckled.

I looked at the clear sky, breathing the smell of the wet earth and the smoky fires the soldiers had started.

"It turned out a beautiful night after all, but I am tired." Brother Gaufredus stood up. "I suppose I'll have to fight the goats for a place to sleep." He walked to the entrance of the hut. "Are you coming, Bernfrieda?" he asked.

"In a moment," I answered. "Sleep well, Brother Gaufredus."

❧ ❧ ❧

Already a week has passed since we arrived in Gerace.

Senda and I have fallen back into a routine. We share a large cotton tent; Gaita joins us when we take our meals; and we wait. There is no word from Robert. He is trapped somewhere inside Gerace, and Rogier is stalking him just outside the walls of the city, ready to pounce on him the moment he comes out. Senda and I have made a peace of sorts, but she hardly speaks to me. She sleeps most of the time; the heat is intense and there are no constant sea breezes here to give us respite. She has never looked so frail, so tired, and I do not want to burden her with the thoughts I put down on my parchment. Perhaps I do not even need to. After all, just writing them down has healed me to a degree. And not knowing what prompted them, Senda may not understand. Later, when we return to the peace of Santa Eufemia, I'll open my heart to her.

❧ ❧ ❧

The sun was high when we finally reached Rogier's camp. A soldier brought a clay jug and a cup to Senda and poured some water for her. He did the same for Judith, but when he turned to Gaita, she snatched the jug from his hands and gulped the water straight from the neck before pouring some over her head and the front of her tunic. She shook her head, laughed, and turned her face to the sun to let it dry.

Rogier and his men had camped in front of the city since Robert had been trapped inside. Every morning Rogier's soldiers halted the peasants who left Gerace to work in the vineyards and fields around the village. No one could go in or out without being stopped.

Rogier was sitting at a trestle table in his large dirty linen tent when Senda and I entered with the others. He ran his fingers through his dark hair in surprise before greeting us. He had not shaven in days. Dark shadows on his cheeks and unusually long hair on his neck made him look unkept. He kissed Senda's hand and smiled at me. When he saw Gaita he hesitated, but nodded in greeting. Rogier smiled broadly when he saw Judith; forgetting himself for a moment, he took her in his arms and kissed her. He turned to face us. "What brings you all here?" he asked in as stern a voice as he could muster.

"We have all agreed — you must make peace with Robert, Rogier," Judith said uncertainly, confused by her husband's tone.

"You of all people? And Arnold?"

"He loved you both. He would want peace between you." Her voice faltered as she struggled to control her emotions. "Your mother said that Robert is sincere in wanting peace. He changed his mind about this — this war after he learned of Arnold's death."

Rogier was unmoved. "What is this about Robert, Mother? When did you see him?"

"Robert came to Santa Eufemia a few days after you brought Arnold's body, Rogier. He was troubled, changed. He wants peace." Senda lied without flinching.

"So Robert shed his false tears over Arnold's grave? And did he cover his head with ashes? Beg forgiveness for his many sins?"

Her head lowered, her arms folded tightly against her chest, Gaita's silence was impressive.

"Nothing of the kind." Senda recited what she had told Judith before. "Arnold's death made him realize what a waste this war is. He wants peace and is willing to give you the land you want. Why don't you believe him?"

"I cannot even count the times Robert has promised peace and land, before going back on his word." Rogier frowned, hands on his hips.

Gaita took a step toward Rogier and spoke in a low, compelling voice. "Robert is trapped in that village. You have the upper hand now, Rogier. You can dictate your terms."

"Robert is in Gerace but no one knows where."

"If he is found?" Gaita asked.

Rogier looked away. "The citizens of Gerace will decide what to do."

"You can ask that he be turned over to you," Senda said. "They are your allies."

Rogier shrugged without answering. He turned to Evisand, who was now his lieutenant. "Bring food and water."

"I shall not eat or rest until this matter is resolved," Senda said.

"Resolved! That is out of my hands," Rogier replied, with a wry chuckle. "It may be days before something happens. Evisand, have a tent raised for Lady Senda and Lady Gaita, and arrange what comforts you can for them."

There was nothing else to do but follow Evisand.

A large tent was pitched in a grove of olive trees. It was stifling hot inside. Evisand brought us a pail of thick broth, cups, bread, a roasted chicken, almonds and a jar of water. We sat on cane stools outside the tent to eat. Senda took a sip of broth and grimaced.

"How can you bear it, Gaita?" she asked her daughter-in-law, who was wolfing down hers.

"Try it with bread." Gaita picked up a loaf of bread, tore it in two and offered one half to her mother-in-law. Senda took it and stared at it.

Gaita soaked her half-loaf with the broth and then chewed the sopping bread. Hungry from the long morning ride, I imitated her. The broth was salty and the bread was gritty; but they were far from disgusting. I took another bite.

"It tastes funny," Senda complained. Gaita shrugged.

"Soldiers' fare. It is made from meat that is boiled, dried and pulverized. Each soldier is issued a bagful; all he needs is hot water to make soup of it. I was seven the first time I tasted it. I have tasted worse." She wiped her mouth with the sleeve of her tunic, picked up a leg of chicken and sank her teeth into it.

Senda stood up. "I can't eat."

Gaita looked up. "Sit. Rest. You look sick. You'll need your strength." Senda sat back slowly and stared at the food. Gaita tore the other leg from the chicken and handed it to her.

"You are a strange woman, Gaita. Not at all like any I have met before," Senda murmured as she nibbled on the meat.

Gaita threw the chicken bone behind her.

"I want Robert back." She wiped the grease from her hands on her mantle. "I want my child to know his father." She patted her belly. "Does that make me strange?"

Senda sat up. "How long have you known?"

"I missed my flux twice," Gaita said matter-of-factly. "You are the first I told."

"Why didn't you stay in Melfi?" Senda held the chicken leg in the air. "Why are you taking such a chance with Robert's heir?"

"Robert needs me now." Gaita stood up. "Nothing will happen to this child. Anyway," her voice hardened. "There will be others."

Senda stood up slowly. "You are foolish, Gaita! You may think yourself brave but you are foolish. Above all else Robert wants this heir; it is the reason he married you. Robert must come to terms with Rogier on his own. He does not need your help." She threw the chicken leg to the side, turned around and went into the tent.

⁜ ⁜ ⁜

"Bernfrieda!" Brother Gaufredus was coming out of Rogier's tent. There were two large sweat stains under his arms, but he was beaming. He hurried over. "Count Rogier needed a scribe."

"Hasn't he a good one?"

"Eusebio the Greek, who is quite put out by my appointment. But there is plenty to do for both of us. Count Rogier still relies much on Eusebio as an interpreter, which I could not do. Latin is my strength."

We walked to the edge of the camp and stopped. We were so close to the walls of Gerace that I could see the bearded sentinel going back and forth, peering in our direction.

Brother Gaufredus whispered. "Count Rogier wants me to follow him to Mileto."

"What? And you have instructed me so well on the evils of worldly powers."

"Well," Brother Gaufredus looked put out. "Isn't that a good reason for a man of the cloth to be close to men of power? To guide discreetly, to point out the right way? Count Rogier may well be the next Duke of Apulia!" He rubbed his hands together. "Who knows where all this may lead!"

To good wine, Brother Gaufredus, to good wine.

⁜ ⁜ ⁜

I saw more of Gaufredus during the next few days. Senda would not budge from her tent and I began to take long walks alone around the encampment. I went in the late afternoon, when the heat was not intense, and my walk usually ended at the spot near the city walls where I had met Gaufredus. There I would sit on a large white rock by a fig tree and contemplate. Sometimes I brought my wax tablet along to record the thoughts that came to my mind. Later I would rework them until they pleased me and I could envision them in my chronicle. I was so intent on my writing one afternoon, a week after Gaufredus told me of his new appointment, that I did not hear him arrive.

"What are you writing, Bernfrieda?" His voice was jovial as he leaned toward my tablet, too quickly for me to hide my writing.

"Can God be felt as a real presence?" he read aloud. He straightened, and tried to look serious.

"Have you ever felt God as a physical presence, Brother Gaufredus?"

He did not answer at first. He took one of the small, unripe figs from the tree and sat by me on the rock.

"God is all around us, Bernfrieda," he began, then stopped and gazed at me. "What an odd sentence to practice your letters."

"I was thinking of the time I had the fever and I thought I was going to die. I talked to God then. I felt His presence. But I was feverish. I have never felt that way since."

He squeezed the fruit open and stared at the squashed halves without speaking. The filaments inside were whitish with just a hint of pink. Sweetness that would never be.

Gaufredus dropped the false seriousness he had try to impress me with. "I felt His presence once, Bernfrieda. I was a child of six and my mother was dying. She had given birth to another child, who died in a week, at harvest time. But she could not leave her pallet. The village women still came and went to look after her and bring food to my father and me, but they were needed in the fields, so they could never stay long.

"They left me in our cottage to watch over her. Her face was as white as her shift. I knew she was very sick, since I always listened to what the women told my father. I would snuggle up at the foot of her pallet and watch her every move."

Brother Gaufredus threw the fig halves away. "She knew I was there, but was too weak to even say my name. She would look at me and then close her eyes. One day, she opened her eyes and reached to me. I jumped up and came round beside her. 'It is so bright. The curtains — ' and she whispered my name.

"'But they are closed, mama.'

"'So bright — ' she said, and smiled. And then she died. I went back to the foot of her pallet and curled up there. But I did not feel alone, I did not feel alone." Brother Gaufredus repeated.

His small brown eyes looked very dark when he turned toward me again. "God was in that room, Bernfrieda. I know my mother saw Him."

❧ ❧ ❧

It is the first day of May, the last time I shall write from Gerace. The soldiers are taking down the tents and packing the mules to go back to Mileto.

Rogier summoned us to his tent two days ago and seated us on cane stools. Across from him a small man, a Greek, cowered on his knees. The Greek was covered with dust and stunk so badly that I thought a herd of pigs must be near.

"This man claims that the Greeks in Gerace have captured Robert," Rogier said.

"Where is he? What did they do to him?" Gaita stood so quickly that the light stool fell backwards.

"That is as much as I could understand, Gaita. Eusebio will be here shortly to translate the rest," Rogier said flatly.

The interpreter walked in, unhurried. He too was small and his complexion was swarthy, with large dark protruding eyes. His pot belly was cinched under a long red tunic with a tasselled belt. He looked around and smirked when he saw Brother Gaufredus, who sat next to Rogier. Gaufredus raised his eyebrows loftily.

Rogier pointed to the small begrimed Greek. Eusebio took a step toward him. He began to translate.

"I am Eustachius, servant of master Basil in Gerace. I tend his garden, feed his animals. I was feeding the pigs, as I do each morning, when a hooded stranger came through the outside gate, limping and bent over a stick. He asked for the master. I tried to chase him away, for he looked like a beggar, but he was angry when I refused. He had an accent. I became suspicious. I ran to the house to warn the master. Basil rushed out, then stopped. It looked as if he was going to kneel. The stranger said something. Master Basil straightened up. He took the stranger to the house. Told me to go home, though I had only begun my work, pretended to go but went to the kitchen instead and waited. Food was ordered. I asked the serving boy who the guest was but he didn't know. I walked to the entrance and peeped inside. The stranger was sitting in the master's chair. I saw plainly that he was not crippled, for his legs were stretched in front of him. He was thanking God for master Basil, for he was very hungry and the whole town was searching for him. He said he heard the cries call out a price on his head. I knew then who the stranger was. Five gold solidi would be paid to anyone who had information. I ran to the captain's house and told the guard I knew where Robert Guiscard was hiding. The captain saw me immediately and when I told him he called out the guards. I never saw so many men assemble so quickly." Eustachius shook his head, and Eusebio cleared his throat impatiently.

"They surrounded the house and shouted for Basil to turn his guest over to them. But a few minutes later someone spotted him trying to take shelter in the church. The crowd caught him and stabbed him with his own knife.

"His wife Melita appeared on the threshold. She is a tall woman, not afraid to speak her mind. She had thrown her black veil over her head carelessly, and her grey hair showed all around her face. She tried to speak but lost her voice when she saw her husband's body. The crowd roared as they seized her —"

"Wait, Eusebio! The man did not say all this," Rogier protested. "I know *some* Greek!"

The interpreter nodded. "Then you realize, my Lord, this man's Greek is dreadful. If I did not improve it, smooth over a few transitions, add an adjective here and there, it would truly be unintelligible. But if my Lord prefers —" He bowed his head respectfully.

"No, go on! But do not embellish so much," Rogier warned.

Eusebio continued his translation.

"They dragged her into the main square and impaled her on a wooden pole." Eustachius stood with his head lowered. No one spoke. He gestured vaguely, then continued.

"The Duke came out of Basil's house. He planted his feet in the gateway. His sword was drawn. I swear there were flames coming out of his eyes. He looked like the archangel Michael.

No one dared be the first to do battle with him. So the crowd surrounded him but stayed at a distance. Then he spoke. He called us his 'dear subjects' and said that he had never hurt the village. He alternated sweet words with threats. He told us his soldiers were waiting for him and that they would destroy the town if he did not return. The crowd wavered. Sometimes they looked ready to jump on him, at other times they retreated in terror. No one in Gerace is very brave, my Lord." Eusebio paused.

"In the end the Duke agreed to follow the soldiers into the town hall. The crowd waited outside for almost an hour. They had all forgotten me, never even paid me the reward. So I decided that I could still earn my solidi if I came to you, for I knew you would pay."

"Very well." Rogier looked at the man with distaste. "Tell him he has earned his solidi."

The interpreter turned to Eustachius and began to speak. I never even saw Gaita move. In a matter of seconds, she had unsheathed her sword and plunged it into Eustachius's side. The interpreter jumped. Gaita calmly cleaned the blade on Eustachius' filthy tunic while he moaned in agony.

Rogier seized Gaita's sword-arm. She did not try to free herself but looked at him defiantly.

Senda cried out and reached out for support. Quickly I steadied her. Gaita turned and looked briefly at her mother-in-law. "He betrayed Robert," she said contemptuously, "and caused the horrible deaths of two good people. For a few coins."

Rogier let her arm drop. He turned to Evisand.

"My horse!" he commanded. "Prepare for battle." He turned to the terrified Eusebio. "Have this mess buried."

"Battle? What are you going to do?" Senda asked faintly.

"I will enforce my claim on Robert, Mother," Rogier said curtly. "I am the one he offended. No one else has any rights in this matter. Evisand!" he called. The young man appeared immediately. Rogier nodded toward Gaita. "Lady Gaita will ride with us, but *without* her sword. And she is not to leave your side without my permission."

"Rogier!" Senda took a step toward her son. "Tell him to ready a mount for me too." Rogier hesitated.

She looks so tired. She should be resting. Perhaps he will order her to stay.

"I will walk into Gerace if you deny me a mount."

Nothing short of imprisonment is going to stop her. She has not slept through a whole night since the wedding. This struggle between her sons will surely kill her.

Rogier nodded his assent. He turned to his wife. "*You* will stay here, Judith."

🐜 🐜 🐜

Rogier stayed behind to prepare for the meeting while we assembled in front of Gerace's gates. Not a very imposing force, since it included three women, two on mules. Senda was so ill she could scarcely stay upright on her saddle. Gaita wore a mailed corselet and carried herself like a vengeful warrior. Among the clouds of dust our own mounts had caused, Rogier's soldiers hastily raised a large canopy in an area approximately three hundred feet directly across from the city gate. Under it they placed Rogier's high-backed chair and several stools. We dismounted and then repaired under the canopy. There was no breeze and the heat was suffocating.

Rogier arrived. He wore a long purple tunic with a gold braided band at the neck, sleeves and hem. His hair had been cut just below the ear in the Norman fashion but he had not trimmed his new beard. He wore his clothes well now that he had lost the slenderness of youth; he had a new air of assurance about him. Senda sat just behind him; I took my place behind her. Eusebio stood to his master's right, Gaufredus to his left. Evisand stood behind Gaita, who sat to the right of Brother Gaufredus.

The gate opened and four men on horseback rode toward us. They halted a few paces away. Three of them dismounted and bowed deeply to Rogier. They were dressed in short peasant tunics; their beards grew down their chests. They wore their hair, curly and shiny, to the shoulders; they all had long prominent noses. I thought at first that perhaps they belonged to the same family. Now that I have seen many more of their race I realize that their resemblance was superficial.

The leader, an old man, waited for the others to help him dismount. He wore a long tunic, with a finely embroidered band at the collar, and split back and front so he could ride. He took his place at the head of the small delegation, advanced toward Rogier and bowed deeply.

"Welcome, citizens of Gerace." Rogier waited until the old ambassador walked to him, then extended his hand for the old man to kiss.

Rogier turned to his interpreter. "Eusebio," he said. "Make sure that you translate *exactly* what I say." He turned toward the delegation.

"You are dear to me because you have always been faithful." He listened closely as Eusebio translated. "It was to request your help against Guiscard that I first came to you. As I expected, you extended your help and hospitality to me when I was your guest, and for that I thank you again. I have had some disturbing news, however." Rogier folded his arms against his chest as he spoke and looked sternly at the ambassadors who flinched under his gaze. "I have heard that you are holding prisoner someone I have been seeking for days. Are you trying to cheat me out of my revenge, citizens of Gerace? I am the one Guiscard offended, and I am entitled to my revenge. You have no right to keep him. Do not presume for a moment that the friendship we have hitherto enjoyed will save you from my wrath if you don't obey me. Tell your captain and your fellow citizens what I have told you and bring me an immediate reply, for I am not disposed to wait long. Go back, now."

Within an hour, the ambassadors returned. Hundreds crowded the sentrywalk of the walls around Gerace. They watched as their ambassadors left the gate. Ten mounted soldiers, Robert in their midst, followed. Once in front of Rogier, the ambassadors dismounted. At a signal from the leader, the soldiers dragged Robert — whose arms were chained — from his horse. Once on the ground, Robert struggled to get up.

"Robert!" Gaita cried out. Evisand was immediately at her side.

Guiscard must have heard her voice; he raised his head, seeming to look in her direction.

"The citizens of Gerace are faithful to you, my Lord," the eldest ambassador told Rogier. Eusebio translated. "The man you want is here." Robert was ridiculously loaded with chains but still looked defiant. "The prisoner is unharmed; you can take your revenge," the ambassador said with an ingratiating smile.

Gaita started; Evisand put a restraining hand on her arm. She hesitated, knowing he had killed his own Lord without compunction.

"Wait!" Robert shouted. "Think before you deliver me to the enemy, citizens of Gerace! *I* am your Duke. My soldiers will take a terrible revenge upon *you* should you cause my death. That man is a traitor and a liar!"

A hush fell on the crowd.

"No one will seek revenge for Guiscard's death," Rogier said, enunciating slowly, forcefully. "His own soldiers recognize I am the strongest. They have come to me willing to recognize me as their new Duke. Guiscard is more cunning than a fox, and more devious than a snake. Listen to him and your ruin is assured, for my soldiers will burn your olives and vines, they'll lay waste to your fields. I shall ride into your town by sundown. Those of you who survive will never be free. You will be watched day and night. I will build a strong fortress for that purpose — there!" He pointed to a hill that overlooked the city.

When the interpreter pronounced the last threat, the men began to speak all at once.

The old ambassador raised his trembling hand. "Enough. Turn the prisoner to the Count of Mileto," he said. The four soldiers dragged Robert forward. Robert threw himself against the two to his right, managing to knock one over to the ground. The other soldiers rushed to help their comrades. Robert fought with his teeth bared like a mountain lion fighting a pack of dogs, but they soon subdued him and dragged him in front of Rogier. They stood looking at each other for a long moment.

"I should have killed you when you first arrived in Melfi, filthy and penniless as a beggar," Robert growled when he had regained his breath.

Rogier studied his brother, his mouth shut tight like a father bent on punishing a child.

"I never wanted what was yours, Robert. Had you treated me fairly I would have served you faithfully." Slowly he unsheathed his sword and lay the point at Robert's throat.

"Let him go!" Gaita thundered.

Robert's face reddened. The point of Rogier's sword nicked Robert's skin; a rivulet of blood spread on the blade. Senda caught her breath. She was ready to throw herself between her sons, but I restrained her.

"Take his chains off." Rogier lowered his sword.

Robert stood, stripped of his mail coat, his clothes in shreds, weary to the bone. He stared at Rogier while the soldiers worked to free him from the chains. Rogier sheathed his sword.

"Will you believe now that I have no ambition to rule Apulia, nor to claim any land that is rightly yours, Robert?" With that, he stepped forward and embraced his brother. Speechless, Robert stood still, then returned the embrace.

"If you want peace, you'll have peace, Robert," Rogier said. "I will not fight you, but I must have what is mine."

Robert grasped Rogier's shoulders. "You have my word, Rogier."

"Robert! Rogier!" Senda called.

The brothers turned in her direction. Senda took a step toward them, faltered and then fell before I could grasp her.

Rogier ran to his mother and took her in his arms. Robert called for a litter and helped Rogier to lift her on to it. The men brought her back to our tent. Senda never lost consciousness completely and, after a glass of strong wine, she revived.

"Bernfrieda! O, Bernfrieda, they are at peace. At peace." She whispered so softly that I guessed her words more than heard them.

Rogier and Robert waited a full day, until Senda seemed completely recovered, before they started back to Mileto.

THE ABBEY OF SANTA AGATHA
1063

*Fredesendis, mother of Robert Guiscard, is buried there
[at Santa Eufemia].*

— Orderic Vitalis, transl. Marjorie Chibnall: *The
Ecclesiastical History*

CAPUT XVII

The Abbey of Santa Eufemia
On the eve of the Feast of St. Juvenal (May 30)
In this year 1062 from the Incarnation of our Lord
The words of Bernfrieda

When we went back to Mileto, Rogier and Judith gave a great feast of thanksgiving. Senda presided over the festivities in the great hall, sitting at the head table, next to her sons. But her happiness only lasted two days. On the third day of the celebrations, she was standing talking to Judith in her chamber, when she clutched at her brooch as if to tear it off. I rushed to her and prevented her from falling. She was senseless for what seemed hours; when she woke up, her left side was dead, and she could not speak. There was little improvement over the next few days, in spite of the fact that Gaita sent for the physician Alphinus from Salerno to cure her. He stood over her for half the mark of a candle before he faced us somberly.

He ordered that she be given a draught made with saffron, mace and castor ground in equal parts and mixed with wine. He said it would relieve the paralysis. Two days passed, but Senda did not improve. Alphinus showed concern on the third morning, when he came to see her. He ordered cooked millet mixed with almond oil and sugar, to thicken her blood.

I was sitting by Senda shortly after Alphinus left when Robert and Rogier came to see their mother.

"How is she, Bernfrieda?" Rogier asked in a hushed voice. Robert stood behind him, his arms folded against his chest, as was his manner when he wished to conceal his feelings.

"Not well." I leaned over Senda and adjusted her pillow. "There has been no change since you last spoke to Alphinus."

They stood there in silence.

Just looking at them made me so angry. I did not think of consequences. "You caused her illness!" I said through my teeth. "She is dying because of what you put her through. You *both* caused this.

"You have never given thought to the sorrow you caused her when you fought. Go on, celebrate your peace now, but remember that your mother will die because of your selfishness."

"Hold your tongue, Bernfrieda." Rogier was clenching and unclenching his fists, as Tancred had when he was angry. "You do not know what you are saying." He stalked out of the room. Robert came forward, and my anger left me. Strangely enough, I did not fear him. He took my arm and pulled me away from the bedside.

"You must know," he said roughly. "Where does she hide it?"

Her message to the Pope! I do not dare feign ignorance.

"It is in Rome, in the hands of a trusted man, instructed to deliver it to the Pope if the peace between you and your brother is broken."

There were many small wrinkles around his eyes, as there had been around Tancred's when he first came to Granville.

"I will have your eyes put out," Robert hissed.

"I know nothing more."

He leaned over me and took me by both shoulders. "Did she tell the truth, Bernfrieda?" he asked. His hands dug into my flesh until the pain became unbearable. I closed my eyes and clenched my teeth.

When he released me, I looked up at him. "You are Tancred's son."

Robert was inscrutable as always, as if what I told him mattered little.

A guttural sound made us turn toward Senda. Her left eye was closed but her right eye was wide open, watching us.

Robert turned and hastened from the room.

❧ ❧ ❧

Senda lay for another week in the semi-darkness of her makeshift chamber in Mileto, unable to speak, communicating with her one live eye. She understood what I told her, and would close and open her eye to respond. I read the last chapters of my chronicle to her, straining my eyes in the light of the single candle Judith had allowed me.

Robert and Rogier agreed that she should be buried at Santa Eufemia. And so we all returned to the Abbey with her body.

❧ ❧ ❧

I began grieving while I put away Senda's possessions. Before the guests arrived for her funeral, I had to clear her room for Robert's use. Her prized possessions — the silver decanter and cups, her silver comb and her mother's fateful mirror — I put aside, to be packed in the chest which Robert would take with him after the funeral.

I sorted the clothes which she had bequeathed to me: *The old brown tunic she wore every day at Granville. So worn! How many times we huddled in the great hall! Not all bad times . . . the laughter . . . the plans we made. . . . The saffron she wore when Father promised her to Tancred . . . when she went to see my Lord Abbot. I had let the fabric out a little under the arms after she stopped nursing Rogier. . . . Those long talks while we embroidered and weaved in her chamber at Hauteville. . . . She treasured my advice then. . . . The long walks on the beach here at Santa Eufemia. . . . She could be witty . . . her bantering when I wanted to learn to write. . . . her gift of parch-*

*ment I found one day on the desk. . . . No one had ever given me any-
thing so precious.*

I put the clothes, and the unfinished tapestry, in a basket for
me to take away later.

Her fur-lined mantle from Tancred. *She had worn it a lot more
than Muriella had.*

Tancred's sword: *Guillaume brought it from Italy . . . never used
in battle . . . his moment of pleasure when he received it . . . the hilt's
secret hiding place.*

Tancred's death mask: *Has Robert forgotten? Would he miss it?*

O God, I had forgotten how sickly he looked.

I kissed the cold wax. *If I could only smooth those lines, Tancred,
O, Tancred!*

I put the mask into the chest and lowered the lid.

⁂ ⁂ ⁂

Robert had the marble sarcophagus brought up from Rome.
They placed it between two side altars on the right aisle in the
church. It lies parallel to the eastern wall inside the entrance of
the church, and looks like a small house, with its pitched marble
roof and marble joists. The busts of Saint Eufemia and Saint
Lucy rest at each end of the roof so that they face the mourners.
In the center there is a mock door flanked by Doric columns
supporting a pediment much like a Greek temple. Senda would
have been astonished by her elaborate resting place. Tancred is
still buried at Hauteville, after all, with only a wooden cross to
mark his grave.

I did not pray over her tomb. I just talked with her, as I do
with God. I told her that I was sorry we had not made our peace
properly; that even as she was dying I had not been able to tell
her what was in my heart. And I told her that the peace between
her sons has not been shattered. I know that is what she would
most like to know.

The truth is I hoped she could not read into my heart. I had
taken care of her from the time she was a baby. I suffered with
her when Adeliza tormented her, when her mother ignored her,

when she lost Guillaume. But as I watched her, helpless on her pallet, pale, with purple circles around her closed eyes, I finally realized that what I felt for her was merely compassion. She had taken my love for granted, as she had taken everyone else's. How ironic that I would arrive at that realization at the end of her life.

When had I stopped loving her? When Tancred first looked at her with love? When she held Rogier in her arms while mine were empty? No: it was when I first saw her mother's cruelty renewed in her. After that moment, I was in the company of strangers. I grew as cold as the stone seat in the alcove. Now, three things sustain me: my conversations with God, however cautious; the completion of this chronicle; and the friendship I feel for Brother Gaufredus.

The priests say that God's love is eternal and all-encompassing. I find comfort in speaking to God, but I do not feel the warmth I felt when I was little and I knew my mother was there. Nothing compares to loving a human being, or being loved by one. Yet human love does not last. Has my fate been so different? Senda was loved by Tancred, Guillaume, her children. Now the first two are dead and her children have other loves stronger than the one for their mother. Love is ephemeral. A succession of moments, soon gone. Love's memories are all that endure.

. . . In the second battle the Count (Rogier), seeing that the soldiers were afraid of the great numbers of enemies, comforted them . . . and while he was speaking those words a knight in shining armor on a white horse appeared in their midst holding a flag with a cross in one hand. The Normans seeing the apparition cheered and shouted "God, God!" and "Saint George, Saint George!"

— Gaufredus Malaterra, transl. by John Julius Norwich: *Historia Sicula*

CAPUT XVIII

The Abbey of Santa Agatha in Catania
On the eve of the Feast of Saint Rictrudis (May 12)
In this year 1063 from the Incarnation of our Lord
The words of Bernfrieda

It is just past Prime and it is already hot. It will be scorching in a few hours, but in the cool *scriptorium* I will be able to work until I tire. It is uncanny how similar the cloister and the *scriptorium* are to those of Santa Eufemia. Everything else is different. The church, for example, has been converted from a Moorish mosque, though masons are busy trying to make it look more like the churches of Normandy.

I arrived at the Abbey of Santa Agatha a week ago with a few brothers from Santa Eufemia, and I have yet to see Gaufredus. Summoned by Rogier, he left for Troina, Rogier's temporary capital, before I arrived here. The brothers I questioned said that he won't be back for at least another week.

The monks speak of Gaufredus in respectful, hushed tones. The first time I saw their awe, I almost laughed out loud; but being Rogier's chronicler gives him a special status here, as re-

flected in the consideration the brothers gave me. They housed
me, not in the guest house for travellers, but in a separate small
cell on the first floor, not in the common dormitory. It is the first
time I have ever had a room to myself. It has a small window
that faces Aetna, the fire-spitting mountain that looms over the
city of Catania. I have a stool, a pallet and even a small desk.
Gaufredus's idea, no doubt. All this attention from the brothers
makes me uncomfortable, as if at any moment someone could
point a finger at me and shout *begone!*

The Brother Hospitalier, Anselmo, took me to the *scriptorium*
the day after I arrived. He led me to the cubicle I would share
with Gaufredus, with my own desk and high-backed chair. How
delightful! Fresh sheets of parchment, quills, ink, sand — such
an abundance. An old manuscript waiting to be copied, a life of
Saint Lucy, from Monte Cassino. Anselmo delicately hinted that
I could begin copying from that manuscript if I wanted to keep
busy while waiting for Gaufredus.

I thanked him and he took his leave. Gaufredus's absence suits
me well, for I must finish this chronicle. I worried that I would
not trace my letters well, after a whole year's idleness. But it took
just a few lines for my fears to be forgotten.

The short time the Normans have been in Catania after
wrenching it from the Arabs has not changed the character of
this city. It still feels alien, exotic. Perhaps it is the open sensual-
ity that pervades everything here. During the long days the light
is blinding; the air scorches. Smells can be putrid, or bewitching,
with scents so sweet they are straight from paradise, heavy with
the fragrance of jasmine and orange blossom. Myriads of small
white four-petaled blooms cover the large bush that climbs on
the open arcades outside the *scriptorium*.

It is time that I explain how I came to Catania.

🐦 🐦 🐦

After Senda's death, Robert donated the village of Sembiase
to the Abbey of Santa Eufemia in remembrance of his mother. It
was indeed a princely gift, for the village lies east of the Abbey

midway up a hill surrounded by well-kept olive groves, fertile vineyards and gardens.

The grey monks were delighted; I benefitted indirectly. They gave me a pallet in the guest house for foot travellers, instead of lodging me with peasants in the village outside the walls. Robert's gift had made them feel generous. The understanding with the monks was that I would have a permanent pallet at the guest house in exchange for helping tend to the visitors' needs. It had been difficult to adjust to the lack of privacy in the dormitory and the bustle and noise of the guest house where children cried, older people moaned, and late arrivals disturbed even the short peace of the night. But I was grateful the monks let me live inside the Abbey rather than send me to one of their villages to pick olives or bake bread for the rest of my life. That would likely have been my lot, after I was excluded from the *scriptorium*.

One spring morning, two weeks after Senda's death, I stopped in the cloister, savoring the quiet. The lavender and the sage in the center garden were in bloom, and the bushes of thyme were clustered with tiny flowers. I picked a lavender sprig and inhaled its sweet scent. How many of these had Senda and I picked — bunches and bunches to lay in chests between clothes . . .

Brother Gaufredus had wasted no time after returning from Mileto with Rogier. I found him in the *scriptorium*, hard at work. He mumbled a greeting in response to mine but did not raise his head. He was trying to finish the life of Saint Godelive before following Rogier to their next destination, Mileto. As Rogier's scribe, his only duties now were to take care of his master's correspondence. He could have been outside enjoying the sun! Yet there he was, copying from an old manuscript.

I sat quietly by his side. He asked me to resume work on the life of Saint Agatha, which remained unfinished since I had deserted the *scriptorium* the previous winter. He looked up when he realized I was not working. He stared at the stack of parchment in my hands. It was my chronicle. I knew it was not finished, that I needed to write a last chapter, but I wanted to make sure that what I had written would at least be safely stored in the *scriptorium* before Brother Gaufredus returned to Mileto with Rogier.

"Before she died, my Lady asked that you store this in the *scriptorium*, Brother Gaufredus."

He carefully took the bundle and ran his fingers over the top. "The sheets of parchment she bought over a year ago. What did she use it for?"

I shrugged.

He leaned back in his chair. "Is it — is it about — you know — ?" he stammered.

I looked at him without speaking.

"The annulment?" he whispered.

"What annulment?"

"You know of what I speak." Brother Gaufredus fidgeted in his chair. "The problem with Lady Alberada."

"I have no idea, Brother Gaufredus. I am only doing my Lady's bidding. She asked that it be stored in the *scriptorium* after her death. If you do not want to do it I'll ask the Abbot —"

"No!" Brother Gaufredus clutched the manuscript and turned away from me, afraid that I would try to take it from him.

He stored my chronicle deep under a whole stack of ancient books in the room that opens over the cloister walk, where manuscripts are kept. I kept a close eye on him, lest he be tempted.

"So you do not know what is in that manuscript?" He picked up his quill but gave me a surreptitious glance. *He does not believe me. Could he suspect the truth?* "I thought you told me she gave it to one of her sons."

"I truly do not know what to tell you, Brother Gaufredus. She gave it to me just before she died."

"Well — whatever it is, it will lie here for a very long time." He shrugged and resumed his writing.

I watched him, hunched over his manuscript, his tongue protruding slightly. This might be the last time that I would see him at work. He was my teacher. After our adventures in Gerace, he was also my friend.

After a while he looked up and glanced at the life of Saint Agatha in front of me. "I am glad you agreed to finish it, Bernfrieda. You do good work." He lowered his head over his parchment. Three days later, he left with Rogier.

✤ ✤ ✤

I expected to continue to work in the *scriptorium* after Brother Gaufredus left for Mileto. But I was due for a shock.

The new *scriptorium* monk's hair was thin around a large tonsure so perfectly round it suggested the work of Nature. He was bent over the parchment, and when he raised his head and looked in my direction he squinted through small, bloodshot eyes.

"What do you want, good woman?" His voice was unfriendly.

"I — came to work on the life of Saint Agatha."

"You what? Oh, you must be Bernfrieda."

He did not offer the stool by his side; nor did he offer his name.

"I am working on it just now." He looked at me with mild curiosity.

"What — what should I do then?" I stuttered.

"Why, go and do whatever women do. You were not expecting me to continue the arrangement you had with Brother Gaufredus, were you?" He was sincerely surprised. "God knows it was an odd one! Brother Gaufredus had no choice, of course; I understand your late mistress insisted on it. Rich ladies have the strangest ideas." He picked up the quill and resumed his copying.

I turned and walked back to my quarters. Besides resuming work on Saint Agatha, I had hoped to get some parchment to properly finish my chronicle. I turned to God. I talked to him, knowing that he might not listen. Hadn't the priests always said that patience and resignation were dearest to Him? I could not resign myself to a life without writing; but only a miracle would change my situation.

Three weeks ago Rogier returned to Santa Eufemia with Brother Gaufredus. I was preparing pallets for the night when he came into the guest house.

"Bernfrieda!" His eyes were round with surprise. "What are you doing here? I thought you would be in the *scriptorium*."

He listened in silence, pulling on the short curls on his cheeks and shaking his head, as I told him how I was sent away after he had left. "Brother Hugo was always a fool," he muttered. "I will demand my cubicle back for the duration of my stay. Come with me."

He preceded me to the *scriptorium*. Brother Gaufredus sat in his chair and I on the stool by his side. He made no attempt to pick up the quill but kept toying with his beard or fingering a roll of parchment. Then he clasped his hands, his fingers intertwined and leaned back in his chair.

"What do you consider important in a chronicle, Bernfrieda?"

I looked at him, taken aback. It was an odd question from someone I had not seen in a year. *Has he broken the seal and read my manuscript after all?*

"The truth," I finally said.

"And what is the truth, Bernfrieda?"

"The truth is recording each event to the best of one's recollection."

"Wrong," he said. He smiled when I frowned. "A chronicler has an awful responsibility," he said. "For he must teach, not just record events. People who listen to the lives of the blessed martyrs, for example, need to know that life is a struggle between good and evil and that good always triumphs, even when it appears otherwise. If the chronicler needs to embellish what happened in order to make that point, then he should, for his purpose is a holy one. And *that* becomes the truth."

He has not seen me in a year, has not written or even inquired about my well-being in all that time, and now he is pontificating?

"And when contemporary events are recorded?" I picked up a quill, to keep my hands from revealing my irritation.

"Even more important! We know, for example, that Count Rogier is in Sicily to wrest it from the Saracen heathens. A just war. When a chronicler describes those battles, his first duty should be to show the goodness of Count Rogier's purpose. Would it be wrong then for him to mention that Saint George himself guided the sword of our count during the Battle of Cerami? Certainly not!"

"Would Saint George help the Normans smash children's heads against walls, rape and impale women, starve old men and whole families when they burn their fields?"

Brother Gaufredus stared at his quill. "Those things are inevitable in war. Do not forget that the enemy is heathen."

"And the innocent, who are killed now?"

"You did not listen to me, Bernfrieda. They are not innocent, they are infidels doomed to the flames of hell."

I tapped the quill against the edge of the ink horn. *He would burn my chronicle if he ever read it. The chronicler wants to record the best about humankind? To confirm that life is not really as squalid as it is? A chronicle should not, then, mention adulterous love? Should not show how miserable the peasant's life truly is? And who would find uplifting what Evisand did? Killing his Lord and escaping without punishment? Yet was not he truly just in his actions?*

Brother Gaufredus picked up the parchment in front of him and handed it to me. "Read!" His voice trembled with excitement.

The message was addressed to Brother Gaufredus Malaterra, from Rogier, summoning him to the Benedictine Abbey in Catania which Rogier had just established, to write the chronicle of his conquest of Sicily. I reread it to be sure.

Finally I put the parchment on the desk. "I thought you liked being Rogier's scribe, being close to power."

"Bernfrieda, you have no idea of what it is like in Sicily — following Count Rogier in his conquests — long marches under the heat of a sun so scorching that the earth burns through the soles of one's boots — ambushes by the godless Saracens," Gaufredus cleared his throat. "Two weeks ago one of them ripped my tent with his scimitar and jumped in just as I was about to retire, only to die at my feet with an arrow in his back — I can't begin to tell you all that I've been through.

"I have been close to power, that is true, but there wasn't a day I did not long for the coolness of the *scriptorium*, the smell of old parchment —" he inhaled deeply, with a satisfied smile on his face, and leaned back in his chair. "Really, Bernfrieda, what business has a man of the cloth in the middle of a battlefield?"

"But Brother Gaufredus, that is where a man of the cloth can do most good, to bring the comforts of the Church to the wounded and dying —" It was hard not to smile.

"You forget I am not a *priest*, Bernfrieda. I am merely a poor Benedictine monk." Brother Gaufredus waved his hand in front of his face as if to chase away a fly.

"I was trying to tell you that I found the solution to my dilemma shortly after Amatus sent Count Rogier a draft of his chronicle. He asked me to read it to him. You should have seen how intent Count Rogier was as I read! He asked me to reread passage after passage, as if he were trying to commit them to memory. He was particularly impressed by the comparisons with the Greek gods Amatus had made. This lasted for days. Over and over I had to reread Amatus's words — and between you and me they are not his best. Then a week later Count Rogier called me. He held Amatus's chronicle in his hands and I headed for my desk, resigned to reread to him for the tenth time. But my Lord sat there, in his chair, immersed in thought.

"'Would you be able to write a chronicle like this, Gaufredus?' he finally asked. I almost jumped to my feet. 'Of course, my Lord!' I said. He looked at me with the trace of a smile.

"'Very well then, Gaufredus' he said. 'You are to write the chronicle of my conquest of Sicily.'

"I was intrigued of course. But the last thing I wanted was to follow him from battlefield to battlefield. I discreetly pointed that out to him. The parchment could be lost or destroyed or — God forbid it — never finished if I were killed by a stray arrow." Gaufredus was round-eyed with earnestness.

"He agreed to send me to Catania. I would have preferred Santa Eufemia, of course, but he insisted I stay in Sicily where he could more easily summon me to his headquarters at Troina."

"Brother Gaufredus, I am happy for you."

He nodded and looked at me without speaking for a few moments.

"I would like you to help me write such a chronicle, Bernfrieda."

I was sure I had not heard him correctly, and pretended to be absorbed with an ink stain on my sleeve.

"Well? You can come in two weeks, copy from my drafts, or take dictation. What do you say?"

To write again? To feel again the shiver of excitement and fear in front of an empty page?

"I can't, Brother Gaufredus," I said after a moment.

"Why not?" He was astonished.

"You want me to copy, to take dictation. I am tired of writing other peoples' words. I want to write my own."

Brother Gaufredus stood up, unable to contain his indignation. "You? A woman?"

I nodded. He sat down just as abruptly, nonplussed.

"I can't believe you'd prefer to serve in a dormitory full of stinking travellers."

"I will come. But I want *some* freedom. I could accompany you to Troina, for example, or wherever Rogier will summon you. It would help your work; two witnesses are better than one."

"Well . . ." he considered me. "I taught you well; you *are* the best scribe at Santa Eufemia," he said, as if talking to himself. He was silent for some time.

"Well . . . if writing your own words is so important to you, Bernfrieda, I may let you do so, under strict supervision of course. And as for coming with me, I do not mind the company when I travel."

"I was thinking . . . O, Brother Gaufredus, I am old!"

"I would not take you with me if you were young. It would be too much of a distraction." Brother Gaufredus actually chuckled. "And you still learn fast. I'll teach you how to write a chronicle."

But I am even more experienced than he! I have already written a chronicle. I can record Rogier's conquest honestly. Gaufredus won't. He is too careful to keep Rogier's good will. If Amatus's chronicle was full of flattery, Gaufredus's will be full of miracles. He can write his chronicle. I will write mine. There will be all the parchment I need in Catania — Rogier is generous.

When I began I only wanted to record Senda's past. I soon found out that I could not ignore the present.

Sicily! New, intriguing, mysterious. Rogier battles the Saracens, the Byzantines, yet has not destroyed Messina and Catania and the other Moorish cities he has conquered. He has even begun to adopt their customs while he is in Sicily. Senda understood him; he would not just destroy. Sicily might become a land where Saracen, Byzantine and Norman can come to terms.

"Is there something else? Why are you not speaking?"

Here I will leave only a well-tended grave — and memories. But those I can take with me. "No." I said. "I'll be ready when you send for me. But Brother Gaufredus — you must give me back Senda's manuscript."

Gaufredus opened his mouth and then closed it.

"It can be stored at St. Agatha," I said.

Gaufredus shook his head "What is the difference, Bernfrieda? She did not want anyone to see its contents."

"It would be safer if it were out of Robert's grasp altogether."

"Ah, then it must contain the truth about the annulment! I am glad you reminded me, Bernfrieda. Here, you keep it until we are in Catania; I do not want to have anything to do with it as long as we are in Robert's territory." Gaufredus hurried to look through the shelf where he had stored the sheets of parchment, creating a cloud of dust in the process, and handed my chronicle back to me.

When Gaufredus left, I quickly filled in all that happened since last May. I finished as the first shadows of the evening were entering the cubicle. I touched the soft page and saw the faces of the people I had called to life. Mauger, Alsinda, Lady Mathilda, Adeliza, Senda, Tancred . . . Tancred. They were all there in the room with me: The last pale smile on my mother's face, the deep worry line on Tancred's forehead, Senda's mocking eyes as she fingered Queen Emma's Missal. . . .

My thoughts have been worth preserving after all. The darkness is advancing but I do not feel alone. The written word has gifted me the past and now it will gift me the future. Peaceful years within the cloister in Catania, quiet hours filled with writing, open doors, and friendship. *Who knows, Brother Gaufredus, we may be drinking some of that good wine together.*

GLOSSARY

Adeliza: Daughter of Mauger and Mathilda. Senda's full sister.

Alberada: Heiress of the Buonalbergo family, a Norman family which settled in southern Italy. First wife of Robert Guiscard.

Alferio: Apprentice knight at Mauger's house.

Alice of Conques: Wife of Mauger, brother of Fredesenda.

Alsinda: Bernfrieda's mother.

Amatus: Monk at the Abbey of Monte Cassino. Author of the *Ystoire de li Normant,* a contemporary chronicle about the Norman conquest of southern Italy. A part of the chronicle was devoted to Robert Guiscard and his achievements.

Apulia: Region in southerm Italy (Puglia). The Normans settled there shortly after they arrived in Italy. From Melfi, their capital, they launched the conquest of Calabria held by the Byzantines, and of Sicily, which was held by the Saracens (Arabs).

Armand: Bernfrieda's oldest brother. Illegitimate child of Mauger and Alsinda.

Arnold: Son of Hawise Giroie and her first husband, Robert. Full brother to Abbot Robert, and half-brother to Judith.

Bernfrieda: narrator of *The Words of Bernfrieda*. Half-sister and companion to Lady Fredesenda (Senda) of Hauteville.

Byzantines: Subjects of the Empire of Byzantium. At one time the Byzantines owned most of southern Italy but at the time of the Norman conquest their holdings were generally limited to the region of Calabria.

Dreaux: Son of Tancred of Hauteville and his first wife Muriella. He became Count of Apulia following the death of Guillaume *Bras-de-Fer*. He was assassinated in 1051.

Evisand: Serf belonging to Richard de Walchelin. Husband of Hirtrude.

Gaita (Sichelgaita): Daughter of Guaimar, Prince of Salerno. Second wife of Robert Guiscard.

Gaufredus Malaterra: Benedictine monk first at the Abbey of Saint Evroult in Normandy, later at the Abbey of Santa Eufemia in Calabria and finally at the Abbey of Santa Agatha in Sicily. Author of the *Historia Sicula*, a chronicle of the conquest of Sicily by Rogier.

Gerace: Small Byzantine village in the Calabrian hills where Robert found himself trapped by Rogier.

Geva: Wife of Haremar and mother of Mauger. Senda's and Bernfrieda's grandmother.

Gisulf: Son of Guaimar, Prince of Salerno and brother of Gaita.

Goda: Senda's best weaver, mother of Jourdain.

Guaimar: Prince of Salerno. Legend says that he was the first Lombard prince to requested the help of the Normans.

Guillaume le Batard "The Bastard" (William The Conqueror): Duke of Normandy and later King of England. It is said that prior to the battle of Hastings, William inspired himself and his men by listening to the stories of Robert Guiscard's conquests in southern Italy. Jealous of his absolute power, he probably was

angered by the independence shown by Abbot Robert. Histori-
cal accounts, however, do not tell the true reason of his anger
toward the Abbot.

Guillaume Bras-de-Fer Son of Tancred of Hauteville and his first
wife Muriella. The first of the Hautevilles to go to southern
Italy. A very popular warrior and leader, he was elected first
Count of Apulia by the Normans in Italy and was the first
Norman to use Melfi as his capital. He was succeeded by
Dreaux, Onfroi, and then Robert.

Haremar: Senda's and Bernfrieda's grandfather.

Hauteville: Small Norman village that belonged to Tancred.

Hawise: Daughter of an important Norman family, the Giroies.
Married to Robert de Grantmesnil in her first marriage, and to
William of Evreux in her second marriage. Mother of Abbot
Robert, Arnold and Judith.

Henry: Son of Alsinda and Mauger. Brother of Bernfrieda.

Hirtrude: Serf and concubine of Richard de Walchelin. Wife of
Evisand.

Jourdain: Son of Rogier and Goda.

Judith: Daughter of Hawise and William of Evreux. Wife of
Rogier.

Lombards: Germanic tribe who settled in the region of Campania
(in southern Italy) after the fall of Rome.

Mark (Bohemond): Son of Robert Guiscard and his first Norman
wife Alberada. Robert declared him a bastard after the annulment of his first marriage. Mark feuded with Robert's son by
Gaita (another Rogier) most of his life. Between the two, Mark
proved to be the true successor of Robert Guiscard. After the
first Crusade, he became known as Bohemond of Antioch.

Mathilda: Bride of Mauger. Mother of Adeliza, Fredesenda and
young Mauger.

Maud: Wife of Serlon, Tancred's first-born by Muriella.

Mauger: Father of Senda and Bernfrieda.

Mauger: Son and heir of Mauger and Mathilda.

Mileto: Small fortified Calabrian hillside village. Rogier used it as his capital until his death.

Odo: Benedictine monk. Senda's scribe.

Onfroi: Son of Tancred and Muriella, his first wife. Half-brother of Robert Guiscard. Third Count of Apulia. Died in 1053.

Raoul: Visiting chaplain to the Granville house.

Richard: Father of Alsinda. Brother of Haremar.

Richard de Walchelin: Adeliza's husband and an intimate of Duke Guillaume (William the Conqueror).

Robert de Grantmesnil: First husband of Hawise of Giroie and father of Abbot Robert and Arnold.

Robert de Grantmesnil: Abbot of Saint Evroult and then of Santa Eufemia. After this powerful and influential nobleman angered Duke Guillaume — for reasons that have remained unknown, though the author provides a motive in this account — he had to flee Normandy. In Italy he was befriended by Robert Guiscard.

Robert Guiscard: Eldest son of Senda and Tancred of Hauteville. He joined his stepbrothers in Italy and eventually succeeded Onfroi as Count of Apulia. Later he received papal recognition as Duke of Apulia. His nickname "Guiscard" means "the cunning." Contemporary chronicles exalted his intelligence, daring and great political skills. An exception is the account by Anna Comnena, the Byzantine Princess, daughter of Robert's worst enemy, Emperor Alexis of Byzantium. In the *Alexiad* Robert is described as the adventurer he probably was.

Rogier, Count of Mileto: Senda's youngest son. More reflective and prudent than his brother, yet as daring and courageous, he became very popular among the Normans in southern Italy. Robert felt threatened by his brother's popularity and tried to curb Rogier's power by denying him land. Eventually this led to the conflict (which is historically true) described in this novel. While Rogier never challenged Robert's supremacy, it was Rogier's son, Rogier II, who established the Norman kingdom of southern Italy, eventually taking over Apulia and all of southern Italy. The Norman kingdom survived for one hundred and fifty years after Rogier's death in 1101 and terminated with the death of Frederick II in 1251.

Santa Eufemia: Benedictine Abbey founded by Robert Guiscard in Calabria. With Santa Eufemia, Robert hoped to build an Abbey that would rival the great Abbeys of Normandy such as the one at Saint Evroult and Bec. In spite of his cruelty and lack of scruples, Robert was a religious man; the support of an Abbey was paramount to him and his Normans.

Santa Agatha: Benedictine Abbey founded in Catania by Rogier. Here Gaufredus Malaterra wrote his *Historia Sicula*. Saint Agatha, a virgin and martyr, was tortured and killed by the Romans. She is the patroness of Catania.

Saracens: The name given to the Arabs who settled in Sicily. The Arabs dominated the island of Sicily for two hundred years, after taking it from the Byzantines.

Senda (Fredesenda): Second wife of Tancred of Hauteville. Nothing is known of her from contemporary chronicles other than that she was of noble birth and that she was buried at Santa Eufemia. Senda's family of origin as described in this novel is fictional.

Serlon: First-born of Tancred of Hauteville and Muriella. There are conflicting theories about the primogeniture of Serlon; some scholars believe that Guillaume *Bras-de-Fer* was Tancred's first son.

Serlo: Son of Serlon and Maud.

Saint Evroult: Benedictine Abbey which became one of the most powerful in Normandy.

Tancred of Hauteville: Minor Norman knight. The episode of Tancred slaying a boar single-handedly is reported in several chronicles, as is the story that he married again after he lost Muriella, in order not to sin.

SELECTED BIBLIOGRAPHY

The Words of Bernfrieda is a work of fiction. In writing it, however, I have consulted several primary and secondary sources about the Norman conquest of southern Italy. Following is a partial list of books for further reading.

PRIMARY SOURCES:

Amatus of Monte Cassino, 1965. *Ystoire de li Normant.* New York: Johnson Reprint.

Comnena, Anna, 1979. *The Alexiad.* Translated by E.R.A. Sewter. London: Penguin Classics.

Gregory of Tours, 1988. *History of the Franks.* Translated by Lewis Thorpe. London: Penguin Classics.

Malaterra, Gaufredus, 1882. *Historia Sicula* in Patrologiae sursus completus. Series Latina, vol. 149. Paris: Garnier Freres & G. P. Migne.

————1954. *La Conquesta di Sichilia.* Translated by Frate Simone da Lentini. Palermo: Centro Studi Storici Siciliani.

Trotula, 1981. *Medieval Woman's Guide to Health.* Translated by Beryl Rowland. Kent: Kent State University Press.

Vitalis, Orderic, 1969. *The Ecclesiastical History.* Translated by Marjorie Chibnall. Oxford: Oxford University Press.

BOOKS OF GENERAL INTEREST:

Bittle, Berchmans, 1957. *A Saint a Day.* Milwaukee: The Bruce Publishing Company.

Bloch, Marc, 1961. *Feudal Society.* Translated by L.A. Manyon. Chicago: The University of Chicago Press.

Brown, R. Allen, 1984. *The Normans.* New York: St. Martin's Press.

Chalandon, Ferdinand, 1960. *Histoire de la domination Normande en Italie et en Sicile.* New York: Burt Franklin.

Coulton, G. G, 1960. *Medieval Village, Manor and Monastery.* New York: Harper.

Crawford, F. M., 1900. *The Rulers of the South.* New York: McMillan.

Delarc O. 1883. *Les Normands en Italie.* Paris: E. LeRoux.

Duby, Georges, 1983. *The Knight, the Lady, and the Priest.* Translated by Barbara Bray. New York: Pantheon Books.

————1988. *A History of Private Lives.* Translated by Arthur Goldammer. Cambridge: Harvard University Press.

Gibbon, Edward, 1952. *The Rise and Fall of the Roman Empire.* London: Benton.

Gies, Frances, 1984. *The Knight in History.* New York: Harper & Row.

Labarge, Margaret Wade, 1986. *A Small Sound of the Trumpet.* Boston: Beacon Press.

Norwich, John Julius, 1967. *The Normans in the South.* London: Longmans, Green and Co. ltd.

Smith, Mack, 1969. *A History of Medieval Sicily.* New York: The Viking Press.

Tannahill, Reay, 1988. *Food in History.* New York: Crown Publishers.

ACKNOWLEDGMENTS

I am grateful to Bydell & Brewer, Ltd., Suffolk, England, for permission to reprint maps of "Normandy and Her Neighbors" and "Southern Italy" from *The Normans* by R. Allen Brown, 1984.

My thanks also to the following publishers for permission to quote:

Random House for permission to quote two passages from *The Knight, the Lady, and the Priest* by Georges Duby translated by Barbara Bray, Pantheon Books, 1983.

Harper & Row Publishers for permission to quote a passage from *The Knight in History* by Frances Gies, 1984

Kent State University Press for permission to quote a passage from *Medieval Women's Guide to Health* translated by Beryl Rowland, 1981.

The University of Chicago Press for permission to quote a passage from *Feudal Society* by Marc Bloch translated by L.A. Manyon, 1961.

The Comune di Padova and the Musei Civici Eremitani and Dr. Gianfranco Matinoni and Dr. Varotto for permission to use the reprint of a portion of Giotto's "Matrimonio di Maria" in the Cappella degli Scrovegni for use on the cover of this novel.

Oxford at the Clarendon Press for permission to quote two passages from *The Ecclesiastical History of Orderic Vitalis (Vol.II)* edited and translated by Marjorie Chibnall, 1969.

Penguin Classics for permission to quote two passages from *The Alexiad* by Anna Comnena translated by E.R.A. Sewter, Penguin Classics, 1979.

Quotes from *Historia Sicula* by Gaufredus Malaterra which are so identified and translated by John Julius Norwich and are contained in *The Normans in the South* by Longman, Green and Co. Ltd., 1967

The quotes from *Ystoire de li Normant* by Amatus of Monte Cassino and quotes from the *Historia Sicula* not otherwise identified are my translation.

I would like to thank Jim McAuley for his thoughtful editing of *The Words of Bernfrieda*. My special friend and colleague and editor Lisa Leitz who corrected and re-corrected so many early drafts of the novel with the patience and respect for the text of a medieval scribe. I am also grateful to John Keeble and George Garrett for their help and encouragement.

My heartfelt thanks to the friends and colleagues at Gonzaga University who read and edited the manuscript at various stages of completion: Sister Phyllis Taufen, Associate Professor of English and Dr. Daniel Butterworth, Associate Professor of English. Their comments were invaluable to me. A special thank you to Dr. RaGena C. De Aragon, Associate Professor of history and medi-evalist, for sharing generously her knowlege and passion of medieval women. Thank you also to Sharon Prendergast and the staff of the Foley Center for their help in securing many hard to find sources, Chris Gill for his help in designing the genealogical chart attached to this volume, and Marty Abrahamson and Sandy Hank for their technical help and patience

Special thanks to the friends who read and commented on the manuscript: Françoise Kuester, Sandy Mueller, Faye Bare, Katie Jones Morgan, Richard Kuhling, Dr. John D' Aboy, Dr. Haideh Lightfoot, and Dr. Pia Friedrich.

Finally I would like to thank three people without whom *The Words of Bernfrieda* would have not been written. My mother who passed her love for reading and stories to me. My uncle, Luigi Biancheri, who taught me to love Sicily and its history. And my husband Phil, whose love, encouragement, loyalty, and humor have given me the daily strength to persevere.

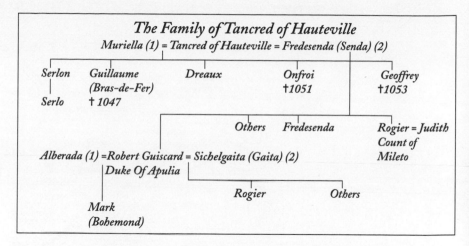

The Family of Tancred of Hauteville

Muriella (1) = Tancred of Hauteville = Fredesenda (Senda) (2)

Serlon | Guillaume (Bras-de-Fer) †1047 | Dreaux | Onfroi †1051 | Geoffrey †1053

Serlo

Others | Fredesenda | Rogier = Judith Count of Mileto

Alberada (1) = Robert Guiscard = Sichelgaita (Gaita) (2) Duke Of Apulia

Rogier | Others

Mark (Bohemond)

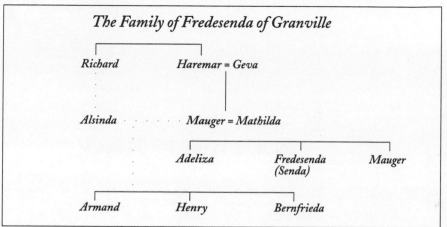

The Family of Fredesenda of Granville

Richard | Haremar = Geva

Alsinda · · · · · Mauger = Mathilda

Adeliza | Fredesenda (Senda) | Mauger

Armand | Henry | Bernfrieda

Judith's Family

Robert De Grantmesnil (1) = Hawise of Giroie = William of Evreux (2)

Others | Robert Abbot of Saint Evroult and Santa Eufemia | Arnold †1062 | Judith = Rogier Count of Mileto | Others

Key

†	Died
=	Married
——	Legitimate Offspring
····	Illegitimate Offspring

Galeria

● ROME

● Palestrina

● Ostia

● Velletri

Ceprano ●   Aquino ●

● Monte Cassino

Terracina

Gaeta

● Teano

S. Agata dei G

Garigliano

● Capua

Bene

● Aversa

NAPLES

Amalfi ●   S A

Sorrento

Termoli ●

S. Paolo di Civi

Bilerno

Fort

SOUTHERN ITALY

0	25	50	75	100 mls
0	25	50	75	100	125	150 kms

TYRRHENIAN SE

PALERMO